all downhill with you

JULIE OLIVIA

Author's Note

All Downhill With You is the first book in the *Honeywood Fun Park* Series. This book can be read as a standalone. There are no cliffhangers.

Please be advised that this book is an **open-door** romance, meaning there is **on-page** sexual content. Mature readers only.

Also, while this book is 98% laugh-out-loud, exciting theme park moments, there is about 2% angst. Be kind to your heart when you read, friends.

Special Note

This book's plot centers around a roller coaster malfunction. However, I feel obligated to note that roller coaster accidents are remarkably rare. These attractions are designed with your safety in mind, and they contain numerous precautions and fail-safes.

All Downhill With You is my love letter to roller coasters. This book is not meant to deter you from theme parks. Please go out there and ride to your heart's content! :)

To everyone who wants to face their fears. It's never too late.

Also dedicated to the VelociCoaster. Yes, I dedicated my book to a roller coaster. It's my book; I do what I want.

Playlist

"Early Morning Breeze" - Dolly Parton
"Honey" - AFTERxCLASS
"Motion Sickness" - Phoebe Bridgers
"Preparedness" - the bird and the bee
"Raining in June" - Olivia Klugman
"Hallucinate (live)" - Declan McKenna
"Vienna" - Billy Joel
"Love Song for the Haters" - Fleece
"You Are My Sunshine" - The Dead South
"Always Forever" - Cult

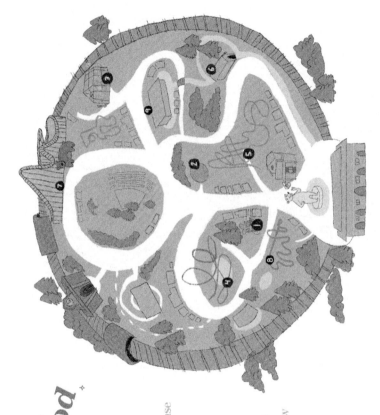

Honeywood
FUN PARK

1. The Bee-fast Stop
2. The Beesting
3. Bumblebee Greenhouse
4. Bumblebee's Flight
5. Buzzard of Death
6. Canoodler
7. The Grizzly
8. Little Pecker's Joyride
9. The Romping Meadow

1

Lorelei

When I see Emory Dawson across the midway for the first time, I realize the world is not a fair place.

I wanted him to match the image I had of a hunch-backed, mustache-twirling, top hat–wearing villain. I wanted him to have a dastardly smile and skinny chicken legs. Maybe crooked teeth for good measure. I'd even settle on him tripping over a twig at this point.

But that is not what I get with Mr. Roller Coaster.

In fact, it's irritating how different he seems from my fictional version. He's not supposed to fill out a suit so well or be that tall. He shouldn't be blessed with rich, dark brown, wavy hair. He's not allowed to have a mysterious gaze that oozes both curiosity and intensity all at once.

The man I'm currently in a million-dollar lawsuit with is not supposed to be on level with Mr. *freaking* Darcy.

Today, Honeywood Fun Park is illuminated by the sunbeams of a bright April morning. The cool breeze comes in through the mountainous air, soundtracked by the spring cicadas and the roar of roller coasters in preseason testing.

It's peaceful, and Emory Dawson stands like the storm showers that will rain us all out.

I can't look away from him. I know I should. I know I'm playing with fire by being in the same vicinity as him. My lawyer would be shooting daggers at me. Literally and figuratively.

But that's why I didn't tell him Mr. Roller Coaster was coming to Honeywood Fun Park this week. Or that I had a meeting with him.

I can handle this on my own ... I think.

He turns in my direction. I feel my hand tighten around the clipboard by my hip—the same hip that's been giving me problems for a few days now. I might only be twenty-nine years old, but the injury aged my pelvis too many years. It's supposed to rain this week, which is why it's twinging. But even if the forecast were favorable, I think my body can sense that it's in danger just by looking at Mr. Roller Coaster.

He is eerily out of place. He has a haircut that must have cost hundreds, and we have a fifty-year-old bear animatronic with matted fur and a goofy smile. He probably owns a high-rise apartment in a city with a million people, and yet we're surrounded by tall Georgia pines in a town with four thousand citizens on a good year.

He looks away.

I don't think he saw me. *Of course the pompous man didn't.*

He probably wouldn't notice anything beyond that beautiful scowl of his. I would be relieved he overlooked me, but I'll be in a boardroom with him in less than an hour anyway, discussing The Grizzly's renovations.

Fred, our park's general manager, knows about my lawsuit. Who doesn't in this town? I'm practically walking around with a scarlet letter on me, except the *A* is for *accident*. Or it's a *B* for *bless her heart*.

When Fred asked if I would meet with Emory Dawson beforehand and teach him about our park, I said it wouldn't be an issue.

But that was before he turned up, looking like this.

I don't know what I was thinking.

Was it pride? Wanting to prove something to myself?

I can't even remember. Heck, I've lost track of what I'm doing right now.

I look down at my small grocery bag full of littered cups and balled-up park maps. It starts to slack.

I've been walking the midway for cleanup. My hands are full of garbage. I look like a raccoon, scavenging for dinner.

Of course I'm holding trash when I meet the king of roller coaster design.

I technically shouldn't be looking out for trash as the marketing manager. It's a Park Services job. But you can always distinguish a seasoned Rides team member by the way they treat the main entrance through the park: the midway. And as a former Rides supervisor, the midway will always be my baby. I would swaddle it if I could.

I was moved to the marketing department after my accident. I'd graduated college with a degree in journalism, so it was a logical progression. The only reason I hadn't moved immediately after graduation was because my love for roller coasters overpowered any career paths I had in mind.

I've been obsessed with Honeywood Fun Park since the moment I passed through those gates when I was three years old. I've been told three is too young to remember something like that, but they don't know what they're talking about. It is my earliest memory. Maybe the park

3

imprinted on me werewolf-style. There have been weirder imprints—looking at you, Stephenie Meyer. Regardless, I knew from that moment, this was my destiny.

All of it intrigued me—the sound of roller coasters roaring on the tracks; the warm hug from the mascot, Buzzy the Bear; the smell of Honeywood's signature all-day pancakes wafting from the in-park restaurant. I loved it all, even when I got a job at sixteen. Even when I started cleaning the blacktop of the midway. Trash bags and all.

Out of the corner of my eye, I see a cup lid I must have missed. I bend to take it, but before my hand reaches it, another much larger hand grabs the lid instead. The wrist is defined and sharp with corded veins and adorned by a watch containing so many intricate pieces inside the transparent face that I'm positive it must have cost well above my recent paycheck—even with the managerial increase.

I follow the arm's length to the crisp, rolled-up white sleeves to the forearm littered with subtle brown hair. I admire the way the fabric clings to his broad shoulders—*don't drool, Lore*—and finally reach the man himself picking it up.

If Mr. Roller Coaster didn't see me before, he sees me now.

Emory Dawson looks at me for one second, if I had to be rational about it. But the moment feels like an eternity as his dark brown eyes trail from my nose to my chin and down to my bent knees and up again. His eyes are swirling pools of chocolate, bright in the beam of morning sunlight shining past our gift shop. The same light casts half his face in relief, highlighting the long Roman nose and the thick, dark eyebrows. He stares at me with such intensity that my stomach flips over onto itself. The clumsy jerk.

4

It feels like cresting The Grizzly's lift hill, barreling down that one-hundred-foot drop.

I wonder if this is the moment he recognizes me. He must see his lawsuit staring him right in the face. The woman who got injured on his roller coaster not once, but twice. By coaster standards, that's unheard of. In fact, it's statistically impossible, and honestly, I should buy a lottery ticket or maybe even look out for falling pianos.

The Grizzly, our wooden coaster with large hills and harsh banked turns, is a product of his company, Dawson Manufacturing. Three years ago, it had a small scrap of paneling fly off and hit me in the arm. The incident didn't make it past our town's local gossip paper, *Cedar Cliff Chatter*. *Thank God*. I only had one month of bruising and a few stitches. I was back on the midway after the weekend.

Not so bad, right?

Wrong.

The second accident happened one year later when the wheels came off the track. My injury put me in the hospital for a couple weeks, followed by minor reconstructive surgery on my hip and pelvis that gave some serious geri- atric *help, I've fallen, and I can't get up* energy. Seriously! I shared my physical therapy time slot with an eighty-two- year-old and her understandable aversion to stairs. I liked her. She brought me Thin Mints every session, and I swear she had a connection to some Girl Scout mafia and their underground off-season cookie sales. I came back to my hometown of Cedar Cliff with a mint chocolate cookie addiction and a partially metal pelvis.

Worst superhero ever.

My real power developed in the hospital bed. I became a wizard at research.

I got in touch with an Atlanta lawyer to investigate why

my accident had happened. He scoured over The Grizzly's previous inspections and maintenance records. But everything was perfect.

No issues had been reported in its twenty-year operating history. My lawyer found nothing that would lead to wheels disconnecting from the track. But with the park not at fault, we were left to research how the ride was made. We shifted our focus to the real culprit.

Enter the Dawson Manufacturing lawsuit.

At some point in the hospital, a bouquet of *get well soon* flowers was sent from Dawson Manufacturing. Probably some *please don't sue us* response.

Too late, buddy.

At first, the research was cathartic. I needed a villain in my painkiller-addled brain. I found pictures of Thomas Dawson—who looked every bit the enemy I needed—but he wasn't the engineer I was looking for. It was his son, Emory, who had built The Grizzly.

I couldn't find any pictures of him, only accolades and achievements.

Fun fact: Emory Dawson is the youngest roller coaster designer in US history, building The Grizzly for Honeywood Fun Park in Cedar Cliff, Georgia, at just the age of sixteen.

Fun fact: Emory Dawson was the CEO of Dawson Manufacturing before he turned thirty. He subsequently stepped down after a few years because ... I don't know ... he got bored of being the king of the world or something? At thirty-six, he is now the lead engineer at Dawson Manufacturing.

Fun fact: I hate Emory Dawson.

Normally, I'd go on a long run to work through it, but I can't do that anymore, thanks to his company. My physical therapist told me it would be a long route to recovery and that, one day, I might be able to run again. That "one day" kept me going.

So, I worked hard. I slipped on my usual *go get 'em* face that had earned me so many medals in high school cross country running. I showed up every day, and every day, I thought of Emory Dawson, the faceless genius villain. He was my Dr. Evil, my Lex Luthor, and my Moriarty. But after a year of consistent therapy and still no running, I realized my physical therapist just hadn't had the heart to tell me running would be impossible without extensive surgery.

I didn't get out of bed for a while after that.

Unfortunately, two years later, we still don't know why the wheels came off the track. And as we search, my lawsuit with Dawson Manufacturing remains.

At this point, it's the principle of it all. The money from the lawsuit is irrelevant to me. I need to know why The Grizzly, a coaster that ran perfectly for twenty years and passed every inspection, suddenly malfunctioned. I need justice for our park. And my insistence has been less than kind to Dawson Manufacturing's image.

So, Emory Dawson must know who I am.

Except as he looks at me now, I feel like he doesn't recognize me at all.

His thick eyebrows scrunch inward, forming a taut line between them. The corners of his mouth tilt downward.

My gut clenches.

Oh, heck no.

He's giving me *that* look.

A look I've seen too many times to count from people in this town.

I curl my lip in, biting it. I don't know what to say.

Mr. Roller Coaster's eyes dart down to my bitten lip,

but he says nothing. Instead, he walks off with the cup lid in hand. There's no, *Hello, good day, just picking up trash,* or, *Hey, you're the woman whose life I ruined, right?*

He walks past the nearest garbage can and underhand tosses the cup lid toward it, landing it perfectly in the open O of the wastebasket's top.

Great. Cool. So, he's smooth too.

Then, he takes one last look back at me with that same expression. It's the one I get from everyone who knows about the accident, my hip, and the fact that I've stayed at the very same park with the ride that brought my life crashing to the ground.

It's a look of pity.

Emory Dawson is the absolute worst.

2

Emory

Honeywood Fun Park is odd.

I'm aware that it's known across the United States—even outside of North Georgia—as one of the must-see tourist places to visit for quirky thrills, but I assume there must be sarcasm in those positive reviews.

Between the old-fashioned bear mascot suits, the rigidly functioning animatronics that haven't been updated since the '70s, and the so-called attraction that consists of wild bees buzzing rampant in an enclosed greenhouse, I'm not sure what to make of it.

Old and run-down? Or a treasured piece of almost-forgotten history?

Depends on who you're asking, but I'm not one for nostalgia. However, the park's general manager, Fred, falls into the latter category of Honeywood enthusiasts.

Fred—with his goofy grin and giant mustache—is a man so enamored with his own park that it's both endearing and off-putting at the same time.

He wraps up my park tour with a flourish of his hands, as if presenting it on a silver platter.

Except to me, the gesture reads as, *Welcome to the next four weeks in our time machine of nostalgia that means nothing to you!*

I do like Fred. I like Fred because Fred likes his park. A man who can be proud of a boat ride with the same music for the past fifty years simply due to the cherished history is a man I admire.

Isn't passion why we all got into this industry to begin with?

"What do ya think?" he asks, his Southern drawl only adding to his barrel-chested, Santa-bellied charm.

Wrong question to ask me.

Honeywood is not a disgusting park. It's just not modern. It's not my style. It's … kitschy.

I open my mouth to speak—to say something nice, *anything* nice—but I hear my name being called instead. I twist on my heel and look over to see the only person I know in about a thousand-mile radius of this small town.

My cousin Orson leans against the iron fence entrance of the park, coffee in both hands, baseball cap turned backward, and a shining grin to accompany it. He's always grinning. I think it's a family trait. At least, one that passed on through my mother's side with her siblings. I, unfortunately, inherited my father's signature Dawson scowl.

Saved for now.

"Emmy!" Orson calls.

I cringe at the nickname.

Did I say I was saved? Never mind. Out of the frying pan and into the fryer.

I give Fred a wry smile—it's forced, and I can feel it—and say, "Hang on a moment."

My shoes click on the cobblestone entrance, uncomfortable and tight around my feet. I should have worn my work

10

boots, but I wanted to make a good impression. Had I known the general manager would wear jeans and a bright yellow polo, I might have thought otherwise. I pass the fountain with a statue of a bear and an oversize bee in the middle, and I feel judged by their stone smiles.

"Can't talk long," is all I say when I reach Orson.

He responds by handing me a coffee with a low chuckle. "Thought I'd say hi on your first day."

"Not too out of your way?" I ask, taking the cup.

"It's Cedar Cliff," Orson says with another laugh. "You can get anywhere within five minutes."

The Honeycomb, his bar that sits one block down from the park, is this small town's watering hole. It's been passed down through the generations, and he finally took over once my uncle and aunt moved down to Florida for retirement. I got lucky he was here. He's the only friend I have in this town.

"Is it everything you hoped it'd be?" he asks.

"I sent you the picture of the animatronic that kept giving me eyes, right?"

"Oh, Buzzy? Yeah, he's even more startling at night."

"A bear named Buzzy? Is that a joke?"

"Wait 'til you see Bumble the Bee."

I sigh.

He nudges me with an elbow from where his forearm rests on the fence. I don't budge.

"Have some humor," he says. "You always get like this when you put on the monkey suit."

He nods his head toward my tailored suit. It's one of three that I invested in after I was told by my father that wearing my gray T-shirts and dark denim to each business meeting was unprofessional.

"Monkey suit is mandated," I say.

"You've at least remembered to smile, right?"

I think back to earlier today when Fred told me they once had to vacate the entire log ride for hours because their bear mascot thought it would be fun to ride with guests. The bulk of his costume and enormous head had weighed down the flume and closed the ride for maintenance the remainder of the day. Even though he laughed about it, I didn't join in.

I found the situation ridiculous.

This whole place is ridiculous.

I take a sip of my coffee. Orson must have added cream and sugar. I wince.

"I smile sometimes," I lie. When Orson laughs in response, I shrug. "I'll try harder."

I won't.

He takes a sip of his coffee, probably loaded up with the same artificial junk.

"Where're you staying?" he asks.

"The parkside hotel," I say. "The Hibernation, I think?"

These names, I swear.

"Darn," he says with a snap of his fingers. "I really wanted a roommate."

"I won't be crashing your bachelor pad, I promise."

"Why? You bringin' Cedar Cliff chicks to your hotel?"

I scrunch my nose. "I'm only here for work."

"Rude," he says. "I'll have you know that Cedar Cliff is full of wonderful, strong women. Gorgeous women."

Cedar Cliff, population *people who grew up here*, has its own type of beauty, I suppose.

It took about thirty minutes of nothing but open fields, followed by another fifteen-minute climb up winding roads in the low mountains, to finally arrive here. But it is lovely.

It's the way the pine trees tower over you, making even the established areas feel buried in forest. The way everything seems both antique and modern all at once with the repainted signs that still hold the old color schemes from the '70s—bright bumblebee yellows and creams. It's the tiny dandelions that sprout between the cracked sidewalks in the historic downtown that seem both hopeful and strained.

I might as well hear banjos in the distance.

I pat the gate and clear my throat. "Right. Good talk. I should ..."

"Have you met her yet?"

I still, meeting his eyes. "Who?"

"You know who."

Yes, I know who.

Lori? Laura? Lauren?

Whatever her name is.

The girl suing me.

The girl who got injured on the first ride I'd ever created. In fact, she got injured not once, but twice—an impossible statistic—and she is out for my blood.

"No," I say. "No, I don't even know what she looks like."

Orson laughs. "You don't know what the girl suing you even looks like?"

"No."

I don't want to know the details. I told my lawyer I didn't even want to see her file. The further away from it, the better.

I had our company send flowers to her as a good gesture. At the time, I was more upset with Honeywood Fun Park for neglecting our ride. Most roller coaster accidents are a result of bad maintenance in the park. It was on them for letting it deteriorate this bad.

But once my lawyer said it wasn't Honeywood's fault—that all the inspections over the years had been passed with flying colors—I started to rethink everything. I haven't been able to sleep more than four hours each night for nearly a year. Seeing her picture would only haunt me more.

My father—Thomas Dawson, CEO of Dawson Manufacturing—has been more involved with the lawsuit. He says this girl is ruthless. She's after every penny we have. She wants to fund herself a new surgery.

The whole thing makes me sick. Her, him, the coaster ...

Not that I'd ever tell my lawyer this, but I don't blame her for suing. Being the heir to a coaster manufacturer, I know that these monsters can hurt. You don't make coasters without trialing them, and I have enough scrapes, burns, and randomly twitching limbs to understand her pain.

The unfortunate fact is that nobody knows why The Grizzly malfunctioned after twenty years. But that's why I'm here—to renovate the ride. To gain back the trust of our clients. To ensure it is safe, moving forward. Maybe assuage some of my guilt, if I'm lucky.

After that, I'm heading home and never looking back.

"Okay, so you've seen no pictures of her," Orson says with a slow nod. "Herculean effort at avoidance, my friend."

"I've got other things to worry about."

"Zeus level."

"Okay, good-bye, Orson."

"She's really sweet, you know."

It bothers me that he knows her, but I'm not surprised. Small town and all. But based on what my father has told me, I'm willing to bet "sweet" is the last thing she is.

"Don't care," I say.

"You might even like her!"

"Stop."

"Trivia at The Honeycomb is tonight!" he calls out, cupping his free hand up to his mouth. "You comin'?"

I don't even hesitate before saying, "No."

I toss my sugary coffee into the garbage the moment I'm out of sight.

3

Emory

F red escorts me into the main offices, a building disguised as a dilapidated saloon in front of the park's entrance.

We walk upstairs and down the narrow hall to a board-room. It's not the normal boardroom I'm accustomed to with floor-to-ceiling windows and digital whiteboards. Instead, there are two skinny windows looking over the park, a long wooden table stained with coffee mug rings, and a flip chart. It's utilitarian. Old school.

When Fred sits in a creaking leather swivel chair, I opt to continue standing instead.

He pulls out his phone and nods at the screen. "Arden says she'll be here in five." He chuckles. "Not surprising. She's always helping out in the mornings."

It was his idea to bring on a so-called park expert for The Grizzly's renovations. Fred said their marketing manager has been with the park since she was a teenager. She would be able to advise on the ride's theme.

Whatever I need to do to get this job done.

I'm only supposed to be here for four weeks. I intend to

scout the place, get the renovation ideas approved by Honeywood's board of directors, and give the rest of the workload to our subcontractors. If meeting with their marketing person speeds up the process, fine.

"So, thoughts?" Fred's words suddenly break the silence.

"Well," I start, "we'll have to close down the Barnacle Bears exhibit for construction but ..."

"No, no, the park!"

"Oh."

Right.

Not the execution of how we'll make the new coaster. The park itself. It's like a new mom asking me if her baby is cute when he came out looking like a newborn Benjamin Button. There's no nice way to say, *Those wrinkles are adorable, ma'am.*

And Honeywood might as well be an old-man baby.

"It's ..." I pause.

Fred is all smiles.

Don't get me wrong; I can partially see what he sees. I know that most people look at that bear fountain statue and think, *Why, that's Buzzy, the buzziest of the buzzy bears!* Or whatever thing they say in Cedar Cliff. I wouldn't know. I'm not familiar with the children's book series this park is based off of. But I understand the draw of nostalgia. It's what our business is built on.

"The park is fine," I only sort of lie.

"Oh." His face falls.

My gut clenches right below my navel, like a hook of a cane trying to drag me offstage. I don't like seeing his thick mustache tilted downward. Nobody likes a sad-looking walrus.

He swallows. "Just fine? Buzzy is a fan favorite. Do you want to ride The Romping Meadow?"

"I'm sure it's wonderful."

Fred's face is now sterner, like a disappointed uncle.

This gets worse every second.

"Emory, we'll be working together to make this park better," he says. "I'd like to know how else we can improve."

I open my mouth, only to shut it again, then say, "I'm only here for The Grizzly."

"Yes, but ... you are a professional. You know what makes a great park."

He's gonna coax it out of me, isn't he?

I was born into this industry and raised in its thrills. I gained stamps on my passport through international theme parks. I understand that you need both a thrilling attraction and cohesive theme to make what we call a "perfect show." But I'm not here to marvel at some piece of history I don't belong to. I'm here to be the good guy, providing hope for a better ride—one ride—not the bad guy, carrying the sore news about their whole park.

But if Fred wants me to be his villain, then fine, I can be that guy.

"Despite its ... charm," I say, licking my lips before continuing, trying to find the words and opting for likely the worst ones, "Honeywood is rapidly approaching a defunct-level park."

Okay, so maybe I shouldn't have said it that harshly.

"Well, we—" he starts.

I barrel on. Too late to turn back now. "It's, quite frankly, outdated, Mr. Louder."

"Call me Fred."

Even when he's getting berated, he's polite. I hate how much I like this guy.

"Fred," I say, leaning forward, splaying my hands out on the table, "updating your star attraction is only part of the problem here."

"Part?"

Don't say it.

Don't say it.

I do anyway.

"I'm curious how your marketing department even manages to maintain hype around such a place."

And there we go.

"Fred?"

A barely audible whisper of a voice comes from behind me, and I turn.

My stomach clenches.

There's the same woman from this morning. The one from the midway, carrying trash.

She walks farther into the room, stopping for a moment with her fist raised, as if she was intending to knock but decided against it.

She's tall. Willowy.

"Arden," Fred says, choking out the word.

Good Lord, I've made a grown man cry.

His voice rises in pitch at the next sentence. "This is Mr. Dawson."

Her doe eyes shift to me. The deep browns of them are almost vacant but in a mystical way. Like she's floating in a dream. Her brown hair frames her smooth face in waves. The length of it hits just above her collarbone, a protruding sharpness to the otherwise softness of the rest of her.

Soft. That's the best way to describe her. Unblemished ivory cheeks with a small tint of pink to them. A full bottom lip that seems ... delicate.

She's beautiful. I noticed it on the midway, and just as

her dreamy eyes stopped me in my tracks then, I find myself staring at her again now, unable to break my gaze.

I hold out my hand. A second passes and then another before she finally shakes it. Her hand is like velvet against my callused one.

But all that softness in her fades.

Her jaw sets. She pushes her shoulders back and tilts her head to the side, furrowing her brow.

"What were you saying?" she asks.

"Pardon?"

"About our park."

I exhale a rush of air through my nose.

I've seen it time and time again—people wanting to outmatch me in a boardroom. She's trying to go toe-to-toe.

Good luck.

"I said it's the most successful, longest-running joke in theme parks today," I deadpan.

She squints a little. Slowly, as if she were trying to get inside my head.

"Maybe if we didn't have defective rides built from our manufacturers, we'd be less of one."

I can feel the heat rising in my chest, and my hand starts to twitch.

I don't have time for this.

It's not that I have bad anger issues—not in comparison to the ones that dominate my father—but I would say that I'm defensive of The Grizzly. Honeywood Fun Park might own it, but The Grizzly was my first solo construction project. My mom calls it *my baby*. While I don't hold that exact type of sentimentality, I'd be lying if I said I didn't feel some form of a tie to it.

"Defective?" I bite out. I put my hands in my pockets, tilting my head to the side and jutting out my chin for emphasis. "It's been fine for twenty years. We don't know why it malfunctioned. But it's being investigated, I assure you."

"Assurances seem cheap, coming from a man who thinks our park is a joke."

"Listen, I'm here to renovate your roller coaster so that your PR mess won't get worse."

"Sounds like you're projecting."

I grind my teeth.

Sure, okay.

Dawson Manufacturing is working through its own horrific reputation since that accident. She's done her research.

"Tell me more about myself. Enlighten me."

She looks away, licking her bottom lip and tucking it in before glancing back at me. I can't help but follow the motion before looking in her eyes once more.

Then, she asks, "You don't know who I am, do you?"

What is this, some type of power move?

I lean back on my heels. I'm like an animal trapped in a corner. I don't even know what game we're playing or how I've lost, but it unnerves me to feel that I have.

"Should I?" I ask, the words as dull and unimpressed as I can make them.

I'm here to improve their park, and this entitled marketing manager can't seem to get her own head out of her ass for two seconds to realize that—

"I'm Lorelei Arden."

My jaw tenses as I process this information, and then it all hits me at once.

I chew the inside of my cheek before saying, "And you think I owe you two million dollars, don't you?"

4

Lorelei

Two million.
Jesus.

I didn't know that number was being thrown around by our lawyers. I thought it was only one million.

All of it almost feels wrong.

Except the man who caused my accident is standing in front of me with the same bored expression on his face that he had this morning. Like he's watching paint dry. Or maybe he's the dull paint drying.

He's a man who clearly believes he has better things to do than be here in Cedar Cliff, and that rubs me the wrong way.

Fred furrows his brow at Emory. "I'm sorry. Will this be an issue?" Fred asks.

"No," Emory says at the same time I chime in, "Yes."

I was okay working on this project, but that was before I found out he was an ass.

Emory continues to stare at me with a blank expression, those thick, well-groomed eyebrows daring me to back out.

"I have zero intention of discussing our lawsuit further,"

he says matter-of-factly, as if he didn't just call out the exact monetary amount of our dealings.

Oh, wait. Yeah, he totally did.

It surprises me how decisive and solid his voice is, like his vocal cords are steeped in the same marble encasing that the rest of his cold demeanor is. I bet he takes his coffee black. I bet he replies to texts with the letter *K*. I bet he answers knock-knock jokes with, *Get off my lawn.*

"Agreed," I say. "But I think us working together might be a conflict of interest."

Emory glances over my canary-yellow Honeywood polo, my denim pencil skirt stitched with tiny floral accents, all the way down to my white Converses, tied with matching yellow laces.

My face grows hotter, the more he evaluates me. His jawline tics. He's even more attractive up close. His intensity is intoxicating.

He's tall, and that's saying something, coming from me. I stand at a good five-eleven. I don't normally have to look up at men. But Emory Dawson is at least five inches taller than me.

His eyebrows pull in, and there it is again—that look of pity. The same look from this morning on the midway.

It sets my nerves on fire.

I was never an angry person until the second accident. I'd worked Guest Services until I was twenty because I could calm down even the rainy-day visitors demanding refunds. I'm cheery. I like that about myself. But leave it to Mr. Roller Coaster to reignite the furious beat of my angered heart.

The night of my life-changing accident will forever be seared into my brain. I remember staring at the stars for what felt like forever as I practically dangled in the seat belt, my hip aching in pain as I was wedged between the broken lap bar and the interior.

It was Employee Night at the park. We all got to experience whichever rides we wanted and as many times as we pleased. We even decided to turn all the lights off to raise the thrill factor. Special changes like that are the best parts of Employee Night.

But on my last ride with The Grizzly, the wheels popped off the track on the second banked turn, and my car dislodged. Thankfully, I was the only one riding. But being alone only made the dark feel that much scarier.

"I think my lawyer would advise me against working with you," I continue.

"Then, why come to the meeting at all?" Emory counters dully.

"Curiosity."

"Well, has your curiosity been satiated?"

"I've seen all I need to see."

"And it took you this long to decide that?"

My hands twitch against my clipboard. I've used yoga as a form of meditation, but now, I wish I had a punching bag. I'd print a picture of Emory's perfect face and tape it on there. It would be excellent motivation.

I look to Fred for support, but he bites his lip, as if keeping in extra words he doesn't want to say.

Oh no.

My stomach drops, and my mind reels.

My best friend, Quinn, has always told me I have a problem saying no.

I blame my passionate parents. My need for approval. They expected the best out of us. I was the kid who sharpened all the pencils before class started, just to get an extra star on the bulletin board.

Fred looks seconds away from possibly saying, *I'm disappointed in you.*

Ugh, it's always worse when authority figures are not mad, but *disappointed.*

Ever since being promoted to a management role, I've known I need to prove myself to him. I might be one of the older team members in this park, but it's still a risk, putting someone relatively young into this role.

Fred is like another father to me, but I also know he wouldn't hesitate to do what is best for his park. If I fail, he won't sugarcoat it. I respect that, but it makes the itch to gain acceptance grow even itchier.

And then there's Emory.

Mr. Roller Coaster looks at me with a sneer, like he's not surprised I'd back out, or maybe it's that he can see my gears turning. He can see how much of a pushover I am. It grates on my nerves.

Fred sighs. "Listen, we don't have to—"

"You know what? No. It's fine," I spout out. "Really. I'm the marketing manager. It's my job."

Emory's eyes do not leave me when he says, "If anyone knows how to market a coaster, it must be you."

It feels like a jab, so I take it as one.

"Why?" I ask. "Because I still rode the same coaster that injured me the first time?"

"Yes," he says. "That's exactly why."

I think I see a twitch at the edge of his lips, like he's fighting a smile. Or maybe not. I bet Emory Dawson couldn't smile even if he tried.

I didn't think I could resent Mr. Roller Coaster more than I had in that hospital bed. But after meeting the real him, I realize he is exactly the villain I imagined.

5

Lorelei

"Oh my God, today was the day, wasn't it? You met Mr. Roller Coaster."

"Shuuuush," I whisper with exaggeration, looking around the bar.

"It definitely was today," Quinn continues at the exact same volume, eyes wide as she tosses her key fob and phone on the long table. Her chair yelps against the wooden floor when she scoots it back and sits down. "Look at that concerned expression on your cute little doe face."

My best friend leans back in her chair and crosses her arms, one blonde eyebrow lifting with a smirk.

"I'm not concerned," I say. "I'm ... determined."

Determined to forget everything about Emory Dawson and enjoy tonight, that is.

It's Wednesday, which means it's trivia night at the bar one block over from Honeywood. I like to get here early and help the bar's owner, Orson, set up for the night. He mostly talks about sports while I'm off-loading chairs, but I like the company. Plus, like Honeywood, everything about The Honeycomb is comforting—the creaking wood floor, the warm Edison lightbulbs strung up over booths and high-tops and picnic tables, and the constant flow of classic '70s music echoing through the speakers.

Trivia night fosters competition between everyone in town. Our five-person team consists of me and my four closest friends. We waver between second and third place, only consistently overshadowed by the rival team, stacked with Cedar Cliff's over-sixty crowd. I swear, our quiet, nearing-retirement mechanic, Frank, is a secret genius.

"We're winning tonight," I say. "No distractions."

"Perfect," she says. "But don't change the subject. Let's get back to your bad day."

I groan. "Oh, come on, Quinn. Look! Mrs. Stanley brought her new puppy! Can we talk about that instead?"

"At least tell me Mr. Roller Coaster was in fact the worst," Quinn says. "And that he looks like some horrible bigwig. Did he have a mustard stain on his shirt? I'm imagining a man obsessed with sauerkraut."

My chest flutters a bit because *man with a mustard stain* he was not.

I haven't been able to get those piercing eyes out of my head since this afternoon. And that jawline. The jerk.

"He was ... all right," I say, averting eye contact.

"Wait, what do you mean, *all right*?" Quinn asks, deadpan. Her crossed arms tighten.

She's onto me.

"I meant that he's on *too much mayonnaise* level," I lie with a high-pitched laugh because there's no way to say, *He's an absolute snack, but only if Gushers had poison injected.*

"You have your bird voice," she says.

"No, I don't."

"You're squeaky."

"I am not!"

Quinn narrows her eyes at me.

Defiance is Quinn's default look. The only time she truly smiles is when she's in costume at work as the poofy-pink-dress-wearing Queen Bee, a Honeywood character with more politeness than Quinn can muster in her day-to-day. But if they allowed the royalty of Honeywood to scowl, she would do it.

Quinn has been my best friend since freshman year of high school after she punched Paul Wallace in homeroom for calling me a tall freak. She's a formidable force. At five foot nothing with kohl-covered eyes and combat boots, Quinn could kick the ass of most people in the room—or at least, she wouldn't hesitate to try. She has a *feel free to say the wrong thing and see how it goes for you* kind of attitude. Fiercely guarded. Fiercely protective of the few she cares for.

The cynical yin to my optimistic yang.

And she can see right through me.

I tap my fingers on the half-empty beer glass in front of me. "It was fine," I say. "I gave him a rundown of our marketing for The Grizzly. I went through the last few campaigns we had, pulled old brochures from my office, blah, blah, blah." I sigh. "We kept it all business, and hopefully, I won't see him again until court or something. I don't know."

"How'd he act?" Quinn asks.

"Pompous." I say this right as our other friend Theo walks up, dropping her overstuffed crossbody bag onto the floor.

Theo is ninety-percent lean, unmoving yoga muscle. But her curly raven-black hair has enough joyful bounce to balance out the rest of her. She's all smiles, all the time. It's why she's a great supervisor to Honeywood's teenage summer employees.

"Who's pompous?" she asks.

"Mr. Roller Coaster," Quinn deadpans.

I bury my head in my hands with a groan.

"Oh my God! Yes! I saw him today!" Theo breathes, ninja-sliding her way into the chair.

I feel my chest tighten. Talking about Emory Dawson in public makes me uncomfortable. Anyone can overhear us, and Cedar Cliff loves to talk.

I wave my hand in the air. "Let's not ..."

"Oh, hey, happy Mr. Roller Coaster Day!"

The fourth and fifth members of our trivia group, Bennett and Ruby, waltz up to our table. Ruby's joyful voice is enough to alert the rest of the mountaintop to our conversation.

I whine out a small, "*Guys!*"

Bennett grabs his usual seat at the opposite end of the table, halting mid-chair pull. "What? Are we not talking about Mr. Roller Coaster?"

Bennett is our resident mountain man. He's the lead supervisor in the Maintenance Division at Honeywood, and it shows. He's built like a man who climbs tall ladders and throws logs over his shoulder. You can see it in how the flannel stretches over the peaks of his arms and over the various cuts he has, such as the small scratch just below his lip. His long black hair rests on his shoulders, and it looks both messy and soft, like some mythical god. His girlfriend, Jolene—the woman we can't convince to hang out with us, no matter how hard we try—likes to call him Aquaman. I don't see it.

"I know he's supposed to be our mortal enemy and all,"

Ruby says, sitting in the seat beside Bennett, "but I still can't believe you got to meet *the* Emory Dawson."

"Mr. Roller Coaster," Bennett corrects with a nod.

Ruby elbows his ribs, eliciting a theatrical, "*Oof.*"

Bennett and Ruby are two peas in a pod. Arriving everywhere together and leaving in the same movement. He moves; she moves. Yet in direct contrast to big, burly Bennett, Ruby is a small ginger. She's petite enough to fit in his pocket, and when she giggles, the sound is sweet and cute, just like her.

"And we're still doing the name? Really?" she asks.

Unlike the rest of us, Ruby doesn't work at Honeywood, but she is an engineer. While she'd be the first to jump on the Mr. Roller Coaster tomato-throwing committee simply because she's a good friend, she's also not going to ignore his obvious talent. To her—and probably most people in the industry—he *is* important.

Plus, in her defense, Mr. Roller Coaster is a ridiculous name we established two years ago when his lawyer referred to him as the king of roller coaster design. We all laughed, and Quinn dubbed him Mr. Roller Coaster. It's a dumb name and only sort of funny at this point, but my friends would have done anything to make me laugh in that hospital bed.

Quinn points a finger over to Ruby. "He deserves the ridiculous name," she says.

"I could think of a different one, if that makes you feel better, Rubes," Bennett chimes in. "Like the Coaster Loser? The Roller Monster? Maybe the Swirling Satan?"

Ruby giggles. "Tornado Testicle?"

"Gross," he says. "I love it."

Bennett and Ruby exchange a small high five.

"Okay, Tweedledum and Tweedledee, let's pull it back," Quinn says with a roll of her eyes and a smile.

"Yes!" Ruby says. "Sorry. So, how'd it go?"

That comment is all it takes to have four sets of eyes staring me down. I can feel the weight of their gazes in my chest as my brain buzzes with what the heck I should even say.

Where do I even start with Emory?

The snark?

The height?

The eyebrows?

"We didn't talk much," I say.

They all groan at once, except for Quinn. She caught my lie.

"Think it's a lawyer thing?" Bennett asks. "Like he's been advised not to talk to you? I would assume your lawyer said the same thing."

I shift in my seat. "Maybe," I say. "Except I didn't exactly tell my lawyer Emory was in town."

Everyone's eyes widen at that statement. I take a quick swig of my beer and look away, as if going, *Ho-hum, I did nothing wrong, friends. Nothing at all.*

"You didn't tell your *lawyer*?!" Bennett asks.

"I didn't ..." I can't find the words, so I blow out air through my nostrils. "Listen, we're not here to judge me, okay?"

But there *are* judging glares.

Bennett has crossed arms. Ruby's lips are twisted to the side, as if she wants to say something but won't. Theo's big, blinking eyes are shocked. And Quinn raises a single, knowing eyebrow.

I want to curl into a hole and disappear. Bury me now. I'll even be buried alive. I don't care.

Theo breaks the ice by patting the table. "I wouldn't have said anything to him either," she says, tilting her head to the side. "Who needs those bad vibes, huh?"

"You're just being nice because you don't want Lorelei to lure you into picking up trash on the midway again, Theo," Bennett says with a barking laugh.

I crack a smile. I know my love for the midway is ridiculous.

And yet ... even Emory Dawson picked up trash. The guy in a suit who didn't have to.

Why though?

That's been bothering me more than anything else. After our meeting, he doesn't strike me as someone who deigns to touch anything used.

So, why did he help?

"Lore," Ruby says from down the table, "what did you talk about with Mr. Roller Coaster?"

I can tell it pains her to call him that. The sweetheart. Bennett notices too.

"All right, all right," Bennett says. "Let's just call him Mr. Dawson or something. Sounds more important."

I laugh. "I don't want to make him *more* important, Bennett."

Theo squirms in her chair and throws an arm up, as if wanting to be called on.

Quinn nods in her direction. "Yes, Theodora?"

"I propose Mr. Eyebrows."

"Mr. Eyebrows?" I ask with a weak smile.

"I passed him on the midway today," Theo says. "His eyebrows are thick, like caterpillars."

Bennett laughs. "Like Eugene Levy?"

"No, no, *much* sexier."

Sexier?!

"Who is sexier than Eugene Levy?" Bennett asks, arms folded.

"Bennett, my dear friend, listen ..."

The table buzzes into conversation, and I settle into the familiar madness.

The five of us see each other all the time, but it still never seems like enough. We're all joined at the hip, like different colors of Play-Doh mixed together over time. Inseparable.

I lean my head back and smile, trying to let the relief of a perfect night with friends wash over me instead of focusing on Emory Dawson.

His gaze.

His ticcing jaw.

His eyebrows, I suppose.

His *sexiness*.

But that doesn't change his attitude. His certified grumpiness.

I don't want to see him again. I don't want to hear his sarcastic words that bite with each flick of his tongue. I don't want a reminder of that lonely night in the dark.

At that moment, my phone buzzes. I glance down.

There's a new calendar event for tomorrow morning, titled Grizzly Analysis.

Scheduled with Emory Dawson.

Speak of the devil ...

My stomach flips, stumbles, and plummets into oblivion, barreling down into a banked turn, like a coaster gone mad.

Today was supposed to be my only meeting with him. We were supposed to discuss Honeywood theming and then part ways. And yet his calendar event illuminates my phone like the fabled bright light before death. I can see the end now.

I almost don't register Quinn's whisper to me.

My head pops back up, and the rest of the table has somehow moved on to the subject of Spice Girls and whether Bennett could be Scary Spice or Sporty Spice. Only Quinn was watching me zone out like I'd just gotten abducted by aliens.

What's wrong? she silently mouths.

I slide my phone over to her, and her mouth drops into an O.

"Drink refill?" she whispers.

I look to my almost-empty glass and nod, taking a final swig of my beer.

We stand, shimmying and sliding past grouped tables and to the bar, where I recognize every face, every genuine smile, every tip of a ball cap, including The Honeycomb's regular, Buck, and his pinched eyebrows.

"Hi there, Miss Lorelei," he says.

I grin. "Hi, Buck."

"You can take my stool, if ya need."

He's only being nice, I tell myself.

But he does this every time, I also say.

"Thanks, Buck," I say, plastering on a smile. "I'm fine standing though. No need to hop off on account of me."

"You're sure?"

Buck is one of a kind under that tattered trucker hat and toothy grin. I know he means well when he glances down to my hip. But that's the thing with small towns. People care. A lot. Sometimes too much.

At first, the gestures were kind. People offered to let me cut in line, so I wouldn't have to stand longer and put pressure on my leg. Guests at Honeywood were less prone to get upset with wait times if I was the one limping down the midway in my team member shirt. Over time, physical therapy allowed me to hide some of my pains in plain sight. The gestures lessened. But some people still treat me like I'm fragile. They still picture that weak woman in The Grizzly's broken car with my hands white-knuckling the lap bar.

I curl my lips in, holding in the tension in my chest and nodding at Buck's offer.

He means well.

He means well.

"I'm sure," I say.

"All right then. Well, tell your folks I said hello. I should go anyway. Be good now."

He hops off his stool, beer in hand, and carries that lie all the way to the opposite back wall, where he stares at me with his eyebrows tilted in.

He's hoping I take the stool anyway.

So, me being me, I do, guilt roiling through me.

"So, what was that calendar event about?" Quinn asks.

It's hard to concentrate when the tension in my chest feels like a fist clutching me for dear life. My body feels heavy, my heart sore from the weight of it all that never seems to go away. The way the town babies me and my injury.

"I don't know," I say, breaking eye contact with Buck, shaking my head. "Just more of Mr. Roller Coaster or whatever."

Quinn is silent, staring through me.

"I just ..." I sigh. "I didn't think I'd be working with him so much. I figured he'd be with Fred, but now, they want me to meet up *again*, and I'll have to see his eyebrows, and it's just ..."

"Deep breaths, lady." Her hand pauses on my forearm.

"Emory gave me *the look*," I say.

"Ah." Quinn nods slowly, her eyes darting to Buck, then back. "He gave you the *sorry you got your hip crushed* look."

"Of course he did."

"God, only an ass would build a defunct roller coaster and look at you like you're the one with the problem."

"I wish I hadn't seen him at all."

"Aw, lady." Quinn wraps her arm around my shoulders. "You couldn't have avoided him forever. But this day does deserve lots of Thin Mints. Tons."

"I don't think they're selling this time of year."

"Then we'll pick up some off brand on the way home."

Quinn understands me. We moved in together right after graduating high school, which was over ten years ago. If Georgia recognized domestic partnerships from extended joint residency, we'd be eligible. It'd make my life much easier if she were my platonic life partner.

I lean my head on top of hers—a natural place, given she's almost a foot shorter than me.

"Minty cookies would help," I say. "But not seeing him again would be better."

She snorts. "The last thing we want is *Mr. Dawson* making you hide in storage closets. You're better than that."

Am I?

I considered hiding in the maintenance building for the next four weeks, but I know Bennett wouldn't appreciate me loitering around while they're prepping for the season.

I can picture it now. *So, what does this wrench do?*

I smile and can feel how weary it must look.

"Ugh. *Mr. Dawson*," Quinn sneers. "I'm gonna kill Bennett for putting that in our heads."

I let out a small laugh. "It's fine, Quinn."

She sniffs, sucking in air. "Lore, be honest with me," she says. "Are you fine? You haven't been coming with me to yoga ..."

"The season is about to start," I say. "You know Honeywood. I don't have time. I have this promotion, the day-to-day, I'm still sometimes helping with Rides ..."

"Yeah, but ... you're less stressed when you go to yoga."

"I feel fine," I say with such a forced laugh that I can feel my face heat from embarrassment. "I'll go back soon. I'm just ... busy, is all. It's temporary. I gotta work hard this season. It's my first one as marketing manager. I don't want to lose everything I've worked for."

She blows out air. "Fine. I'll pass on the tough love for now. But listen to me." She takes my cheeks into her hands, and I can't help but giggle. "You, lady, are a beautiful ray of sunshine. You wear white after Labor Day and pastels on Halloween. Don't let him get you down."

I kiss the tip of her nose because if anyone understands, Quinn does.

"I would never," I say.

"Good," she says with a sharp nod. "Let the sunshine in. Just like the song."

"You know what else would let the sunshine in?"

"What?"

"Petting Mrs. Stanley's puppy."

Quinn rolls her eyes with a smile. "Okay, refills, then puppy time."

We get second place in trivia that night. Just barely and only with the help of Orson, who supplies the sports answer.

It's a good night at The Honeycomb. It always is.

But at the end of it all, when Quinn and I get home and sit on our back porch with books, blankets, and too many off

37

brand chocolate mint cookies, serenaded by the sound of clicking grasshoppers and entranced by the glow of blinking fireflies, I still find myself drowning in the inky sky above.

I breathe in, telling myself that Emory will not be the one to puff out my flame. I even close my eyes and try to drift off elsewhere, but all I can imagine is myself in a clicking car, cresting the peak of a darkened hill before falling into the unknown.

6

Emory

I'm not surprised when Honeywood's parkside hotel, The Hibernation, meets my already-low expectations.

The tiles in the bathroom could use some replacing. The closet door's hinges are wobbly. And there is a mural of Buzzy the Bear giving me a thumbs-up the moment I open my eyes for the day.

Terrifying way to start the morning.

But despite all this, they do know where the priorities are. The mattress practically breathes life into you. The combination of memory foam and their Honeywood canary-yellow blackout curtains almost makes me sleep in.

Almost, if I had the capacity to sleep longer than four hours each night.

After a morning run on the hotel's treadmill—one of only three options for outdated gym equipment—I open the curtains, sip on my Styrofoam cup of coffee, and peer out from the balcony to watch the sun rise over the park. The Grizzly's peak is silhouetted against the morning sun. It's admittedly quite pretty.

I built The Grizzly from scratch at sixteen, and I

personally did the test runs on the coaster on our tens of acres of land at home. We might have had a construction crew for the final installation, but the initial build was all me.

It's hard not to overthink whether the accident was our fault. I've come a long way as a designer and engineer since making The Grizzly, but I know the efforts that went into that build, and at the time, it was perfect.

I sigh, gripping the railing harder, seeing the whites of my knuckles.

But that doesn't change the fact that their marketing manager was hurt. That Lorelei wants to rip our company apart and bury the pieces.

Can I blame her?

"She's a snake," my dad said before I left. "She's taking us for all our money."

After meeting her, part of me agrees.

Granted, the man who told me this is the same man who dilutes most of his blood with alcohol nowadays, so I take what he says with a heaping pile of salt. But so far, with Lorelei coming out the gates, swinging, he hasn't been wrong about her yet. A stopped clock is still right twice a day, I suppose.

Someone stands at the top of the maintenance staircase on The Grizzly, leaning against the railing. I wonder what their maintenance team is doing up there. The ride has been closed since the investigation started. I grind my jaw before shaking it out.

I guess if their day is starting, mine should too.

I pick up my phone to check my calendar events and see a text waiting for me.

Mom: How's it going down in Georgia?

My mom and I share a love of travel. Though, while mine is spent for work, she's off, riding her motorbike across North America. I tell her she's a divorced woman cliché. She says she's patching into a motorcycle club soon. I don't know if she's joking.

My fingers hover over the screen. I normally send my thoughts on local tourist sites or hole-in-the-wall restaurants, but so far, all I have is a two-bit treadmill and a woman out for our blood.

I don't want to talk about Cedar Cliff or Honeywood. I change the subject instead.

Me: Where are you?
Mom: Somewhere in Kentucky. Don't change the subject.

She reads me too well.

Me: Georgia has been fine.

I swing on my blazer, the damn thing tugging at my arms like a straitjacket. I can't wait to get back into jeans and a work shirt, but business is business.

A monkey suit indeed.

Mom: How have you been managing stress?
Me: I run.
Mom: Have you found a yoga studio for your pain?

A biker, obsessed with yoga. She's an enigma, my mom. I adore her for it.

Yoga isn't necessary, but it does help. I have lingering pain from years of construction. I still keep in touch with my physical therapist, Wesley, for occasional sessions. Sometimes, stretching is all I need though.

But I'm not exploring this town more than I need to over the next four weeks.

Me: No.
Mom: I'll do research for you.
Me: You really don't have to.
Mom: I'm sure there's a yoga studio nearby.
Me: Don't you have a motorcycle club to join somewhere?
Mom: I always have time for you. Focus on the silver linings, my love.

She never fails to send this advice, like a fortune cookie with the same slip of paper every time.

My favorite fortune cookie—even if it is predictable.

I suppose when you've escaped the clutches of your ex-husband, it's easy to look on the bright side. I like that for her. Even if I see her less, I prefer she live out her adventures without the tyranny of Thomas Dawson's hammer. After what she went through, I'm happy she's sunny at all.

She's my moral compass I need to grasp on to. Sometimes, I forget that.

I send a GIF of a cartoon storm cloud with big eyebrows because I know it'll make her laugh.

I look at the rest of my messages. There's a text from Orson, telling me that we're watching the baseball game at his place tonight ("No negotiating!") and finally a message from my dad that simply says, *Call me.*

Good morning to you too.

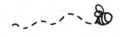

Per my mom, I try to find the silver lining at our morning meeting in Honeywood. Surprisingly, it's not hard.

While Fred and I meet at the front of the park with lazy smiles and travel mugs of coffee, Lorelei's hands are free, and she's running on nothing other than sheer sunshine. Or cocaine. I don't know her life.

She's all smiles, and it feels so different from the woman I met yesterday. But from her sideways glance at me, I realize this happiness isn't for me. It's for the park.

Of course. I'm just the means to her end.

But it's hard not to get sucked in to her orbit.

Lorelei has this cadence in the way she talks about Honeywood. Waving hands, accentuating each sentence; raising her eyebrows when she smiles; and some type of wizard skill at walking backward and narrowly missing benches or trash cans as she points out fun facts about each ride. I'm sure she's given a similar tour millions of times, but it doesn't seem rehearsed. It's passionate.

Her admiration radiates out of her, making her soft features glow, highlighting her pink lips and rosy cheeks. Her brown eyes have a joy to them that I can't help but admire. I don't ask questions. She answers them before I can open my mouth. She knows everything about this place.

But when we finally hit The Grizzly, a storm falls over her mood.

The change is instantaneous.

She trails a hand over the railing separating the queue line from the ride. Every so often, she looks up at it, no doubt at the banked turn on the far side—the place where her life changed forever. As if it stings, she immediately averts her eyes toward the ground and draws her hand back to her side.

My stomach clenches tight. It's like watching a pink

bubble pop. It doesn't feel natural. I feel my own eyebrows furrow, in awe of how, even in despair, she looks like a painting. But then she looks over at me, sees my expression, and narrows her eyes.

Right.

That's the look of a woman with a vendetta. Her cutting glare is all I need to see to confirm once and for all that my father is right. She might have a soft spot for this park, but not me. I'm the enemy.

Just like that, my guard comes back up.

I just need to do my job and leave.

"So, I have a few ideas for The Grizzly's reno," I say to her and Fred. "I'm imagining a launch coaster instead. We'll boost them up the lift hill right out the gate. It's modern, and most rides are doing this to increase rider capacity per hour."

"I love it," Fred says.

I think he'd love anything I said, but that's beside the point.

This is my favorite part of the job—giving the client a mental image of where the ride will be. It's like finally bringing the pot to a boil before we hit the ground running. I love seeing the excitement in the client's eyes.

At least, I would be happy about this if Lorelei were tuned in.

I start throwing my ideas out, and Fred catches each one with enthusiasm. His hands wring together as he waddles this way and that.

I offered a massive discount on construction—a concession dear ol' Dad thought was a terrible idea—and it's the discount that is fueling part of Fred's joy, I'm sure. You don't get this level of work with that cost. You just don't.

Whether my father agrees or not, this is the cure to our

current public relations nightmare. Sometimes, you have to soothe the clients. Sometimes, you have to do the right thing even if you don't know whether the mistake was yours.

Lorelei folds her hands in front of her and stares as I speak, as if she were looking right through me. It doesn't halt my stride.

"Once they go down the lift hill, we can add another launch," I say. "Really amp up the energy."

"Wonderful!" Fred says.

Lorelei remains quiet.

I grind my jaw, trying to stop myself mid-gesture. I went through too much dental work, only to grind them to a nub.

She either doesn't like my ideas or she doesn't trust them. I don't know which makes me more irritated.

"I think it'll be great," I say. "A good standard attraction."

Fred's face scrunches up.

That did not soothe as intended.

"Problem?" I ask.

"Well, we don't want standard, do we?" Fred asks. "We need something that matches our park. Has the feel of Honeywood."

This again.

If this were some park with award-winning hyper coasters in Europe, I might concede, but this is *Honeywood*, for Christ's sake. Some park in middle-of-nowhere Georgia. Theming is important, but for this type of ride? Not so much. I want to make sure it functions well. That's my priority.

"Best you have a baseline for what we represent, right?" Fred continues. "How about Lorelei shows you our other attractions tomorrow?"

"Me?"

It's the first word she's said in five minutes.

I can't help but feel the same anxiety.

She was supposed to be a quick consultant on this project. Not a permanent fixture.

Fred laughs. I find no humor in this, personally.

"He needs to ride them if he's going to understand our thrill level!" Fred says.

Her face is unreadable, as if there's some Southern small-town hospitality she's trying to maintain. She probably wants to push me off the top of The Grizzly. She wants to see me splat on the ground like a cartoon.

"Okay," she says, pasting a smile on her face. "Yes, of course."

Fred calls for lunch with a clap of his hands, wobbling back toward the offices and down the midway, waving to any team members who pass. And I'm left with Lorelei, whose smile has instantly dropped.

She twists on her heel to face the ride again, spending time with it like I'm not even here.

I shake my head.

The last thing I want is to work with her too. We're in a lawsuit, for Christ's sake. But if this is what Honeywood's general manager prefers and what will get me through these four weeks, then I'll work with her.

"This will be a tumultuous relationship if you can't talk to me," I say.

Her eyes flash over. Big, brown, and fueled with heat.

"Tumultuous?" she asks, a spit of fire to her words.

"I believe that's what I said."

"Well, I'm perfectly fine if you are."

Yeah, right.

The tone is stilted, and she might as well have said, *I would rather die.*

Get in line.

I put my hands in my pockets. I would have maybe leaned down to her level, but she's so close to my height that I don't even have to. Kind of kills my usual intimidation factor.

Instead, I take a step closer. I catch a whiff of her peachy perfume, or maybe it's just her natural aroma. Who the hell actually smells like peaches? Maybe it's a small-town thing, smelling like something grown from the earth—something clean and humble.

"You want to play hardball, and that's fine," I say. "But let's not be shy about it."

She narrows her eyes. "Good. There's no need for us to be friends," she says. "I will simply do my job if you can do yours."

"Funny, I thought I was."

Her jaw is set, and her eyebrows are tilted in the center, making a tiny crease between them. It might be cute if she wasn't poised for battle. She should have one sword in hand yelling, *FOR FREEDOM!*

I can't help but straighten up my spine.

Bring it on.

"What's on your mind?" I ask.

"You want to know my thoughts?" she says. "I think it's ridiculous that we're going to have the same engineer who created this coaster that randomly malfunctioned be the same engineer who fixes it."

"You don't know how many teams I have at my disposal virtually."

"I only see you here," she counters.

"And I'm enough for first evaluations."

"You weren't twenty years ago."

"Listen." I take one step forward. She doesn't budge.

"We're the best at what we do."

"Aren't we lucky?" she says.

My teeth grind again.

She tilts her head to the side, chewing at her lip. I inhale sharply at the motion before I realize I'm doing it. My chest feels tight. I immediately glance back up at her.

It's such a simple thing, but her bottom lip is so full that it's hard to ignore what effect that has on me. If she were anyone else, I might have asked for her number by now. Or at least considered it in my head. I'm not exactly one for asking people out.

"I will make the best version of this attraction that we can," I say. "Our company isn't going to be your problem unless you make it one."

She shifts back around, her eyes emblazoned. "You made your company my problem when the wheels ran off the track."

"We don't know what happened," I say. "As far as we're concerned, this isn't on us."

"So your lawyer says," she counters.

"I put trust in people who have education and experience to back up their specialties."

"I put trust in people who have earned it," she counters, taking a step closer.

We're nearly chest to chest. I suck in a breath before I can stop myself.

"If a surgeon botched an operation," she says, "I think I'd second-guess their so-called experience. And so far, you and your lawyer are zero for two."

She turns on her heel and walks down the midway.

And my heart is absolutely pounding.

7

Lorelei

"Everyone has their cards?"

We all hold up our five-by-five whiteboards that have been filled in with various names, situations, and quotes. It is Thursday night, which also means it's reality television bingo night. Nothing is more exhilarating than crossing off a square with the words *I'm not here to make friends*.

Now that I think about it, Emory would do well on a reality show with his outlook on life.

Ruby, being the only one in our group to own a house with more than one bedroom, hosts our shenanigans in her sunken den, next to the open kitchen overlooking the couches and television. I have my place on a barstool, cutting vegetables with Quinn.

"How'd it go with Mr. Roller Coaster today?" she whispers to me.

I can still see those eyebrows furrowing at me with pity behind them. And how, even being only a few inches taller than me, he still felt like a towering presence with his set jaw and impassive stare. Like a statue at a museum.

Emory Dawson is the last person I want to talk about because that means I'll have to figure out how to live my normal life with him now in it.

I shake my head feverishly.

Quinn understands, pulling her thumb and forefinger across her lips in a zipping motion.

I smile and mouth, *Thank you.*

"Is Bennett not coming?" Theo asks, popping a chip in her mouth as she walks by.

"No, he's with Orson tonight," Ruby says, picking at the side of her bingo card.

"Surprising the Wicked Witch didn't claim him," Quinn says.

"Oh, come on, no. Jolene isn't bad," Ruby says. But I see her worried expression.

I feel bad for Bennett's girlfriend, Jolene. I can't exactly blame her for limiting how often her boyfriend hangs out with four other girls. But we've tried to get her to join us too many times over the past couple years. I've personally invited her to movie nights, yoga, and even offered free passes to Honeywood. But most of the time, she doesn't even respond to our texts.

I wish I could be closer to her. We all would like to be. Bennett is like a brother to us.

Ruby is the only one who sees Jolene regularly, but that's the privilege of being best friends with Bennett since elementary school. Jolene might want him to have fewer female friends, but Ruby is like his conjoined twin. She isn't going anywhere.

Plus, Ruby is Jolene's biggest ally even if she doesn't know it. She's too nice to say what we all don't want to admit—well, everyone, except Quinn, that is.

"Jolene sucks."

50

Theo, Ruby, and I all chorus at once, "Quinn!" and, "Hey now!" and, "No!"

"Whatever," Quinn says, waving her vegetable cutting knife in the air. "I'd rather him bail on us for Orson. At least he's cool."

"Says every girl ever," Theo mutters, lifting an eyebrow. "The ladies at yoga are obsessed with him. I know far too much about his ... private life."

"You have zero room to talk," Quinn says with a laugh. "Who was that guy you met from Atlanta the other day?"

"Oh, Big Dick McGee?" Theo says, popping a pepper in her mouth and chewing it obnoxiously on purpose.

Theo is not shy about her active sex life. She relishes in it.

"Yes, your latest one-night beau," Quinn says.

"My sexy adventures are different," Theo says. "I don't spread my seed around Cedar Cliff like he does."

"We talk like Orson has slept with everyone in town," I say. "Name one person."

"Literally all the other yoga instructors," Theo deadpans. "I now know which positions he prefers."

"And how is our bar friend Orson?" Quinn asks. "Talented in the sack as much as he is with making drinks?"

"Why?" Theo asks. "Wanting to try him out?"

Quinn smirks. "Don't project your wants onto me, Theodora."

"Not my type," Theo says, straightening up. "He's shorter than me. Doesn't matter how charming he is."

"Ooh, you said he's charming," Ruby says with a giggle.

"You're curious," Quinn says. "You just won't admit it to yourself."

"Whatever." Theo rolls her eyes. "Bennett can miss

reality TV night with whomever he wants. We'll see him next week."

"Not me and Lore," Quinn says.

I slap my forehead. "Oh, yikes, I forgot."

With my mind distracted by Emory, I almost forgot next week is our preseason family dinner. My parents know they won't see us once the summer season gets rolling.

Family dinners used to be just me and my twin brother, Landon, and our parents up until high school. But Quinn's parents had a divorce that led to many nights of her crashing on our couch. After a while, she became like a second daughter to my parents. Our family events are her family events.

"Oh, saying hi to your best friend?" Theo asks Quinn.

Quinn rolls her eyes hard. So hard that I see the whites of them, and I wonder if they got stuck for a moment.

"I'll be sure to tell the human toe jam I hope he falls from the highest drop ride this season," Quinn says.

Ruby giggles alongside Theo. They think the angsty rivalry between Quinn and my brother is hilarious. And sure, it might be, but once they're put in the same room together, it's like cats and dogs. I think I literally saw fur fly one time. I don't even know where it came from.

Landon works in security at some warehouse in Tennessee. We don't see him as much anymore. But the day he moved, Quinn brought home a cheesecake.

Quinn starts on a rant about my brother. No doubt talking about how he's a human golden retriever—which isn't untrue—but I focus in on Ruby.

She's still a bit distant, leaning against the counter, circling her finger over the bingo card. I thought I was shy and quiet, but when I met Ruby, she changed the meaning of what *shy* even is.

The dynamic of our five-person friend group is never really the same when any one of us is missing—especially when Bennett is gone. Even though we're all close, he's Ruby's social crutch. Her glue. Ruby needs a distraction from Bennett's absence, and unfortunately, I can provide the only thing that might help. Even if it kills me to talk about him.

"So, uh, Mr. Roller Coaster told me about his plans today," I say.

"Oh yeah?" Her head perks up, eyebrows rising.

Knew that'd get her. Her love for engineering will overpower anything.

"Yeah," I say. "He's thinking of adding launches."

"Oh, wow," Ruby says, splaying her hands on the counter. "Hard and fast. I love it."

"Probably how he is in bed," Quinn mutters.

My face instantly catches fire. I don't want to think of that man in bed. He's probably boring and only does missionary and never reciprocates oral. If I had to guess.

So, why does my mind want to imagine the opposite? A dude who takes charge?

It's his strength. I noticed it when we shook hands for the first time. His felt rough with a couple nicks here and there. I wonder if he's still active in the construction process, sweaty and manhandling steel parts.

Don't think about his steel parts.

"And how are you feeling about it all, Lore?" Ruby asks.

I shake my head, clearing my thoughts of his hard, rigid, long steel.

Crap.

"He's just a corporate guy," I say. "Make one coaster, then move on to make the next, you know? Kind of an ass."

"Of course he is," Quinn says.

53

Ruby tilts her head to the side with a sigh. "He's probably been working hard his whole life and forgotten how to develop people skills. Knows more about the numbers."

"Okay, let's not give this dude some imaginary sob story," Quinn says.

"Well, you make one tiny change when it comes to engineering, and the whole thing can get blown apart," Ruby continues. "He's probably more technical-minded and focusing on getting things right instead of being concerned with entertaining people. Nothing wrong with that. I'm sure he entertains fine."

"With looks like his?" Theo jumps in, blowing out a raspberry with her tongue. "Yeah, I don't think he has problems with entertaining others, if you get me."

Ruby raises her eyebrows and pouts out her lower lip, as if to say, *Really?*

"Hey, don't look at me!" I say, holding up my hands.

Theo waves her drink with a grin. "Well, whatever! Fred and I are operating your rides tomorrow, so I'll be the judge of that!"

"Oh, wow, you're working with him again?" Ruby asks, leaning on the counter with her chin in her palm.

"I don't really have a choice," I say. "And it's clear he doesn't trust me at all."

"Who couldn't trust this face?" Theo says, placing her palm out to hover just below my chin.

I laugh. "I don't know ... I just ... I need this to go well."

"It's not like Fred'll demote you," Quinn says with a shrug. "I've been slacking as Queen Bee for years, and he keeps me coming back."

I don't say it, but somehow, this feels different. A management role this high up isn't taken lightly, and he's made that clear from day one. My gut says he wouldn't make me step down. We've worked together since I was a teen but ...

"Freddy's fun, but he is also fair," Theo says. "He won't fire you, but you'd probably go back to Rides."

Quinn's eyebrows rise in understanding.

Rides. Where I'd be working close with coasters. Where I transferred out of after my injury.

I shake my head. "I have to work with Emory if I'm gonna keep this job past this season," I say.

"Then, be cordial," Ruby says. "That's all you can do."

"Or you could make his life a living hell," Quinn says.

"Or you could be cordial," Ruby repeats.

Right.

I can do cordial.

8

Emory

It's nice to get away from Honeywood's property.

I sit on Orson's couch with a water in hand, zoning out to baseball. At one point, he whoops. I wonder what happened in the game. I don't ask but instead take another gulp of my water, emptying the glass. I walk to the kitchen to refill.

The couch shifts behind me, and when I turn, Orson's elbow is hanging over the edge.

"Hey, Dawson."

"What?"

"You're quieter than usual," he says.

"I didn't think that was possible."

"Ha! You're fun when you tell jokes."

"It wasn't a joke."

He narrows his eyes with a smile as the doorbell rings.

I forgot he invited his other friend Bennett. I think he's the head of maintenance at the park. I'm very interested in meeting the man who's been overseeing The Grizzly the past few years. Enough investigations have shown that

Lorelei's accident wasn't Honeywood's fault, but my father has kept me skeptical.

Orson goes up the spiral staircase to the first floor, returning two minutes later with a tall man who might as well be a sports player himself.

"Brought the goods," Bennett says, waving a small six-pack of beer in the air.

Orson looks from me to Bennett. It's a subtle motion, almost imperceptible, but the man beast in front of him catches it.

"Sorry," Bennett says. "Is that an issue?"

"No," I insist, waving a hand at him.

The look of realization when it hits people that I don't drink is my worst nightmare. I told Orson to get beer for the two of them, but he insisted on a dry household while I visited. It's kind—it really is—but the last thing I want is to inconvenience people. I don't have the heart to say that it isn't *me* with the drinking problem, but my dad.

I choose not to drink so that it's one less vice I inherit from my father, but that doesn't mean I mind if others indulge.

I shoot out my hand, trying to break the tension as quickly as possible. "I'm Emory."

Bennett's eyebrows rise to the top of his head. Something tells me he knows who I am.

He slaps his hand in mine, shaking firmly. His palm is practically a bear paw.

"Bennett," he says. "And unfortunately, I've heard a lot about you."

Orson grins and tosses a thumb over his shoulder. "This guy." He claps Bennett's back.

Orson is stocky and muscular, and he's on the shorter side. Probably five-seven, if I had to guess. But next to

Bennett and me, he looks smaller. The good thing about Orson is, he has the confidence to not care.

Orson walks back over to the couch, but not before grabbing a beer as discreetly as he can, which, for Orson, just means he tries to carry it low to his stomach. He did the same motion when he snuck cookies out of our grandmother's jar when we were kids, as if carrying it lower camouflaged the gesture. He shouldn't get a career in robbing banks anytime soon.

Before I can say anything else, Bennett is cracking open his beer with a bottle opener from his rattling key chain. There are enough keys on there to rival a prison guard.

"Your girl, Lorelei, is one of my best friends," he says.

My girl, Lorelei.

My chest clenches at that. That we would even be considered close enough for any form of possession is odd to me. And yet why is my hand flexing in reaction to that? I shake it out.

"That right?" I ask. "And how's her impression of me?"

He shrugs. "That you're an ass."

Orson barks a laugh from his place on the couch.

Lovely.

"Last I checked, you're a tough guy to sue too," Bennett continues.

Orson calls from the couch, "That checks out," before leaping in the air with a holler at whatever goal the team just made before plopping back down.

When I look back to Bennett, his eyes are still fixed on me, one brow lifted.

He would be an intimidating guy if I were the type of man to be intimidated. He's bulky, tattooed on his right arm from the wrist up, winding around until it disappears under his sleeve. The only remotely soft thing about him is the small, thin piece of pink string knotted around his bony wrist.

"So, how're you likin' Cedar Cliff?" he asks.

"I haven't gotten out much aside from this."

"Well, it's got just as much character as Honeywood. I'll tell ya that."

"Born and raised here?" I ask.

"Me and most everyone else," he says with a chuckle. "I'm sure it's a culture shock, huh?"

"Sort of," I say.

"Emory's from a small town too," Orson interjects, a sort of acting participant in the conversation.

When Bennett seems interested with another rise of his eyebrows, I shake my head quickly.

"Again, sort of. There's not much of a town. It's more like a secluded piece of land with a population of me, my parents, and all the backyard coasters we built," I say. "It's the only way we could have too much land for too little money. We were maybe an hour from the closest grocery store. My mom did a lot of gardening."

Bennett smiles. "Mine too."

He seems like a decent guy. I only know this because, like Orson, he's also discreetly scooting the beer closer to his chest, as if to hide it from sight. I feel the corner of my mouth twitch at the oddly good-natured gesture.

Fine. I can try friendship.

"So, what do you guys do around here?" I ask.

"Well, we don't have backyard coasters, but we do have trivia," Bennett says. "We go every week. Me and the girls."

"The girls?"

"Lorelei and a few others. They're all like sisters to me," he says with a laugh, but he falters for a moment before adding, "Sorta."

I don't overlook the weird bit of guilt on his face.

Part of me wonders if he likes Lorelei, and something in me shifts a little, like an itch inside my chest I can't scratch. I don't know why. Lorelei has a home here, a life with friends and people who get to see her bubbly personality.

But not me.

I find myself saying, "I promise I'm not trying to make her life difficult."

Bennett furrows his brow. "Who? Lorelei?" His motion seems stilted.

Who else?

When I say nothing in confusion, he laughs, shaking his head.

"Right. Of course," he says. "Nah, it's fine, man. Lorelei is fine. I'm just protective of them all. But she's a big girl. She can handle herself. Just wait until the park opens. She's amazing in action. They miss her in the Rides department."

"Did she work with the coasters?"

"Oh, yeah," he says. "Adored everything about it. Couldn't stay away from Honeywood if she tried. Just hasn't been able to touch one since."

"Why?"

"Fear, if I had to guess," he says with a deep sigh, absentmindedly taking a swig of beer. I think my silence brings him back because he clears his throat and shakes his head. "But, listen, I didn't tell you that, all right?"

"Of course."

Lorelei's apprehension toward coasters kicks me in the gut in a funny way. I understand what it's like to fear what you love.

I look down, and as if he read my thoughts, my father's name pops up on the phone screen once more.

"Need to take that?" Bennett asks.

"I can call back."

I mute the call right as Bennett grins.

"I can put in a good word with Lore, if you want. I don't think you're an ass yet."

"Yet," I say.

He claps me on the shoulder with his meaty hand and a bellowing laugh. "I guess we'll see."

9

Lorelei

I love the way the sun rises over Honeywood. It crests the statue of Buzzy and Bumble, shining right between where their stone meets, creating a ray of light that highlights the midway like some destined path before a long journey.

I unlock the iron gates to the right of the entrance turnstiles. It's not the staff entrance, but it's early enough in the day that I enjoy entering the park like a guest, observing what they will see. I used to run the length of the park each morning pre-Grizzly attack. Now, I just walk. It's still peaceful.

We have three weeks until the park officially opens, and I can feel the energy start to pick up. In a few hours, the rides will be tested with empty cars zooming over the tracks, only missing their key element of guests' screams.

I lock the gate behind me and walk past the offices, instead opting to go down the left side in the fork, passing our gift shop, The Bare-Naked Necessities; the kiddie coaster, Little Pecker's Joyride; our medium-thrill roller coaster, Bumblebee's Flight; all the way down secret paths to our signature coaster, The Grizzly.

The faded orange beast was the highlight of any guest's Honeywood experience. It had a type of charm to it, regardless of its crippling age and outdated track that led to occasional neck pain for people who had ridden it more than three times in a day. It closed indefinitely once they couldn't find the source of my accident. Too much of a danger to the public.

"Hey, buddy," I say.

I creak open the queue line gate, walk down the single-rider section, and trek up the many, many maintenance steps to reach the top of the first lift hill.

It gets breezy once you hit the twentieth stair, and by the time you're at the crest, it's downright chilly.

I lean against the railing, breathing in the cool morning air. It's only me and the beast this early, and when it's just us, I can almost feel the tension breezing away in the wind.

I can't bring myself to ride him again. I won't even after the renovations are finished. But there's a weird sense of camaraderie between us. I imagine this is how retired fishermen feel about the sea. And, yes, I just compared myself to a crusty, bearded man.

Out of the corner of my eye, I notice someone else at the bottom of the lift hill.

Who in the world would be here this early?

But I instantly know who.

He's tall and donned in denim and a quilted jacket, fitted to a T to his shoulders. He adjusts the coat collar as he looks up at me, and my stomach shifts.

Freaking Emory Dawson.

Do I wave?

I can't *not* say hey; it'd be weird. We'll be working together all day. But also, the last thing I want is for him to—

Right. Okay. Now, he's climbing the stairs. Perfect.

I tighten my grip on the railing.

What do we do? What do we talk about? The weather? I'm not a meteorologist. What even was the forecast today? Also, why in the world does it seem like he's not getting out of breath at all?

Each stair he takes is barely conquered before he's pounding his boots up to the next. He's The Terminator. I'm convinced.

When he reaches two steps below me, he looks up through thick eyelashes. A moment passes before he lifts his eyebrows and I take a step to the side to allow him on the same platform as me, right at the top.

It's silent. I wonder if he can hear my heart pounding in my chest to the beat of *why is he here, why is he here?*

Out of the corner of my eye, I peek him staring out at the sunrise, barely moving, save for a small twitch in his left hand that grasps the railing.

He smells like a candle. Mahogany. Cedar. All the woodsy scents, combined into one. I take a deeper whiff of it. Don't judge me.

"I would have thought," he starts, and I rebalance myself when I jump at the sound of his low voice, "that someone who survived this ride twice would be less inclined to continue going on it."

Shots fired this early? Is he kidding?

No, we're supposed to work together.

Channel your inner Ruby.

Cordial. Be cordial.

"It's a comfort," I say.

There. Personal info. Maybe if I offer up some, he'll do the same.

He pauses for a moment, and then, in a slow drawl, he asks in the most sarcastic tone, "How?"

Screw cordial. I'm taking Quinn's advice to make his life miserable.

"Okay, why are you here?" I spit out. "I would have thought you'd avoid it."

He doesn't say anything, and I'm almost too nervous to look and see if he's offended.

"I'm not ashamed of this ride," he says. "I mean, you guys haven't exactly taken care of it—"

"That's nice. Very polite to insult a park you're visiting."

"Have you *seen* this place?" He turns to me, thick eyebrows raised.

It takes me a second to find my words.

"Honeywood is a sacred landmark," I say.

He scoffs. "For who? Cedar Cliff townies?"

"For America."

"Real patriotic there."

"For theme parks," I correct. "It's a staple. Like Old Faithful or the Grand Canyon."

Another pause.

"You think it's on par with *monuments*?" he deadpans.

I tense at his continued sarcasm.

"Surprised?" I ask.

He lets out a breath of air—or ... is it laughter?

"We've been featured in dozens of magazines."

"When?" he asks. "The '80s?"

Yes.

"Just because you can't see that we're great," I say, "doesn't mean people don't like nostalgia."

"Nostalgia," he says, as if testing the word. "Of what? The failed children's books?"

"They didn't fail," I say with a scoff. Then, I clear my throat. "The movie adaptations did."

Birds, Bees, and Bears, a children's book written by a woman named Honey Pleasure—no kidding—was published in the '70s and subsequently developed into a live-action film. This park was built on the hopes that this new movie, *Honeywood*, would do well. Except it flopped horrifically. The world was not ready for bug-eyed 3D depictions of cartoons. In their defense, the technology wasn't there yet either. It's actually kind of a weird movie. We focus our marketing more on the books.

"Is that why you're here?" Emory asks. "The memories?"

"You clearly don't get it."

"Believe it or not, I know how to make a decent ride experience."

"This *is* an experience," I press. "A fun one. A cherished one. Just 'cause it doesn't have five loops ..."

"Right. Honeywood's lack of thrills is my problem." His toe touches the track. Chips of paint fall off.

"People like simplicity with heart," I say. "We give them that."

"Sure, a good story is important. People like fun thrills. You're telling me, you really don't like the idea of a launch coaster? Instead of a slow-clicking lift hill, you get a boost—"

"I know what a launch coaster is," I say. "I've worked in a theme park most of my life."

He turns to me, staring for a moment. "Why?" he asks.

"What?"

"Why have you been here so long? Don't people stop

working at theme parks around twenty? You're not twenty, are you?"

"I'm twenty-nine, thanks," I say. "What are you, eighty?"

"I'm sure not working at a theme park."

"This might come as a shock to you, but sometimes, people love things," I say. "I love the sounds, the smells, the feel of it all. I love the fireworks on Memorial Day and Fourth of July. I used to love running through the midway each morning. If you don't understand what makes this park special, you never will."

He pauses before saying, "Fireworks?"

"Yeah, the colorful blowing-up things?" I ask. "The things that normally make people happy?"

"I just didn't think people did fireworks outside of the big tourist parks."

"Well, we do. They're special."

"They're loud and not worth the money."

"I don't have a problem with that if it makes people happy."

He grimaces. "Of course you don't."

"Excuse me?"

He looks to me and shakes his head. "We both know why you're still in a lawsuit with me."

My entire being feels like it's shaking with anger. I've never felt so amped up in my life.

"You don't even know me," I bite out. "Don't pretend that you do."

I decide I don't want to spend another second with this condescending man if I don't have to.

"I'll see you at the nine o'clock with Theo and Fred," I say. "Don't fall up here."

"Why? Are you planning on pushing me?"

I scoff. "Sure would solve a lot of my problems, wouldn't it?"

"Are you always this pleasant?" he asks.

"Are you?"

"Always."

I go to leave, but he doesn't budge.

I give a fake, forced smile and shimmy past him to get to the stairwell. I underestimate how bulky he is because I lose my footing, feeling the air whoosh out of me as I start to fall.

Shit, shit, shit!

Emory's hand grabs my puffy jacket in a fist, pulling me forward and letting me fall against him.

We're chest to chest, breathing the same panicked air. I can see every bit of him now—how his pretty-boy face is actually rugged and rough. There's a small scar on his cheek, another faint abrasion on his chin with dark stubble shrouding it.

I inhale right when I meet his eyes and quickly pull away, sidestepping to the right of him, pausing before the first stair downward.

"Don't touch me," I wrestle out.

Wow, good one, Lore.

"You're welcome for saving your life," he says.

His tone makes my blood boil. Everything about him— from his gorgeous looks to his arrogant demeanor—irritates me.

I say the first thing that comes to my mind.

"Well, I'll have a bad hip forever because of your clever ride, so how about we call it square?"

I'm not proud of it. In fact, I cringe the second the words leave my mouth, but the anxiety of the near fall, combined with how he overwhelmed every part of me, urged the words forward like a bad sickness over a toilet bowl.

It takes a moment before his eyebrows contort further, dragging inward. God, that look. The look I can't stand.

Pity.

I descend the stairs with my now-shaky hand clutching on to the rail, wondering how in the world we're supposed to work together.

10

Lorelei

"I'm sorry, but *this* is not the Mr. Roller Coaster I saw," Theo hiss-whispers. "I thought suit-wearing Eugene Levy was hot but—"

"Theo, stop with the Eugene Levy."

"I mean, Mr. Dawson, *hello*."

"Theo, he'll be back any second!"

She grins. "What, like you didn't notice the tiny bit of super-manly chest hair at the top of his shirt?"

I cross my arms, walking toward the door where both of us lean out the doorframe, like two floating Muppet heads. We tilt them to the side as he bends over to place down his wallet and keys in the hallway locker.

"Stop staring," I whisper, dragging her back in my office.

He's not in his usual suit. Today, Emory is wearing well-cut denim with a leather belt, worn with aged lines of light and dark brown. He has on a heather-gray T-shirt that is fitted around his broad chest and shoulders. With each step, you can see his abs constricting, showing exactly how built he is underneath.

Emory walks in two seconds later with his hands in his

pockets and a blank stare on his face. He almost looks like a normal human instead of a corporate drone. I prefer the suits. They reflect his stone-cold heart better than this getup.

After he implied that I was suing him simply for the money, my nerves have been on fire. And given my last sniping remark, he doesn't seem like he's any less on edge either.

Theo reaches out her hand. "Theodora. Call me Theo. I'll be one of your operators today, Mr. ..."

"Dawson."

I expect a further correction—*Call me Emory!*

I'm not surprised to find that's not the case.

"Fantastic," Theo says with a grinning nod.

She's never been deterred by sullen, sour men. She's normally the one who breaks them down, melts their hearts into putty for her to knead and mold.

But Emory just stares at her with a blank expression.

Her lips tip up, and she swings the key fob around her finger.

"What's first?" she asks. "Fred is busy, so we can only do things that require one operator for now."

"Oh, I can take Fred's place. I'm not riding today," I say. "We can start with The Beesting."

"Darn, I love seeing you on that ride," she says, letting out an easy laugh. "Your screams are hilarious."

"Sicko," I say with my first smile of the morning.

It's hard not to smile around Theo. I notice Emory beside me furrow his brow. I bet he's disgusted by any form of happiness.

Well, Mr. Man, you *disgust me.*

We push out of the office's saloon double doors and onto

the midway right as Emory says, "You're not riding with me?"

His voice almost makes me jump. Not to mention, the ... implication.

Me and Emory? Riding ...

No.

Stop.

"You're learning today," I say, probably a bit too short. "I'm just the tour guide."

"How can you market rides you don't get on?"

Even Theo's eyebrows rise up to the top of her hairline. She just keeps swinging her keys on her finger, as if she were a fly on the rope of our boxing match.

"I've ridden them before," I shoot back to him.

"How long has it been?"

"I can remember how a ride feels," I say.

We stand in front of The Beesting one minute later. It's a classic drop tower with seats encircling the whole of the ride. It raises you high in the air and accelerates you downward, so you experience the weightless freefall. Emory walks to one of the many open seats.

"You know, Lore," Theo chimes in, "I'm operating anyway. Why don't you go have fun? When *was* the last time you rode this one?"

I couldn't twist on the heel of my sneaker any faster if I tried. This ride isn't a difficult one for me. In fact, most attractions are not a problem. It's the roller coasters that I avoid. But I don't want to ride because then I'd be one hundred feet in the air, alone with Emory.

I'd rather be forced to eat pudding with a fork.

"Lorelei, come on," Emory's bored voice calls from the ride. "We don't have all day."

I want to yell at him that we do, but that's beside the point.

I narrow my eyes at Theo, as if to say, *See if I agree to loan you a tampon next time*, but it's an empty threat.

"Okay, fine, fine," I say.

I grab the seat next to Emory—because I know it'd be weird if I didn't—and strap into The Beesting. Once I give Theo the thumbs-up, we instantly rise, my breath catching with it.

From the top of the ride, we can see a lot of Cedar Cliff —the historic downtown area and a couple neighborhoods. There are crowds of trees, some distant mountains, and the highway beyond, filled with what look like Matchbox cars.

It's in that moment that I realize just how close we are for the second time this morning.

I immediately look away.

He doesn't speak.

Neither do I.

But Ruby's little voice echoes through my ears.

Cordial.

Be professional.

So, I ask, "Do you like these rides?"

"Oh, so you're nice to me now?"

I know I was a jerk on The Grizzly. But so was he.

"I'm trying to make conversation," I say.

"I don't think we should be talking unless it's work-related."

"Coming from the man who walked up the million steps to my coaster this morning and talked to me about nothing."

"Your coaster," he whispers, almost like a breath with the wind. If it wasn't so quiet this far up, I might not have heard it at all.

I say nothing, swallowing instead, trying not to glance down.

Why the heck hasn't Theo dropped us yet?

"What do you think makes a coaster thrilling?" he asks.

"What?"

"The marketing manager should know, right?" he continues. "What do you think makes a coaster great?"

"You're the expert," I say.

"Answer the question."

"I don't know." I look down. *Huge mistake.* "Heights?"

"It's testing the limits," he answers.

"You test the limits too far maybe." All sense of reasonable talk leaves my mind with the anticipation of the drop. I sound like a person pleading for their life.

"You never know what will happen if you don't," Emory answers. "That's the risk of my business."

That comment does me in. Not the nerves of our height, but the callous, unfeeling way he said that.

"Really spoken like a true businessman." I can hear the edge in my voice, and I don't know if I've ever mustered that much poison on my tongue. I feel guilty about it, but I'm too worked up to care anymore. "I don't like being collateral damage to your risks, Mr. Dawson."

"Watch it." His tone shifts completely, a harsh edge to it, a bitter taste.

My comment hit a nerve. And for some reason, my stomach drops. Not because the ride does—because it still hasn't—but because of the sharp way Emory's word came out. I can feel it in my gut. Then, much to my disdain, right between my thighs.

"Don't speak to me like that," I say.

He scoffs. "I can see why you're in marketing. Just

putting on a face for the public. But up high, with nobody around, you're not afraid to show your true colors."

My chest feels on fire. He's infuriating.

"Sorry I'm not nice to the man who keeps insulting me."

"Sorry I'm not nice to the woman trying to drain our company dry. I'm sorry for your accident. I am. But—"

"I'm not after your stupid money, Emory!" I say, huffing out air. "I just want to know what happened. So, if those are my true colors, then so be it. Maybe my true colors don't mix well with your blackened heart."

The air gets ripped from around us. It's silent as his eyes roam my face. Searching. But for what, I don't know.

He finally says, "I'm not a fish."

"What?" I bite out.

"Fish can be blackened," he mutters. "I can't have a blackened heart because I'm not a fish."

"Funny," I deadpan. "Well, you're o-*fish*-ally an ass."

"No, my humor is e-*squid*-sit."

I narrow my eyes. "Did you just ..."

For a moment, I think his eyes dart down to my lips and back up. There might even be a twitch at the edge of his mouth.

My insides twist. I swallow.

In a split second, it feels like my bottom has dropped out, and every nerve in my body that's been building in my gut gets whooshed out of me as the ride finally falls.

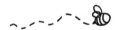

We make it to the first of our track-based roller coasters next, Little Pecker's Joyride. It's a kiddie coaster with barely any height or thrill to it. The instant we arrive at the station, I do not follow him on, but instead step to the side.

He raises an eyebrow. "No?"

I shake my head. "My leg can't handle a lot of bumpy things," I lie. "I'll be the other operator since Fred is busy."

I feel my heart settle in my chest, and even Theo shifts from one foot to the next, crossing her arms and leaning against the operator booth's doorframe.

I don't want to admit my fear to Emory. I don't want to explain the way my stomach clenches up tight and how my airflow feels like it stops in my throat, not allowing oxygen to reach the rest of my body. It doesn't matter how many times I try to breathe heavy, dragging in mouthfuls of air; nothing seems to fill the hole in my chest at the top of that lift hill.

When I went to group therapy, they used to tell me it was likely a panic attack. But part of me wonders if maybe I'm just defective now—a product of the fear ingrained into me, incapable of enjoying the thing that once felt comforting.

"I know the ride just fine," I say.

His eyebrows tilt in, and, God, I wish he could stop looking at me like that for even one second. It's like he thinks I'm pathetic and small. It hurts even more because I know I am.

I punch the second button with Theo that sends Emory off on the ride without another word or glance in my direction.

"Boy, he's a delight, isn't he?" Theo says with a snort.

"Delightful as pulp in orange juice."

"Those pants are misleading."

I sigh, and she rubs my back.

"Sorry for leaving you guys up on The Beesting," she says. "I thought maybe y'all needed time to talk."

I grumble, "I think it only made things worse."

Now, I know he makes puns.

We watch the lone, rigid figure of Emory cycle through, looking like someone put Frankenstein's monster in a little red wagon.

We try The Romping Meadow, our boat ride, next. We don't talk when we bob into the water and under the cave entrance. We only hear the soft waves. The cool air of the enclosed area sends chills down my spine.

I should probably say something—be some form of a gracious host—but I'm keeping my hands and feet inside the bitter-emotions vehicle at all times. The embarrassment of not riding the other attractions digs itself deep inside me.

Colorful lights pour from the ceiling, highlighting the singing animatronics. Honeywood's mascot, Buzzy the Bear, holds a fish. The bees float around him on strings, and he sways back and forth, back and forth, all on repeat.

"We can't work like this," Emory suddenly says.

When I don't respond, he continues.

"I've got a job to do," he says. "So do you. Am I right?" I nod, but he must not see it because he bites out a small, irritated, "Come on, Lorelei. I'm trying here."

"Yes," I say. "Yes, I do. I ..." *Cordiality means opening up. Just do it.* "I just got promoted actually. I need this. I'm here for the long haul."

"But you won't ride coasters?"

I grind my teeth. "It's complicated," I say.

"Is it The Grizzly?"

I gulp. "Yes. He just hurt me two times too many. He's like a blind animal that doesn't know what it's doing."

He pauses before muttering, "You think of rides like animals?"

"They are in a way," I say. "He doesn't know any better."

All I get is a small, "Hmm," and in the dark, I can't see what his expression is, even when I try to squint.

I continue, "I only want what's best for the park ... even if you *do* think Honeywood is all a load of bull."

"I want to fix whatever turmoil we've caused," he says. "Did that ever occur to you?"

He does? He feels guilty?

"No," I say.

"We need our PR fixed just as much as your park does," he says. "Your ... the ride's ... two accidents are making us lose contracts. Let me do my job; I'll let you do yours."

Never mind. So, it's not about fixing my—or even Honeywood's—turmoil. It's about bettering his company's reputation.

Business, business, business.

"Fine," I say.

He stares for a bit too long before looking away.

"Good," he finally responds.

Emory clears his throat, and when I look over, I see his hand extended. I glance up at him. He's staring at me, those intense eyes boring through to my soul. It's the expression that rarely seems to falter unless he's giving me the look of *oh, this poor girl*. But he isn't doing that now. He's all hand-shakes and contracts, like the good suit that he is.

I place my palm in his, my much-too-slender fingers getting engulfed in his large hand. They're callous at the fingertips, and I can feel the veins running along the back of them.

My stomach flips.

I shake once.

His hand lingers in mine, the warmth spreading up my forearm and to my elbow. For a moment, I think his pinkie trails a line along the outside of my palm, but he pulls away before I'm sure.

My heart pounds for the rest of the ride.

We don't talk much after that. Attraction after attraction passes, and our day finally ends in front of The Grizzly.

I've already resigned myself to another pitying look from him when we pass. But to my surprise, he doesn't do that.

Emory stands there, staring at me.

"You built the ride," I say. "If you feel so confident that it's safe, go for it. We still inspect it every day and send a train through to keep it maintained. We haven't found anything."

"No," he says.

"What?" I ask.

"I won't ride it if you can't."

"Why?"

And for a weird moment, his breath is shaky on the exhale.

"I've got a lot of work to do." He swallows before he nods and says, "I'll see you next week, Lorelei. It was nice to meet you, Theo."

He walks away, hands in pockets, and I'm burning with too many unanswered questions.

11

Emory

The phone call starts like throwing knives.

"Emory."

"Dad."

"How's it going down there?"

"Fine."

The calls with my father are not filled with laughs or inside jokes. We don't talk about the sports game on television, and he doesn't give parental advice.

Thomas Dawson and I have business-only discussions, and that's that.

I'm pacing my hotel room, trying to avoid the stare of Buzzy's mural with the mocking thumbs-up.

I ignored my dad's calls for a week, and that was too long for his taste.

Sometimes, I try to pin down the exact moment our relationship changed. Maybe it was when I was ten years old and I first smelled his breath reeking of bourbon. Maybe it was when I was fourteen and he told me I wasn't smart enough to be an engineer. Or maybe at sixteen, when he realized I was. Maybe at twenty-five, when he took back the

CEO position after making a full recovery in the hospital. Maybe it was when I was twenty-eight and I realized he'd shoved Mom.

I have some memories of him laughing. I remember the time he, Mom, and I rolled in the grass with tears in our eyes after he launched himself into a tree with the backyard zip line.

"You can make a loop, but not a straight line!" she said.

My mom never let him live that down.

The only time she didn't bring it up was when she walked out.

The jokes were over at that point.

I would have followed had she not asked me to keep making coasters.

"This is your calling," she said.

I wouldn't have seen his face for one more day if I hadn't promised to carry on the legacy of grassy knees and a sense of adventure in the Dawson family—in Dawson Manufacturing. But our foundation was already shaken before Mom found her freedom.

I took over the company far too young when he went in the hospital. He hid away from the eyes of the press. He didn't want them to see the cracks in the Dawson Manufacturing armor. I think our increase in profits during his absence pushed him to get better. Medically, I know that doesn't make sense. But anger is a powerful motivator. Next thing I knew, I was demoted, and the tone of a loving father never saw the light of day again.

"When're we tearing that thing down?" he snarls through the speakerphone.

It's eight o'clock at night and way past his sobriety time.

"End of summer," I say.

"Fantastic. Come on home."

"I have three more weeks here," I say, picking a piece of lint off the honey-yellow curtains.

"That's ridiculous," he says. "You don't need to go through great lengths for that park. It's just some hick town off the map."

He doesn't understand the nuances of this business, and he never has. Once Mom left, he was loaded with the duties of public relations, and he's flubbed it since day one. Thank God he's excellent at creating the rides rather than selling them. And thank God I'm better at both.

"It's a hick town that'll get us clients again if we help out," I say.

"Bah, we're fine with what we have."

"You haven't seen the sales numbers."

"I have," he says. "And I know exactly how much you're selling this coaster for. That isn't helping."

"We might be losing out on some money," I say. "But it will pay off once our reputation returns."

I don't say that it's also the right thing to do. I don't say that it might help me sleep again, knowing that nobody else can get injured for a problem we can't seem to diagnose. I also don't mention that Lorelei is starting to get to me.

I've seen tons of people fear roller coasters. It doesn't matter that you're statistically more likely to get in a car accident. People fear the loss of control. It's natural.

But the way Lorelei looked at The Grizzly today? It just felt wrong. And the fact that all she wants is to know what happened ... that changes things for me.

"Come back here to do real coasters," he says. "That Swedish park wants your ideas. I told them you're working on inventing a new launch system."

That Swedish park. And he wonders why he's allowed

to stay at home instead of attending client meetings. He offends everyone he meets.

"I'm using the new system for this park."

He sputters and scoffs. "Wasted talent."

"It'll help soothe whatever damage we've done to Honeywood. To Lorelei."

"Lorelei?"

I pause, feeling my heart stammer in my chest. I shouldn't have said that. But I can't back down now.

"The girl," I clarify. "The girl who got injured."

There's another moment of silence.

"Did you meet her?" he asks.

My teeth grind together again.

I realize I don't like him talking about her. Not one bit.

"No," I lie. "I don't think she works here anymore."

"Probably couldn't handle the pressure," he says.

I grip the balcony railing harder.

"Probably went to crawl back to her hole, where she came from."

I can feel my chest tighten and my cheeks redden.

He's only saying it to get a rise out of me, and I know it.

Unfortunately, it's working.

We both have tempers. Our similarities are something that bites at my core each time we talk.

"I'm sure I would feel the same way if I had my hips rammed into the side of a train," I bite out.

Even the thought tosses my stomach.

"That's the park's error," he spits out. "They should have checked those track wheels regularly in maintenance."

I nod even though he can't see me. I don't speak to clarify that they *did* pass inspections. He knows they did. He's just drunk and angry.

"Don't feel bad for that park, Emory," he says. "It's their fault. We did nothing wrong."

I let out a quiet, "I wonder if we did."

"Don't," he snaps.

I look out at the dark park below, the only illumination from the round lamps. It's hard not to compare these conversations to the ones with my mom, where all she does is convince me to go to yoga. Or even Lorelei, with her silly puns.

The side of my mouth twitches into a small smile.

"How about we just add a top track?" he asks.

Good feeling gone.

I inhale, trying to steady my breath, but I can feel my blood pressure rising.

Sure, adding a steel top track on top of a wooden roller coaster would look good for a lot of reasons. It's more durable over time. Maintenance costs are lower. It's a smoother experience. Plus, adding a new track on The Grizzly would ensure that whatever caused the wheels to detach would no longer be an issue.

On paper, it's great. In fact, I imagined part of my rebuild would involve adding steel. But we're looking to overhaul our soured image, not look like we put lipstick on a pig.

"We need something that stands out," I say. "I was going to add a launch or two. Modernize it."

"No," he says. "Change of plans. Just add a steel track on top of the wooden bases. That's it."

"That's gonna make us look even worse," I say through clenched teeth.

"We're barely making money on it anyway," he says.

"Ever think it's not exclusively about the profits?"

"Says the man doing this to gain clients," he says. "I see right through you, son."

I slam my fist against the railing with little force. I know there's no arguing past this. He wants me back in town. He wants me to make his coasters for him while he sips on whatever poison he likes outside the workshop. And I'm the sucker who will do it.

I have to maintain our company. My mom's pride and joy. My dad's wreckage. The steel rails will fix any safety concerns, but something in me still feels uncomfortable about it. But who am I to argue with the CEO?

"Fine," I say. "We can send the contractors afterward, and they'll handle everything else. We'll just add the steel track on top. No major rebuilds or feature changes."

"You'd better guarantee that and not get roped into something more."

I grind my jaw further. He's pushing me, but I don't argue. Because even though most of our employees know I'm more competent, at the end of the day, my dad is the owner. He's the one who can fire me, blackball me from the industry, and they'll say nothing.

They'll always side with the king.

12

Lorelei

My parents live five minutes from me. You can access any place in Cedar Cliff within that window. Honeywood, the library, the hairdresser, our single gas station, and even our local breakfast place. But even with such easy access, my mom prefers home-cooked family meals.

Quinn and I pull into my parents' gravel driveway, surrounded by a sea of colors.

Louise and Jack Arden are Cedar Cliff's main supplier of flowers. Their home acts as a floral shop storefront with wooden signs wrapped in vines that say, *Park here!* and, *Live, Laugh, Love.*

Believe it or not, my dad contributed that last one.

He does indeed live, laugh, and love ferociously.

We walk in the side door with the screen slamming behind us. The house already smells like an amalgamation of different spices and warmed butter. The wooden flooring creaks as we toe off our shoes in the mudroom. I can already hear The Rolling Stones humming through from Dad's speakers in the den.

Quinn and I find him in his massive armchair, giving us a sleepy wave. The man hasn't even had turkey yet, and he looks like he's seconds away from nodding off. The room is decorated in memorabilia from our youth—my old track and field trophies, my brother's football jersey, and framed pictures of our family in matching white turtlenecks on the beach.

We're cringe, but it's cute.

Quinn and I bend to hug him, his long arms wrapping around us.

"Go scare your mother," he whispers in my ear.

I nod, understanding my assignment, and drag Quinn along with me. We tiptoe through the dining room and into the kitchen.

My mom is at the stove in her frilly apron. Her wild red hair is tied up in a bun, glasses near the tip of her nose. The frames are connected to a colorful beaded necklace that wraps around her neck. Her denim pants are patched with different squares of patterned fabric. She's a walking art market.

I've always heard a good relationship consists of one exciting person and one boring person. I firmly believe my parents took that advice as gospel.

Even though Mom is turned toward the oven, distracted as she stirs the pot and moves her hips side to side to the beats of "Gimme Shelter," she still calls, "Don't even try it, kids."

She turns with her kind, dimpled grin. She always gives us this look, like she hasn't seen us in fifty years even though it's only been a couple weeks. Her arms shoot out, and we both barrel into her.

A hug from your mom is one of the most comforting

feelings, especially when she smells like fresh cookies. No, really, I swear it seeps out of her pores.

Quinn gets a little kiss on the cheek after Mama holds her face in both hands. Leave it to Mama to bring out a rare smile on Quinn's face.

"Doin' all right, girlie?" Mama asks.

"Yes, ma'am."

This place is comforting after the week I've had with Emory.

"Hey, Toe Jam."

"Sup, Barbie."

Well, it would be comforting without the background noises of my brother and Quinn fighting. But even that carries some bit of comfort to it as well.

I turn and wave to my brother, Landon, who leans against the doorjamb. Like the rest of our family of giants, he's tall. But that's where our similarities end. We're fraternal twins, so he's got Mom's warm smile and dimples, whereas I inherited Dad's dazed look and subtle waves in my hair.

"How's Tennessee?" I ask him.

"Boring," he says.

"It's 'cause they have you now." Quinn snorts.

"Don't be jealous," he says with a tilt of his lips.

"Kids, please," Mom says. "Would you mind setting the table and fighting in the dining room instead?"

All three of us grab some plates and utensils and go into the dining room with the long wooden table and quilted place mats already arranged.

"So, any preseason park drama?" Landon asks. "I need some happiness. Too many of my team have quit for higher-paying jobs. *And* my laundry machine broke."

"Wow, a real shitstorm," Quinn says with a smirk.

"Finding joy in my misery?" he snarks back.

"Of course."

He grins. "I need some cheering up with Honeywood drama."

For a second, I wonder if I should even bring up Emory. I don't want to spoil the evening with talks of lawyers and mean comments thrown in his direction.

Not that I care if someone talks dirty about Mr. Roller Coaster.

Then again, when have I ever withheld something from my brother? He'll figure it out anyway. Somehow, he always does. It's a twin thing.

I bite the bullet.

"Mr. Roller Coaster is in town," I whisper.

"What?!" Landon practically booms, and both Quinn and I shush him.

"Quiet! Mom and Dad'll hear," I hiss.

"Yeah, that kinda seems like something everyone should know," he whispers back.

"Yeah, well ..."

Landon nudges Quinn with his elbow. "Have you seen him?"

Quinn scrunches her nose at his thick arm still extended toward her. "I will next week. Theo says he's a real pill though."

"Oh, great," Landon says with a snap of his fingers. "Then, you should get along with him well."

"Ha-ha," she says with her excellent deadpan laugh, rolling her eyes with the sound.

My brother and Quinn couldn't be more different if they tried. Landon has always been the goofy jock. He was all laughs while she was all scowls. Landon was in every sport in high school; Quinn was in every art program. He was the popular golden retriever, and she was the loner pit bull.

They fight, but I think somewhere deep down, they care for each other. But only if you squint really hard and use a magnifying glass.

"You're gonna at least tell Ian about Mr. Roller Coaster, right?" Landon asks. "There might be things you can and cannot say."

"No, I'm not gonna tell my lawyer," I mutter. "I don't want to cause drama where it's not needed. He's here for a few weeks, and then he's gone, and we'll probably never see him again."

"Except in court."

"Shush, Landon."

He holds up his hands. "Your funeral if Mom finds out."

"But she won't, right?" Quinn asks, lifting an eyebrow in Landon's direction.

He sends a playful grin. "I'm not a snitch."

"Good," Quinn says, and before I can stop her, she whispers, "But I am. Landon, Lorelei hasn't been going to yoga."

"Quinn!" I whine, and then it's their turn to simultaneously shush me.

"Tell her to go," Quinn whispers. "She'll listen to you."

She grabs the forks from my limp, stunned hand and places them around the table.

Quinn's right. I hate when my brother gets all stern, and right now, Landon's once-smiling, bearded face falters into a downturned frown.

Dang it.

"Lore, why?" he asks.

"I'm ... fine," I mutter. "It's all fine. I've just been busy."

"You have to go back," he says.

"No, it smells like patchouli and sweat," I say. "And people stare."

"Your leg needs it. Promise me you'll go."

"No."

"Yes."

"No."

"Don't make me move back to Georgia and force you to go."

Yoga does help with my pain. But I can't go to hot yoga in anything more than the shortest of shorts. I can't hide the massive scar spanning from my upper thigh to my hip.

Thanks a lot, Grizzly.

Let's just say, I used to like bikini season a lot more until that ride had something to say about it.

"Two can play at this game," I say. "Maybe I'll bring up to Mom that you're looking to date, Landon. Let her set you up with people."

"You wouldn't dare," he says.

Quinn snorts. His head jerks over to her.

"All right!" Mama storms into the dining room, clapping her hands together. "Turkey is done, gravy is on the stove, and ... wait, what are you three talking about?"

Landon, Quinn, and I stare at her for a moment, then back at each other before devolving into useless mumbles.

It's Dad who finally saves us, coming in from the den and saying, "Dinner ready?"

I leave to wash my hands before Mama tries to pry, but I still hear my brother's quick whisper of, "You'd better go back to yoga, Lore."

13

Lorelei

Honeywood pre-opens two weeks early for private corporate events, and pre-opening day is always my favorite day.

There's something in the air—the buzz of the first guests waiting at the gate to come in, the roar of the coasters, and the first slew of college kids ready for their fun summer job. Sure, they might all be horny, single, and ready to mingle, but they bring the energy.

Fred gives a rousing speech, and some of the teens jump on the fountain to pat Buzzy's stone belly as we pass by. Then, we wait in two lines on either side of the midway, waving yellow pom-poms like a bunch of overgrown cheer-leaders. Everyone is encouraged to attend if they can. Every project is on hold for the first ten minutes of opening. Every email can wait. It's just us and the park guests.

The gates open, and we start handing out maps. It's a slew of *good mornings*, *welcomes*, and *if you need anything, let us knows*.

We're all smiles, good vibes, and happiness.

I should have expected Emory would be the storm

cloud looming over it all. He seems gloomier than last week, if that's even possible. I wonder what's changed.

He's handing out maps with a stern look that says, *You'd better not lose this or else.*

If it were up to him, he probably wouldn't be helping. Technically, he doesn't need to be. But you try saying no to Fred's opening-day enthusiasm.

A child walks by with her thumb in her mouth, eyes darting around at our swishing pom-poms. She's scared by all the noise. I get it. It's a lot to take in. I try to get to her before Emory's grinchy attitude can sully the day further.

I reach into my side bag's pocket, rustling around for my stash of Buzzy key chains, and extend one out to her. Her face transforms into a giant grin, and the tears glistening on her cheeks are only a memory.

Day saved.

All I get from Emory is a curious glance.

It's not my responsibility to make sure he's enjoying himself. I'm here as a colleague, and he is not my guest at the moment.

Another little girl jogs up. But, boy, she picks the wrong person, going straight for Emory.

"I want a key chain too!"

She doesn't frown or get scared of the tall man with the stern look. Instead, she grins up at him, and when I look over, he's lowering himself down into a crouched position.

I blink for a second or two because he's got this weird thing on his face.

Is that ... a smile?

My heart practically stumbles its way into a faster rhythm.

It's handsome. *So* handsome. Not that Emory wasn't good-looking before, but a smile on him is like watching clouds whisk away. The tiny crinkles near his eyes deepen. Lines edge along the outside of his mouth. I'm so in awe that I don't realize he's nodding toward my bag and holding out his hand.

"Got a key chain for her, Lorelei?"

The little girl grins up at me. I dig in my pocket, stunned as I tug out a key chain of Buzzy. I place it into Emory's hand. My fingers glide over his palm for just a moment. It's rough every time we touch. It feels like the epitome of a hardworking man.

I can't help but gulp, feeling the tension twist deep in my stomach.

Emory dangles the key chain into the girl's tiny palm.

"Thanks," she whispers out, a blush rising on her cheeks.

What?

For Emory?

For his smile?

For how he showed one single inkling of kindness?

She runs back to her parents with the speed of a bumblebee in flight. I wonder if maybe she just had some type of awakening in her. A first crush that she'll never forget.

The mysterious guy at Honeywood.

When Emory rises back up to his full height, I glance over at him.

The smile is now gone, but the intensity of his gaze seems just a little less bored. Less perturbed by the spectacle of Honeywood's opening ceremony.

Holy hell. Emory Dawson might have a heart.

At least he would if he didn't walk away in that instant.

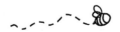

Around mid-morning, I'm back in my office, catching up on emails when Quinn's head pokes in my office.

"Hey, lady," she says with a grin.

Fully decked out in her Queen Bee costume, Quinn is drop-dead gorgeous. The dress with puffed sleeves is a soft shade of pink that she'd never be caught wearing out of the park. With eye shadow and heavy blush, she is no longer the woman who wears black and makes fun of life. She is radiance personified.

Queen Bee is the only face mascot we have. All the others are fur suits of Buzzy or Bumble. A few years ago, we tried out a side character from the books, named Ranger Randy, but that was a disaster. He had thick thighs and short shorts. The moms were more excited about him than their children. After one—okay, fifty—too many phone numbers scribbled on napkins, we stopped featuring him.

Now, Quinn operates alone most days. I think she prefers it.

"On break?" I ask.

"Yes. And covered in sweat. You?"

Southern weather slingshots across the board with no rhyme or reason, and while yesterday was cool, today, we might as well be on fire. Honestly, I imagine hell is just a mid-July Georgia scorcher.

"Sweat meter is at a solid ten," I say.

And as those words come out of my mouth, Emory appears in the doorway.

Fantastic.

Humidity does me no favors. My hair is in a messy bun, and I've already had to apply deodorant for the second time. Plus, I cleaned up the glitter confetti from the midway, so I'm pretty sure I look like a midnight performer at Dripping Honey.

"Lorelei," Emory says as I'm swiping away the specks of glitter. My efforts halt. My name on his tongue is like butter. "Conference room in five?"

I look at the clock on the wall.

"Our meeting isn't until eleven," I say.

Emory pulls up his wrist, looking at his intricate watch. "You can't do ten minutes early?"

His face is blank, fueled by a sort of bored expression.

I open my mouth to counter, but not before Quinn blurts out, "Wow, you must be ... Mr. Darson?"

"Dawson," he instantly corrects, his frown twisted in a way that is the exact opposite of the smile I saw him give the cute child this morning.

Well, it couldn't last forever, I suppose.

Quinn tilts her head to the side with a small grin. She knew what she was doing.

"Ah, right. Dawson," she says. "My bad."

He doesn't give her any additional moment of consideration before turning his head back to me with raised eyebrows.

Interesting.

How in the world is he focused on me—sweaty, hair tied in the messiest of messy buns—when my best friend is literally in full Queen Bee makeup, painted up to look as beautiful as humanly possible?

Yet here Emory is, staring at *me*. Expectantly. Not giving her a second look.

My face heats up, and this time, it isn't due to the Georgia weather.

I find myself saying, "Uh, sure, yeah. I can go now."

Quinn lets out a bored sigh. "It's always work, work, work with you," she mutters in a faux sarcastic way, throwing me a half-smile.

"We'll still get lunch," I say, and I can't help myself when I add, "Of course, if the meeting can be over ten minutes early since it's starting ten minutes early."

Emory's eyes slide over to me, and for a second, I think the edge of his mouth tugs upward. I think.

I'm getting lucky with these partial smiles today.

"We'll see," he mutters.

Is that a joke? Is he joking?

"If not," Quinn interjects with raised eyebrows, "I'll see you at trivia tonight."

"Absolutely."

When she walks out, Emory doesn't acknowledge her exit. I bite the inside of my cheek.

"You could have been nicer," I say.

"Why?" he asks. "Should I know her?"

I shake my head, grabbing my notebook off the desk and walking toward the doorway.

"She's just my friend. It's fine."

His eyebrows twitch toward the middle, and my chest constricts instantly. Is he seriously pitying me when I tell him I have a friend? Is that so unbelievable?

"You look like a disco ball," he says, picking off a bit of glitter from my shoulder.

I stiffen. I still feel a ghost of his fingers on me.

"Let's go," I say, taking another speck of glitter off my skin as well.

Who am I kidding? You can't get rid of glitter. It's like trying to return a gift to the gift horse that already galloped away.

97

He throws his open palm toward the doorway as I walk through the threshold.

At our meeting, he's back to the Emory from day one.

No smiles that show he can be compassionate toward children.

No little gesture of solidarity.

Not even one tiny inkling of *something* that shows he's remotely human at all.

Beep-boop, must process business.

"I've had a change of plans," he says.

Kindness does not compute.

"I'm thinking we don't tear the whole coaster down."

I'm snapped out of my thoughts.

"Wait, what?" I ask.

"I think all we need is a steel track. It's relatively quick to throw on."

My mouth hangs open, but all I can think of is how in the world I'm going to tell this to Fred—to communicate that we're not getting what we're paying for, but instead just a small update to make the ride smoother.

It's the expectant look on his face that spurs me forward. As if it's a challenge on whether or not I can rise to the occasion. I refuse to look weak in front of this man.

"Why?" I push.

"It makes the most sense."

"In what world?" I ask. "This feels like a step backward."

"It'll be safe."

"It has literally nothing we've talked about so far," I say. "No launches. No Honeywood-specific theming …"

He waves his hand. "We'll add trees."

"*Trees*? Are you kidding?" I let out an exasperated breath. "I feel like I'm getting pranked right now."

I see his fist clench on the table. The whites of his knuckles show.

"If this is all you had in mind," I say, "why have I even been here?"

"Please," he says, a hand rising midair.

Please?

"Just let me do my job."

I lean back in my chair.

Please?

Something isn't right with him. This is not a man that pleads. This is not a man who asks. He takes.

"Only adding a steel track won't make people feel more comfortable," I say. "Isn't that the whole point?"

"It'll fix the safety issues and make the ride smoother," he says. "If that doesn't make the people of Cedar Cliff comfortable, I don't know what will."

"Why make the change now?" I ask.

"Why are you fighting against safety? Out of all people, you should be on board."

"Don't use that against me. Why is this so last minute?"

"Why are you so concerned?"

"Why are you avoiding my questions?"

His palm slams on the table. It's hard enough to make me jump. He stretches out his hand and inhales sharply.

"I'm here to get your top attraction running again," he says. His tone bites. It's sharp. "That's it. That's the best we can do. Take it or leave it."

He blinks at me, clenching his jaw tighter.

I'm speechless.

What happened this weekend that made him like this? We never really got along, but part of me thought maybe we had an understanding or ... *something*.

Fish puns, if anything.

Julie Olivia

Now, he's all business. And I don't see him budging. Not with the fire in his eyes.

"Fine," I say, the word practically whispered.

"Fantastic."

When I tell Fred later, he won't be happy. But neither am I.

This doesn't feel like the right thing to do. So, why is he pushing it suddenly? What else is going on?

Or maybe there isn't anything else.

I should have known a coaster engineer would be well versed in rollback.

14

Emory

My father's decision to only add the steel track doesn't sit right with me, but when has anything felt correct since I got here?

I'm barely putting in the effort, but if I get one more call from him about coming home and working on the next biggest and best coaster for some park in Germany or Canada or literally anywhere other than this "hick town," then I'm going to go nuts.

At least his attitude is counterbalanced by the texts from my mom. She likes to send the occasional pictures of her leaning against her bike, giving me a thumbs-up in front of some landmark in the Midwest.

It balms the ache a little.

It's best if I get the job done, make sure the coaster is fit enough to draw Honeywood's usual crowd, and get out of here. But more importantly, it's making sure nobody ever gets hurt again on this new refurbishment. Not when they're drawing crowds with young kids.

The more I look at The Grizzly, the more I wonder what went wrong.

Or maybe it's the more time I spend with Lorelei.

I've been holed up in the conference room, creating the final business plan for this simple revision. I have one meeting a day with Lorelei, and she only supplies the essential information when I ask. Most of the time, she's on the opposite side of the conference room, typing away with her own work. She's cold. Not at all how she is when I look out the window, watching her talk with her coworkers.

She's a different person with them.

Beautiful, beaming, and laughing.

Always laughing.

I'm envious.

She says she's not suing us for the money, and I believe her. I couldn't ignore the desperate look in her eyes when she said she just wanted answers.

I do too.

I stay cooped up in the hotel after meetings, running out my frustrations on the treadmill, and only occasionally dropping by Orson's place. Bennett is sometimes there too. He's quiet, like I am, which I appreciate. We're two soldiers on either side of the embodiment of extroversion that is Orson Mackenzie.

I swear, if Orson tells me to smile one more time, I'll kill the guy. Cousin or not.

It's an endless loop of days drifting by. Wake up, run, and stand on the balcony as the sun rises. I lean on the railing, watching that same ant-sized dot climb The Grizzly's lift hill. Lorelei, whether she knows it or not, watches the sun rise with me every morning.

I wonder if she knows she's no longer alone.

I wonder if I could get any freaking *creepier*, Jesus Christ.

"Stop being weird," I say to myself one morning, which honestly only makes me feel weirder.

The Buzzy mural continues to give me a thumbs-up, as if to secure that opinion. He's encouraging, even in the worst of times.

I call my mom. I need somebody to level me out. I don't expect her to answer, considering she's likely one time zone behind me. She does.

"Emmy!"

Just the sound of her voice is enough to still whatever rushing waves were pounding over my heart.

"Hey, Mom." I can hear the roar of other voices behind her and the clinking of utensils. "Where are you? A diner?"

"Yeah, somewhere in Louisiana, maybe?"

"Sounds nice."

"I'm wrapping up, so hang tight, baby."

I already feel better. Willa Dawson is a hurricane in life, but when it comes to me, it's like I get to see the eye of it all. Calm, comforting. A respite from the rest of the world.

I imagine she exits the diner because the sound of voices fades away to birds.

"So, you rang?" she asks. "Tell me all about the past week."

"Oh," I start, but I can't finish. Something stops me. There's too much—the insistence on the coaster's changes from Dad; the fact that I suddenly feel weird about everything in Honeywood; and how Lorelei isn't how Dad described her.

It's all meshing together in a mess of inconsistency.

"Uh-oh," Mom says. "Silence ain't good. What's wrong?"

"I'm feeling ... off."

"You're *always* that way."

I let out a weak laugh. I can't help but smile, feeling my eyebrows cinch together in the middle. My mom used to say I looked concerned whenever I told her I loved her, like I couldn't fathom such an emotion. I can't help it. It's like her happiness spears my heart. That cold, hard thing must be concerned, I suppose.

"My head just feels crowded, I guess," I admit.

"Well, lucky for you, I did some research on yoga studios in Cedar Cliff."

"Mom, I said not to—"

"I took the time to do the research, so you're going," she says. "They only have one studio called Yogi Bare. That's cute. Isn't that cute?"

I hear the rumble of her bike in the background, like a growling titan behind her.

"I don't want to leave this hotel room. I don't need the locals figuring out who I am."

I don't want to run into Lorelei.

"Sorry, you're going," she says. It's not a question anymore. "You don't have to redo your chakras or whatever, son. But it'll help you clear your mind."

I groan, but once the conversation is said and done and she sends the address, I stare at it for a solid ten minutes before deciding to go to tonight's class.

Mom ends up being right. Again.

The stretching does help my sore muscles from so many years of manual labor. I feel each bend, stretch, and breath cool into my muscles, tugging at my brain like taffy and leaving it out to dry. But in those quiet moments in Savasana, I don't think about my dad or mom or The Grizzly. I think of another person.

Lorelei.

I've noticed on particularly overcast days, she walks with a slight limp. It's nothing too noticeable, but our walks down the hall slow to a pace where two of her steps no longer match one of mine.

On the second corporate event Honeywood held, we had an unfortunate thunderstorm that caused delays for most of the rides. The entire staff was helping with crowd control, running this way and that to redirect guests toward the indoor shows or dark rides.

Despite being in operations and relegated to the offices, she insisted on joining in with Rides efforts, as if she couldn't contain herself.

On that stormy day, Lorelei seemed pained to walk anywhere. Her right leg had a significant delay after each left step. But she still corralled those crowds like a cowgirl with a lasso.

She loves Honeywood.

Each and every morning, at seven sharp, Lorelei takes a leisurely walk down the midway, circling through the loop near the entrance of The Canoodler tunnel, down the too-steep incline, and ending at The Grizzly, where she ascends the stairs to the peak of the lift hill.

Maybe it's conquering a fear for her. Maybe it's showing the coaster she's an alpha or something weird. Who knows?

She's a breed of person all her own.

At the end of each day, her biggest concern should be turning off the lights to her office and locking up behind her. But at eight o'clock every night, she starts the rounds with the cleanup crew, guiding those part-time teenagers with a type of gusto she never offers me.

And I feel my heart rate rise at how easy she smiles at them. Her laugh with the crew seems effortless. It's almost mystical, the way she smiles when she chooses not to look dreamy, like she's perpetually mid-joke with those white teeth on full display.

She doesn't seem to carry the world on her shoulders; she looks like she dances with it instead.

At least in front of others. Not me.

Never me.

They love her. Absolutely and thoroughly.

And she smiles. Until she ascends the top of that hill the following morning.

I still watch from my hotel balcony—feeling like a total creep—as she stands there.

I see the tension in her jaw during meetings when it's just her and me.

The hurt.

The anger.

And I can't help but wonder ... just how bad did I hurt this woman?

And could it have been prevented?

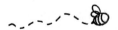

I spend too much time in my hotel room.

It's meant to be welcoming with its Bumble the Bee alarm clock and the encouraging Buzzy the Bear thumbs up mural. But for me, the room just feels like some cell where I come to ruminate. I am a prisoner, and I'm losing sanity. I'm just waiting for this last week to end. To go home to another miserable place.

I'm a total joy. I know.

My cell phone rings next to me, and I flip it over.

Orson.

"Hey," I answer.

"Get out of that hotel room and come down to The Honeycomb." Orson's normally jubilant voice is harsh on the other side of the line.

"I don't drink," I answer.

"We have water."

"I'm fine up here."

"Emory, you don't do anything in this town."

"I hang out with you. I go to Yogi Bare."

"Barely. Come on. You can't leave until you've done something fun here."

"No."

"Damn it, Emory." He lets out a heavy exhale.

Did I hit a nerve? Did I flap the unflappable?

"I'm trying to be nice here. Get out of your head. Fred dropped by the bar and said you're a total bummer."

I sit up on my elbows in bed. "Wait, Fred said that?"

I'm surprised by how much I care about that man's opinion.

"Come on, big guy," Orson says. "Down the stairs and one block over. The bar is right there." I almost say no once more, but then he says, "You'll blend in with the crowd anyway. It's trivia night."

Trivia night.

Lorelei will be there.

I remember Queen Bee—whatever her real name is—saying she would see Lorelei there. It seems like everyone at the park frequents The Honeycomb on Wednesdays.

Part of me wants to see her in her natural habitat—among the Cedar Cliff locals with a smile instead of the scowl she reserves for me.

I run a hand through my hair.

God, am I sick or what?

This woman is suing my company for ungodly amounts of money, and yet ... and yet ...

"I'll be there in five," I say.

I put my book on the side table, turn off my lamp, and descend the stairs to no doubt make an ass out of myself.

15

Lorelei

When Theo shakes my forearm and points to the bar, I initially think she's pointing out Mrs. Stanley's puppy. But that happiness is completely shot down when I see him.

Emory.

Heather-gray T-shirt—*God, does he wear anything else?* —and black denim that looks even better on him than the day-to-day blue jeans.

He's leaning against the counter while Orson folds over the opposite side, forearms resting on the bar top. I wonder if they know each other. Orson is skilled at making friends at the drop of a dime, but to think he knows Emory so well this quick would be a feat, even for him.

How is Mr. Roller Coaster still closed off and surly, even in The Honeycomb? There's bluegrass pumping through the speakers, rolling laughter from the other trivia teams, and the to-die-for on-tap lagers.

Yet Emory holds a glass of water with a deep-set line between his eyebrows, as if the thought of having fun is vile.

Mrs. Stanley's puppy attempts a sniff at his crotch. He

pats the dog's head impassively. Then, he looks around the bar, eyes narrowed, as if searching for someone.

"Oh, I didn't know Emory was here," Bennett says from the opposite side of the table. "Let's invite him over."

I jerk my head over to him and am relieved to see the rest of my friends do the same with a full chorus of, "What?" and, "Bennett, seriously?" and, "Why do you hate Lorelei?" and, "Are you nuts?!"

He holds his hands up with a chuckle. "Hey now," he says. "What's the worst that could happen?"

Ruby laughs. "Uh, Lorelei might kill you."

"I wouldn't—" I start.

Quinn interrupts, "If she won't, I will."

"Come on, y'all," Bennett says. "He's probably just lonely. Look at the guy."

We all turn to stare at once.

"Yeah, he does have an *old man feeding the pigeons* kinda vibe," Theo muses.

"Good," Quinn and I say at the same time.

Though, while she looks proud of her statement, my gut instantly clenches. My mom didn't raise me—or teach Quinn either—to be so cruel. Especially to someone new in town with no friends.

And yet I wonder how Mama would react if she saw him here. The guy we've come to villainize. The guy who has been nothing but sour since day one. I don't think even she, the Mother of the Year, would be so quick to allow him to sit with us.

Jeez, I sound like Regina George.

Next thing I know, we'll be kicking him out for not wearing pink.

But his harsh turn from helping Honeywood to doing

the bare minimum was like a kick in my gut. And yet I'm supposed to be taking the high road?

"C'mon, Lore," Bennett coaxes from the other end of the table.

I throw him a sidelong glance, but he grins and tilts his head, as if to say, *You know it's the right thing to do.*

The right thing.

Isn't that the whole point of my lawsuit? To do the right thing? To figure out what happened? For justice or something?

But what justice is there in letting some man suffer in silence? Even if he is a total grump.

I exhale in defeat, get up, grab my empty glass of beer, and raise my eyebrows at Bennett, as if to say, *Fine. See? I'm still a decent person.*

I can feel my heart pounding as I approach Emory. He's like a stalking panther, large and lean, seeming both relaxed and yet somehow also on edge. I can feel the fifty *predatory wild animal* red lights going off around him, screaming, *Danger, danger!* to my little prey brain.

Against my better judgment, I ignore said alarms and stop in front of him.

His eyes meet mine, and he doesn't blink.

Neither do I.

"Would you like to sit with me and my friends?" I ask.

He looks to my table, where Bennett is giving him a wave. He returns it.

Emory glances back to me, twisting his mouth to the side and looking down into his water glass.

"Are they putting you up to this?" he asks.

"Against my will completely."

"Ah. Your Southern hospitality really is charming."

My stomach twists, but I bite the inside of my cheek and take another deep inhale.

In, out.

I say, "I'm thinking I need to be the bigger person from time to time."

"Must be difficult."

"It's sure easier to be bigger than you."

His thick eyebrows rise to the top of his forehead, and I consider that I might have just implied he has a small penis, and before I can brush it off, I try to stammer out, "I didn't ..."

But when I avert my eyes and instead look down to the floor, I see the way his pants fit him so well, and my face feels hot. The way the denim hangs over his crotch makes me wonder if it's a fold in the fabric or if that's really his—

Get it together, Lorelei!

When I look up, one eyebrow is lifted.

He totally saw me checking him out.

Emory pushes off the bar, getting far too close to me in the process so that I can smell his woodsy-candle scent. "Sure, I'll join you."

Joy.

When we sit back at the table with my friends, Theo scoots over, reaching behind her to ask another group if they can spare an additional chair. Of course she slides it between mine and hers so that he'll be forced to sit next to me.

Great. This gets better and better.

Emory sits, and his long legs look like they need to stretch out farther. But Quinn sits across from him and doesn't allow room. Instead, he rests one thigh against mine, and it's all I can concentrate on.

"Everyone, this is Emory," I say. "Um, Emory, this is ...

everyone. You know Theo and Quinn. And apparently Bennett?"

I tilt my head to the side, and Bennett nods.

"Baseball watching buddies," Bennett says.

I see a subtle nod from Emory in response.

Ruby scrunches her nose. "Since when?"

"I don't tell you everything, believe it or not," Bennett says to her with a grin.

"That's Ruby," I say to Emory. "She's also an engineer."

"That right?" Emory asks her.

He actually sounds interested. Maybe he's trying to be nice.

"Yes," she says from down the table. I can feel the nerves coursing through her from here. She's picking at the corner of our trivia answer sheet. "I'm working for Dominion at the moment."

Emory's eyebrows furrow. Dominion is another manufacturer. I wonder if Mr. Roller Coaster is competitive.

"At the moment?" Emory counters. "Are you looking to leave?"

"I ... yes," she says. I'd feel better if she wasn't looking at him like he was some mythical god. "I'm always looking for something new."

"With Dominion, I bet so."

Definitely competitive.

"Heh. Yeah."

And then it's quiet because what do you even say to that?

"So, Emory, how are you liking Cedar Cliff?" Theo asks.

"It's fine."

"Fine as in ..." Quinn leads.

113

"Fine as in ... small town," he says. "Not a ton to do, I guess."

"Have you been to Chicken and the Egg?" Theo suggests. "It's a really good breakfast spot downtown."

Emory shakes his head. "No, not yet."

"Do you read a lot?" Quinn asks. "You could try the used bookstore. It's one block from there."

"Oh, and Dripping Honey has wet T-shirt contests."

"Theo!"

We all burst into laughter at that. Emory only has a small twitch of a smile, but mostly, he looks at all of us as if observing aliens.

It's weird. He's normally so confident, but tonight, he seems awkward, like he can't figure out how to navigate this group. I don't know why. For once, my friends are behaving. Theo is practically feeding him questions; Quinn, though quippy, is at least attempting conversation; and Ruby is legitimately wiggling in her seat, no doubt wanting to ask him more about engineering.

But Emory doesn't say anything after that initial conversation. Time passes, and he only nods at our conversations, contributing nothing to trivia and only giving me short glances.

Great.

By the third round, his leg has relaxed against me more. We both have longer limbs, so it's difficult not to bump one another. But his thigh hasn't moved since he sat down. I've noticed that it's hard. Strong. He clearly works out.

With each passing second, it's like the weight of it gets heavier against me. I wonder if he's relaxing into it. But when I look at him, he's always looking elsewhere—in the crowd, at the trivia host, at the televisions with the questions. He doesn't talk. All he does is sip his water. I wonder why he's not drinking, but I know better than to ask.

Finally, after another round of questions, where Emory just sits there and clenches his fists by his sides—jeez, he's practically white-knuckled—Quinn says something that makes my jaw drop.

"So, I've gotta ask, has Lorelei pitched The Hornet yet?"

No, no, no.

I stumble and fall. Metaphorically, of course. Because I'm sitting.

"Oh, come on, guys—" I start.

"The Hornet?" Emory asks.

Of course, *now*, he talks.

"Oh yeah!" Ruby says with a smile. "She's been sketching it for years."

"You're not an engineer," Emory says with all the grace of a blunt weapon.

If my stomach didn't drop before, there it goes now.

"Yes, I know that," I counter with a bite.

I'm not normally this harsh with someone. I don't know what it is about Emory that brings this out of me.

No, wait, I do. It's the fact that he's a freaking douche nozzle.

I pull my thigh away from his. Admittedly, I miss the warmth. I think I even see his own expression falter at the motion. But I'm probably just imagining it.

Theo, trying to recover—bless her—says, "She was supervising all of the Rides department for a while. She knows her stuff."

His eyes turn to me again. My face heats. This is more humiliating than if my mom were here, showing baby pictures.

"What happened?" he asks.

The table goes silent. We all know what happened.

"I left for the marketing department," I say. "That's all."

Emory narrows his eyes, as if considering something. After he speaks, I know he should have considered harder.

"Why make sketches if the ride can't come to fruition?" he asks.

"Do you have to be so blunt all the time?"

"I'm practical."

It's silent, and then I hear the faint sounds of Ruby asking, "Um, so does anyone know the answer to …"

"It's salmon," Emory bites out. "So, why the change to marketing?"

"Oh, so now you know the answer to trivia questions."

He breathes out air through his nose. "They're not hard."

"You've been closed off all night, but you've known the answers all along?"

"You guys figured them out."

"That's condescending and rude," I say. "How do you not see that's rude?"

He blinks, as if wondering if it was rude, before asking, "Are you going to answer my question?"

"God, do you know how to be a person *at all*?"

I heave out a sigh and stretch out my hands. They felt tight, and I know I must have just been clenching them, like his own irritation from earlier had seeped into my bones.

When I look back to the table, there's a mess of uncomfortable people. Theo is wide-eyed and biting her lower lip, Quinn is glaring at Emory, Ruby is scribbling down *salmon* on the answer sheet, and Bennett has his mouth pursed to the side, as if disappointed that he suggested this whole thing in the first place.

But Bennett can't help that Mr. Roller Coaster here should be more aptly named Mr. Butthole.

The silence is broken by the buzzing of a phone I don't recognize on the table.

Emory reaches out to flip it over.

Dad is on the caller ID.

It breaks me out of my heightened nerves, settling me back in reality.

My own dad would be so disappointed in my actions right now.

"I'm sorry," I say, apologizing more to my friends than Emory. "I'm just ... ugh." I scoot out my chair and stand with every intention to get fresh air.

"No, I'll go," he says, running a hand through his hair, ruffling the edges from smooth and proper to something a bit messier. I've never seen him do that. "I need to take this anyway."

He stands, and suddenly, we're much too close. This bar is packed, and the tables are cramped. There's nowhere else to stand. We're toe to toe.

Our eyes meet, and neither of us moves.

I find that I can't breathe. His brown eyes are caught on me, lodged like a fire in a locked house. But I'm not extinguishing it. I'm letting it burn.

He's so close that I can see his gaze flickering between mine. I can see every single tiny hair forming a five o'clock shadow on his stiff jawline; I can see how that same jaw tics. His eyes drop to my lips. His tongue darts out to swipe across his own, and my stomach plummets. My thighs clench tighter.

Jesus, when was the last time a man looked at me like *that?*

I part my lips to say literally anything to end this stare-off, but Emory cuts on his heel and pushes out the fogged front door.

I sit back down, my heartbeat steadying and my breathing leveling out again.

I look over to my friends. Their blank stares cause my stomach to flop once more.

"What?" I ask.

Ruby clicks her tongue and waves the answer sheet in the air. "You know, I think I'll take this up!"

"I'll join you," Bennett quickly says, placing a hand on the small of her back as they leave their chairs.

"I should get a refill," Theo says, ducking her head as she gulps down the remainder of her drink and scoots out from her seat as well. "I'll see if Orson is free."

"What?" I stammer out. "Why is ..."

I look to Quinn, who brings her beer pint up to her lips.

"What?" I ask.

"Don't say *what*, all innocent-like," Quinn says. "Even I got a little hot, seeing that."

"What in the ... what are you ..." I sound like an idiot, blubbering out useless words.

"Oh, that man *feels* for you. Maybe it's hate, but boy, does he love to hate you."

My whole body tenses.

"No. Absolutely not," I say. "Did you not just see him? Were you not here when he just spent the last round being freaking Eeyore? He doesn't feel anything."

"Yeah, sure, the dude has problems," Quinn says, tilting her head side to side before taking one long gulp of her drink and setting it down on the table. "But I think you might be ninety-nine percent of them."

Emory does not return after his phone call.

16

Emory

Lorelei is pretty when she smiles.

And it bugs me that I realize this as I'm rushing to finish my presentation for tomorrow.

I've locked myself in the conference room, hunched over the table with a laptop, my tablet, and loose sheets spread everywhere like a madman. I got off a call with our other engineers one hour ago, and while they were smiling, I could tell they weren't impressed by our new idea. But being the former CEO as well as the owner's kid grants me immunity. Nobody wants to risk their jobs arguing.

Maybe Orson is right. Maybe I should just smile more.

Maybe I should laugh, like Lorelei does with her friends.

I lean back in my chair, running a hand through my hair. It's a habit I've picked up in the past week. It's the only thing that can relieve the tension coursing through me.

All I can think about is how Lorelei laughs.

And how she doesn't laugh with me.

Not ever.

As if summoning the dreamy girl herself, I hear her

voice down the hall. It's higher, happier, and floatier than our last conversation. She must be with any of one of her four friends.

I can't show my face around them. I know how I acted last night, and I'm not proud of it.

But I did learn some things—new tidbits about the mysterious woman I've been working with for weeks and somehow know nothing about.

With me, she's headstrong. Stubborn. Infuriating.

But with everyone else, she's kind. Happy. Forgiving.

I wish I could see that side of her.

No. You're leaving tomorrow.

I just need to get out of here in one piece. My plan is to present this dumb top-track idea, and then I'm gone. I will only see her again in the inevitable courtroom.

That's that.

Except I hear her talking.

I get up from the table, stalking—*okay, bad choice of word*—across the room toward the door, where a small window peers into the hallway.

They're just out of view.

If Lorelei were walking with Bennett, I could handle that conversation. Even Theo is too nice to shoot an insult my way. But Quinn ... not so much. She's small, but I wouldn't be surprised if she socked me right in the face.

I can't gather who it is or what they're saying, but I hear a good-bye and see Lorelei turn the corner.

Like some pervy kid sneaking a peek in the middle-school locker room, I run back to my chair, leaning my forehead in my palm right as she walks in, pretending like I wasn't just eavesdropping.

"Oh," she says, stopping mid-step. "I thought maybe you were at lunch."

Did she really not want to see me that bad?

"Just wrapping up things," I say. "I got another 3D mock-up from our art guy."

"I'd like to see," she says. "I haven't even looked at a final design."

She's not wrong, and my gut clenches at this knowledge.

She wants so much more for this roller coaster. But this one won't be modern and pretty. It will be safe. It's the minimum viable product, as we call it. It will get the job done.

For all intents and purposes, I'll be off the hook.

But that doesn't mean I don't feel bad whenever she asks about it.

"I've got a business to run," I say. "I can't put everything past you." I know how crappy that sounds, so I at least throw in, "You're probably busy anyway."

"I've made time in my schedule for this project."

Her face gets more settled in the lines around her brow. The frown on her face. I recognize that irritation. It's around me all the time.

But regardless, something keeps nagging at me from last night. Her friends mentioning some ride of hers. The thought that maybe she does want input.

I shake my head.

Whatever this fascination I have with her needs to stop. I need to go.

"I'll present to the board tomorrow and be out of your hair in no time," I say.

She narrows her eyes. "That's not the point."

I roll my shoulders back. I just want to get out of here. I need to. And she's going to make it as difficult as possible, isn't she? With the way she stiffens her own spine and how she has the audacity to cross her arms.

121

It's maddening. It's ridiculous. It's admirable. And part of me wishes one of my own engineers could muster up the gall to stand up to me like she does.

"What *is* the point?" I ask.

"I've taken time out of my already-busy preseason schedule to help you make us something that is unique to this park," she says. "Because this park *is* a unique park. And I don't think you're delivering on that promise."

"It's a good coaster that your guests will be thrilled about. That's all I can offer."

"Didn't you once tell me storytelling is important too?"

I stand. "Listen here—"

"Don't patronize me, Mr. Dawson."

Mr. Dawson.

I stop on the spot, the balls of my feet practically burning through the carpet. My chest aches. My fist curls, then splays out, stretching out the tense muscles.

Something about her calling me that sets my nerves alight. It sends my heart pounding.

"Fine," I say. "Let's pretend you actually know what you're talking about. You, in marketing. More than me, twenty years of engineering. Let's assume, okay?"

"Real good job at staying professional."

"I think we're getting past that."

"Then, continue."

"If you knew what you were talking about, maybe I would take your layouts. Hell, maybe if you had spoken up and talked about your sketches or whatever it is you put in your notebook, The Yellow Jacket—"

"Hornet," she corrects.

I remember. I'm just an ass. She already thinks that, so why try to change her opinion?

"You haven't told me any of your ideas," I say. "Not a

single one. So, you can't stand there and act like you deserve something you haven't worked for."

She purses her lips before licking her bottom lip and chewing on it.

I have to hold back my swallow.

"When you attack me for only being in marketing, what possible incentive could I have?" she asks.

"Making your park better, like you said," I counter.

"At this point, I'd rather you just be gone."

"Ah, that's the end goal, right?"

"The earlier, the better."

"Good. We're on the same page now."

We stand there in silence, her arms tightly crossed over her chest. She's trying to stay calm, but I can feel the energy radiating off her. I know because I feel it too—a live wire electrifying every nerve in my body from just looking at her.

I've never met a woman so invigorating.

Her nostrils flare on an exhale, and she shakes her head, letting out a sharp laugh.

"Fine, work on the thing by yourself," Lorelei says, throwing her hands in the air. "I *can't wait* to see it crash and burn tomorrow."

The sarcasm practically bleeds from her.

I open my mouth to retort, but she's already twisting in place to face away from me. And as she turns on her heel to leave, my eyes catch it right as it happens.

It.

The fall. The stumble. Whatever *it* is.

I watch Lorelei's whole body veer to the right and slouch.

Without thinking, I rush forward, placing a hand on her hip to catch her, burying it inside the curve of her waist, halting her in an upright position.

She slams her palm on the conference room table just in time to steady herself.

"Are you all right?" I ask.

She doesn't answer, and my blood pressure rises. My stomach feels tight, and tension rolls against my temples.

"Lorelei, what the hell just happened?" My tone is sharper than intended, but I can't help it.

Quiet as a mouse, barely audible, she whimpers, "Please let go of me."

And that's when I realize that my hand is still on her. My thumb is gripping the fabric of her shirt, but the rest of my fingers are clutched right in the dip of her waist, sprawling over her bare skin.

Lorelei is smooth under my coarse palms. Smoother than newly sanded wood or curved coaster steel. I shift my fingers just slightly, and tiny goose bumps form across her skin.

I jerk my hands back to me, and the sting of her touch still lingers on my callous hands—my worker's hands that have been cut, burned, and decimated over the years by working with raw materials, only to be haunted by the ghost of her silken waist.

"What happened?" I ask.

"My joint locked up," she says. "It's supposed to rain tomorrow."

She straightens her back. I can see her subtle tilt toward the left. I wonder if she's favoring her good side. I reach out to catch her again but pull my hands back once she seems to have her balance.

"I'm sorry," I say. "I was just trying to help."

I can feel my eyebrows furrow inward. She's so determined. So beautiful in her strength.

"Are you kidding me?" she bites out. I've never seen her

this angry before. Her eyes look glassy. "I don't need your help, Emory. Or your pitying look."

My mouth opens, then shuts.

"Pity?" I echo.

"Just present what you have tomorrow and get it over with."

It's not until she's out the door that I realize my heart is beating fast.

Beating for her.

17

Lorelei

It's storming the next day, which means a bad day for the preseason guests, but also an inevitable bad omen for Emory's board meeting presentation.

It's been raining too much lately. My leg is killing me. My hip is irritated. And now, I have Mr. Roller Coaster in our conference room, showing off the most generic refurbishment imaginable.

The board of directors came in with loud voices and bad jokes. I forget that the corporate guys only see money signs. And the way they're now sitting in their seats, practically reclined with hands steepled or pens clicking, tells me they don't see what Fred and I see.

On paper, the new top track is great. It makes the ride smoother. The Grizzly will get a fresh coat of paint. And we won't have to close the ride for another season. The board of directors is nodding and grinning with every bullet point.

But Fred isn't.

They don't know coasters like we do, nor do they understand the soul of this park.

But Fred does.

Emory's heart isn't in it, and I can see Fred's disappointment. He doesn't smile when he looks to me either. I wonder if he's also disappointed in me. My job was to incorporate more theming, and Emory threw all of that out the window by only adding top track.

The board of directors asks Emory questions when he's finished, and he answers them with finesse. Emory is a professional after all. If he's good at anything, it's business.

"Did you enjoy your stay?" one of them asks while packing up.

He nods. "Yes, thank you."

They pause, and I can tell they're waiting for some compliment about the park, but Emory doesn't relent. He just nods cordially and shuts his laptop.

Of course.

They slowly file out with Fred leading their charge, but I stay.

I wait as Emory puts the laptop in his backpack.

"May I help you?" he asks, not even looking up.

What happened to the Emory who handed that little girl the key chain? My whole world is shattering, and this man is just standing there. Job well done. Pat on the back. Move on to the next project.

"Let me get this straight," I say. "You stay here to learn the park. To make us a coaster that fits our brand. You make me endure you for weeks. And then you give us some generic ... thing?"

Emory's eyes dart up to me. I can see him searching my face.

Heck yeah, I brought the thunder, Mr. Roller Coaster. You mess with Honeywood, you mess with me.

"It'll be good for the park," he says.

"So, you don't deny it?"

"I did my job."

"No." I stiffen my back and look him dead in the eye. "No, you half-assed it."

He narrows his eyes.

Emory finishes the final zip of his backpack, like an end punctuation to his sentence, straightening up and slowly walking toward me.

A shudder runs over my spine.

"You want to run that by me again?"

"You gave us subpar work, and you know it," I hiss with more gumption.

Another step closer, almost a foot away now, with his hands in his pockets.

I move forward as well. So that he knows I'm not afraid of him. Because I'm not.

"What do you want me to say, huh?" he asks with a tip of his chin.

"That you'll redo it."

He lets out a weak laugh. "I don't have time for this," he says, turning on the spot, his fancy shoes clacking on the hardwood floor.

"Time for what? You're screwing us over, you know," I say, then spit out, "Again. This is the real Emory. This businessman with no heart for anything but money."

He halts mid-step, turning and looking at me.

I must have hit a nerve.

"Money?" he asks.

Emory's eyes are ignited. He looks furious. It only makes my own temper rise.

He opens his mouth to speak, but voices carry down the hall to us. He huffs out a breath, running a hand through his hair, messing up the neat style he had. Irritation is apparent in every motion.

"Don't do this," he says through gritted teeth, shaking his head. "Not on my last day."

"I'm sorry, did I offend you, Mr. Dawson?"

He looks from me to the hallway with the voices of our board members and then over to the closet door next to us.

"If you want a fight, let's fight," he whispers. "But I'm not doing it out in the open."

I look to the door, then back. "Worried about your reputation?"

He scoffs, his lips tipping up in a sarcastic smile. "Aren't you?"

I open my mouth, only to clam it back shut.

He's not wrong. We can't argue out here. I already have Fred disappointed in me today. I don't need more issues popping up.

I storm to the storage closet, ripping it open. Emory rushes in behind me. I knock my back against the shelves as we crowd in. He slams the door behind us.

There is only room for one person in here. We're practically standing on top of each other, his cedar-whatever scent engulfing us both. He's intoxicating.

This was a bad idea, but I'm committed now.

It's pitch-black inside. I can barely see anything in front of me, but I feel a brush of his hand ghosting along my face. I inhale sharply.

He pulls the single lightbulb's string, and it clicks on.

Emory looks just as irritated as he was before, but this time, his scowl is closer. Mere inches from me.

It'd be even worse if we were caught in here in this position, so I turn in the small space and twist the lock on the door.

"Listen," he says. "I'm not the only one with things to

lose here. You really want to be caught fighting with the person who is changing your park?"

He leans in. I can't help but lean my own head back, hitting the shelf behind me in the process.

"The person you're *suing*, in case you've forgotten?"

"You abandoned the launch idea," I say. "Adding just a steel track is a disgrace, and you know it. If you're truly here for penance, then you're doing a bang-up job of it."

"How do you know it won't market well?"

"It's a fine ride, sure," I say, my chest aching at the admission, but I continue anyway. "But even you once said that I know this town. I know this park. This is the bare minimum. We don't do that here."

"I'm just doing my *job*," he says again. The words sharp on his tongue. Biting. "This is my *job*, Lorelei. How many times do I have to say that?"

"You're being a corporate asshole," I spit back.

"I've got to get home, and this was the doable outcome for the time I had."

"We're paying you for good work."

"Not exactly."

My stomach twists.

"What ... what are you talking about?" I ask.

"I'm doing this for peanuts," he bites out. "If it were up to our CEO, I wouldn't even be here."

"Then, why are you here?"

"To do the right thing," he says.

"The right thing?" I pry.

"Yes, for you," he says. "The girl who got injured. Twice. So, I hope you're happy."

I grind my jaw.

He hopes I'm happy?

"God, you're the absolute worst sometimes," I say. "Do you know that?"

"Go on," he says with a jerk of his chin. "Tell me how much you hate me. Really."

I can feel my heart racing and a sting of tears behind my eyes. I'm so angry that I'm getting emotional, and that only makes me more livid.

How dare he make me cry!

How dare he!

"Seriously. Go on," he coaxes again. "You don't say shit to anyone else, but I know you're not a pushover. You've never held back with me. So, go."

"Screw you."

"You first."

I reach for the handle, but the subtle turn in my hips in this small, enclosed space pinches the nerve running down along my pelvis.

I wince and let out a whimper. I can't help it. It's all the rain and the storms.

"Is it your hip again?" he asks.

Like the drop of a hat, his tone is calm. Gentle. This only infuriates me more.

"Like you care," I bite out.

He inhales sharply. "You actually do hate me, don't you?" He says it like it's fact.

I don't hate anyone. I never have in my life, but standing here, looking at this man, I wonder if I could.

"You're an asshole," I say. "You know it, and you don't even care. You just say things to hurt people. If you care so much about doing things, then maybe find out what happened with The Grizzly."

"Wear and tear happens over the years—"

"For the first accident, it did. But the second accident? Come on."

His jaw tics, but he doesn't say anything.

"The wheels got caught." My voice cracks, and I hate myself for it. "The wheels got caught and went off the track, Emory. Honeywood has passed every inspection for twenty years. So, don't give me this bullshit about wear and tear. I want answers."

He's silent, but then he does the last thing I can handle.

He gives me *that look*.

His eyebrows pull toward the center, a tiny crease forming between them.

And I can't take it anymore. My heart pounds in my chest, and I don't think I've ever been so angry in my life. Not when I sat under the stars in complete darkness as my hip pressed into The Grizzly's car. Not when I was trying to recover in the hospital. Not when I knew I could never run again, no matter how much physical therapy I tried.

My blood is pumping and roaring through me like the very coaster that hurt me.

"Don't you dare," I snap.

"What?"

"Don't you dare look at me like that again. With pity. With ... disgust. How fucking dare you!"

Emory's eyes dart between mine. I can see everything this close. The flecks of green in his deep brown eyes. A small scar on his cheek. The tiny abrasion on his chin, blending in with the stubble. The small twitch in the corner of his mouth.

And in that moment, something shifts.

I see it in his eyes first, how they relax a little. They trail down to my lips, linger for one second, then two—much too long—and then slowly make their way back up to my eyes.

The temperature drops, and every nerve in my body feels it.

I pull my own lip in, chewing on it, unsure of how to move.

The dead silence is only accentuated by my shaking exhale.

And before I can take another breath, he steals it from me.

Emory Dawson kisses me.

His lips press against mine. Suddenly. Out of nowhere.

His rough hand grabs the nape of my neck, snaking into my hair as he deepens the motion.

The initial kiss is punishing, but as he swipes a tongue across my lips, it is soft. Gentle. A question. A plea. Maybe even an apology.

I can feel his stubble against me, his inhale as his lips caress mine, and the tiny, shaking exhale that follows, breathing life into me.

So, I kiss him back.

I open my mouth, welcoming him in.

I turn off my mind and let myself sink into his touch.

And it's wonderful. Horrific. Impossibly amazing.

Our lips move in furious tandem. The rhythm comes natural to both of us. His mouth lays claim to mine, and I fight it with the desperation of my own tongue dancing with his.

And I am—desperate as hell—kissing him back.

He devours me more each moment. Each kiss after kiss after kiss.

My chest is ablaze, my whole body lighting like fire, sensitive to every touch. Every tug of my strands, every exhale against me.

I trail my own hand up his hardened chest, running over

the buttons of his white collared shirt, over the column of his corded neck, and to the curve of his stubbled jaw. He's everything and nothing I imagined. Composed yet unhinged. Asking yet demanding with his touch. My other hand finds its way to his hair, gripping it at the same time I fist the fabric of his shirt, trying to pull him even closer, as if that could be possible.

Emory takes a step forward to close the nonexistent gap. My back hits the shelving, causing pens and other stupid objects to clatter to the floor. I stumble, and his hand tightens in my hair while the other grips my hip, clutching it in his grasp to steady me.

His hand trails down my side. There's nothing nice about it. It's not sweet. It's heady. He fists my fabric in his hand.

I whimper into his mouth.

He growls back like a starved animal.

God.

My thighs shiver, my knees wanting to give out with the noises we're making. The heavy breaths, the small sighs I can't hold back any longer, the reciprocating moans he returns when I do.

I melt into him. Into the sound of his longing, letting the apex between my thighs grind against the hardness beneath his zipper.

And then ... it ends.

Just as quickly as it started, Emory breaks the kiss. He jerks his hands away from my head and waist, leaving me limp against the shelves. We're still chest to chest, taking heavy breaths, my breasts pushing against him with each subsequent exhale.

Our eyes search each other's for a second. I don't know

what to say. My mind has been washed of anything but him and that kiss and my need for more.

He breaks the silence first.

"My apologies."

Then, Emory reaches down, swiftly unlocks the door, and rushes out.

I try to follow, but by the time I lean out, he's already out of the conference room and down the hall, taking long strides and running a hand through the same hair I had in my own grip not even seconds ago.

I stand there, only able to blink and watch as he whips around the corner, away from my sight.

I reach up and run a finger over my bottom lip. I can still feel the sting of him. I think, at one point, he might have bitten me, and I missed it.

What in the world just happened?

18

Emory

"Wow, you look like shit."

"Shut up."

Orson laughs.

I'm having a hard time finding the humor.

I *do* look like shit. My hair is a mess because I can't stop running my hands through it. I'm sure the area under my eyes looks heavy and sleep-deprived. And it's because I am.

It's just before seven in the morning, and we're at Slow Riser, a coffee shop in Cedar Cliff that has so far only seen me, a couple older people reading the newspaper, and now, my cousin, who is scanning me head to foot. I've been here since they opened at six.

Orson plops into the booth across from me. His eyebrows rise, and he looks expectant.

I don't know what to say.

I'm miserable?

I couldn't stop myself?

At least, not with her.

Lorelei Arden is everything. She's the steady rise of a lift hill. She's more exciting than the anticipation as you crest the top. She is the thrill of the downhill, the rush of anxiety through your chest, the harsh banked turn, the dip in the track, the grip from the brake run.

And I couldn't help myself.

I just couldn't.

But that is my problem.

Among others.

My entire being burns for Lorelei. It burns like the big dumpster fire that I am.

I didn't sleep last night. My normal four hours was stolen by the thought of Lorelei and the massive mistake I'd made in kissing her.

The woman who hates me.

The woman who is *suing* me.

I need to get my head on straight, and the only person I could think to call was Orson.

"Well, I'm here," he says, giving a wave to one of the old women nearby, who waves back to him.

His baseball cap is on backward, covering his shaved head. I never realized how much younger he looks even though we're only a couple years apart. Maybe the joy of small-town nightlife gives him radiance and youth. Or maybe all my crappy decisions make me look older.

Lorelei's words bounce through my head, just like they have for the past eighteen hours. *"You're an asshole. You know it, and you don't even care."*

I open my mouth to talk—still not decided on what I should even say—but thankfully, I'm saved by someone else who stops by our table.

It's the barista. Orson stands and hugs her, asking how her morning is. His laugh is contagious as he talks. She laughs with him, and her cheeks get pink. She touches him on the arm.

I wish socialization were as easy for me as it is for him.

Everyone knows everyone in Cedar Cliff. It's me who is the odd one out. The most familiar person I know is some old woman named Mrs. Stanley, who frequents the yoga studio I've started visiting two doors down from here.

Almost everything in Cedar Cliff is "two doors down" or "one block over" or "just a five-minute drive."

Even when Orson agreed to meet me here this early, he added, "I'll need to hit up the farmers market down the street anyway."

Down the street.

It's a type of familiarity I've never had with anywhere that wasn't my workshop.

I kind of like it.

Eventually, the barista offers to take Orson's order, and he asks for coffee, making it a point to request creamer after eyeing my cup of plain black. I order another cup as well.

Orson clicks his tongue at me after a couple moments. "Are we just gonna sit here or ..."

"I just need to think," I say.

"You needed me for that? I mean, I'm flattered but—"

"No, I needed a friend."

His mouth opens into a huff of laughter. "Wow, I think that's the first time you've ever called me that."

I lean back in my chair, lifting my hands above my head and sighing.

Orson's mouth twists to the side as he grins. "Having a crisis, Emmy?"

"Can I ask you something?"

"It's either that or we talk about the weather."

I swallow, looking outside. It's sunny today. Lorelei's hip might not be hurting. I can find solace in that.

The barista drops off our coffees with a wink in Orson's

direction. He thanks her, returning the gesture. But it doesn't seem skeezy. He's genuine. Nice.

"Am I a bad person?" I ask.

I didn't think Orson's eyes could grow bigger, but they do.

"No ..." he says, dragging out the word. "No. You're ... pensive."

"Pensive?"

"Stern."

"That's not better."

"Yeah, okay, but," Orson says, waving his hands, as if finding the words in midair, "you're a nice guy underneath it all."

"No, I'm not."

"You mean well. You have a lot of Aunt Willa in you."

My mom. The kindest person I know. My heart feels lighter with his words.

He clears his throat. "So, what, you're just lonely?"

"I'm not lonely," I shoot back. But, God, am I? Why else would I have called him? "I just ... need to distract myself."

He twists his lips to the side. "Are you running still?" he asks. "Or doing yoga? Meghan down at Yogi Bare says you've been a regular."

"Do you know all the women in this town?"

He points a finger at me with a grin. "That is an insinuation I don't appreciate."

"Name me the instructors."

"Unfair."

"Come on. Do it," I say. "I know you can."

He grins back at me, holding up his hand and counting down the fingers. "Meghan, Jenny, Allie, Theo ..."

"Oh God, don't tell me you've slept with Theo too."

"No," he says, halting me with his hand in the air. He

looks like a deer in headlights before shaking his head. "No, she's ... no." His face reddens. "No, I haven't."

I sip my coffee.

Touchy subject. Got it.

I bring my cup down right as he starts to stumble his way through the next sentence.

"So, anyway, tell me why you need a distraction."

I stiffen.

How do I tell him I kissed Lorelei? How do I say I feel like I've made both a mistake and also a wonderful discovery? How do I say I'll never forget that kiss?

I don't. That's how.

"I did something," I say.

"What did you do?"

"A complicated thing."

"You're going to keep it vague?"

"Yes."

He sighs. He twists the bill of his baseball cap forward.

"Okay, so ... what *can* you tell me?" he asks. "Or what do you *want* to tell me?"

I sip the last of my coffee before setting it down and tapping my knuckles on the tabletop.

"I think I need to stay in Cedar Cliff longer," I finally say. "I need to rework the ride."

Orson's face transforms into a disbelieving smile.

He barks out a laugh. "Who even are you?"

I sigh, grabbing my new cup the barista dropped off and tossing it back like a shot of espresso.

It burns like hell.

I cringe.

"Apparently, I'm not fully *here* this morning," I say. "That's who I am."

"So, why make a change?"

Lorelei's words ring through my head again. *"You're an asshole. You know it, and you don't even care."*

"Because it's the right thing to do," I say. "Because it's what I came here to do. To give Honeywood a *great* coaster. Not just an added top rail or some small changes. The Grizzly needs an overhaul. And if I want my company to survive with integrity, then I need to start making some executive decisions."

He lets out a high-pitched, "Hmm," in response.

I narrow my eyes. "What?"

"You're kinda sounding like a nice guy."

I sniff. "Well, this is important."

He smirks. "Honeywood is important to you?"

My stomach shifts. I'm sure it's just the overabundance of coffee. I don't respond.

Orson shakes his head before twisting his cap back once more. "I knew you weren't all suits under there," he says.

"Screw the suits," I say.

"Yeah," Orson says with a grin, "screw the suits."

19

Lorelei

"Wow, look at you! So flexible!"

Quinn and I cut a glance over at Theo, who is mid-handstand.

"Showoff," Quinn says.

"No! You're just out of practice!"

If she were anyone else, I'd say Theo is in fact showing off, but that's just not her style. She's the type to compliment your puny progress and genuinely mean it—even if I am barely reaching past my knees with my stretch.

"I'm so proud of y'all," Theo says. "I can't believe it took so long to get you back here! Lore, that stretch is only gonna make your leg feel better over time, I promise."

I feel my chest heat at the comment before echoing her initial, "You're right. I'm just out of practice, is all."

We're at Yogi Bare, the only yoga studio in Cedar Cliff. Their specialty is hot yoga, a type of relief my leg desperately needs at the moment. The studio is packed with Honeywood team members, taking advantage of the free time before our official opening day.

I've been avoiding coming here for months. But after last week ... I could stand to clear my head.

I keep replaying the same clip over and over.

Emory Dawson kissing me. His hand in my hair, tugging with just enough roughness to give a girl something to beg for.

How hard he was against me.

How much my own body betrayed me by wanting it just as bad.

When I went home that night, I locked myself in my room after telling Quinn I didn't feel well, and I ended up touching myself before my back even hit the mattress. My body hadn't been so heated in I don't know how long. Maybe since the accident. I orgasmed three times.

Three.

Without a vibrator.

All to the thought of how his lightly stubbled jaw had felt in my palm, to how he'd pushed me against the shelves, to how everything had felt like pleasure and punishment, all rolled up together.

I'd kill him if I didn't want to kiss him again so bad.

Except I can't. He left town after last week's presentation.

That was it.

Good-bye.

Sayonara.

So, yoga it is.

"Oh, good morning, Mrs. Stanley!" Theo gracefully dismounts from her handstand with a partial cartwheel before walking over to the shuffling older woman, who both Quinn and I wave to.

"God, I wanna be like her when I'm older," Quinn

143

mutters, clicking her tongue. "What's she now? A hundred?"

I laugh. "Eighty-one."

"And still going to yoga, wearing that."

Mrs. Stanley used to run a day care in town. She was the watchful eye for most of us born and raised in Cedar Cliff, and even though she is starting her eighties, the lady still has enough spunk to wear shorter shorts than I can manage along with a cropped tank. Her sagging, wrinkled boobs threaten to dip below the hemline, but her workout gear really tucks those puppies in.

While Yogi Bare encourages the least amount of clothes possible for some of their classes—it's kinda their thing—I've never been in less than my wicking tank top and bike shorts that hit just above my knee. These shorts hide my thigh scar.

"No fear at all from that old bird," Quinn says in awe, giving her head one last shake.

To live without fear. What a feat. I wonder how many people Mrs. Stanley has kissed in a closet. I wonder if she was the bold one who instigated or if she was the pushover who kissed them back.

"Oh shit, oh shit, oh shit."

"Language. Jeez, Quinn," I say. "Mrs. Stanley is right there."

"The words warrant it because oh *shit*, Lore. Look!"

I follow Quinn's bugged-out eyes and nodding head toward the parting curtains that separate our room from the lobby.

And there he is.

Emory Dawson.

Can a woman get no peace in this town?!

To top it all off, he's in a tight white tee and gray sweatpants—gray sweatpants that hang artfully from his hips and leave almost nothing to the imagination. Just below the knotted drawstring is a nice, healthy, thick bulge, and by God, if that is him *not* erect, then how in the world—

I glance up at his face, and he pauses on the spot. He's staring at me, no doubt watching as I just checked out his freaking *wiener*.

My chest, my face—every single thing about me grows hot.

Emory's jaw is as tight as I've ever seen it, and those eyebrows are reliably turned inward with the tiny crease between them.

He's late, so the only space available—unless he wants to be dead center in the front of the class—is right next to me.

So, he spreads his mat up at the front, in the dead center.

"What the absolute heck is he doing here?" I hiss-whisper to Quinn, watching as Emory says hi to Mrs. Stanley, as if they were BFFs.

Since when is he best friends with someone?

I look down to my own mat. "He was supposed to have left town by now!"

I feel my stomach trip over itself. As if it reached stairs at the end of a hallway and forgot how to walk and just barreled down without any grace whatsoever.

Quinn's head tilts to the side. "Oh boy."

And when I follow her gaze back to him once more, he's taking off his shirt.

I mean, every other man in here isn't wearing one. Why should he?

Dang it, Yogi Bare!

Nobody else is built like him. Nobody else has broad

shoulders that shift with every movement. Nobody else has those upper-middle-of-the-back muscles that are thick and probably hard as rocks. Nor do they have lean biceps and even stronger-looking forearms, littered with manly hair and corded veins.

My mouth is drier than the desert, but my bike shorts are not.

"All right, it's eight on the dot," Theo says with a clap. "Let's get going!"

Quinn has to whack my arm to get me breathing again.

I stand on my mat and look straight ahead.

Don't look at Emory, I tell myself.

Except I end up watching Emory the entire class.

We're all sweating and holding poses that my shaking legs can barely maintain. But Emory is a yoga god, twisting into Warrior Two, showing off his smattering of brown chest hair in all its glory.

Good Lord.

He's not supposed to be so gorgeous.

He's not even supposed to *be here*.

Yet by the end, I'm less concerned with that and more concerned with how fast I can get into a cold shower.

We pack up, me rolling my mat in silence as Quinn continues to whisper, "Holy moly, that was next-level porn."

"Quinn!"

"Is that weird to say? It's weird. Sorry. Yes. We hate the guy."

I gulp and nod my head. "Correct. That is ... correct."

Hate is a very complicated word at the moment.

When I have my mat rolled under my arm, turning to leave, he's already standing in front of me. He looks less angry than when he walked in, but his jaw is still ticcing. That jawline that I felt in my palm not even three days ago.

"How are you?" he asks.

How are you? Is he kidding?

"I'm ..."

I don't finish.

He's wearing his shirt again, but it's sticking so close to his sweaty chest. It might only have spots of sweat, but he could be competing in a wet T-shirt contest as far as I'm concerned. And he's winning. Gold medals. Every single ribbon.

"Right," he finishes for me.

I nod in response, rolling my bottom lip in to chew on it. When I find his gaze, it's pointed directly at that motion before snapping back up to my eyes.

If he looked south even more, he would be able to see how hard my nipples are. The traitors.

"You're supposed to be gone," I blurt out.

At that, Quinn looks between us and says, "Yep, meet you at the car, Lore."

Thanks a lot, best friend.

Then, it's just us. Us and the few lingering people, but mostly ... us. Not standing nearly as close as we were in that closet, but close enough. So near that I can smell his mix of cedar, mahogany, and sweat. Pure man smell.

"I was supposed to leave," he says. "But I have other ideas."

My stomach flips at the statement. There's no way he's talking about me when he says that, is he? If so, he shouldn't sound so seductive when he says it, but ...

"For The Grizzly," he amends. "He deserves better."

The words echo through me. *He.* The ride.

I don't realize I haven't replied until I see him slowly grinding his jaw.

He glances down to my lips and back up one final time before leaving me with a parting, "I'll see you at Honeywood, Lorelei."

He walks out the door. I stare at his tight butt the whole time.

20

Emory

If I could capture a snapshot of the look on Fred's face, I would.

His mouth is open like a gutted fish, and he keeps blinking, as if he can't believe what he's hearing.

In his defense, neither could my dad when I told him I might be here for the rest of the summer.

"Are you fucking with me?" he said.

"No. They need a full rebuild, and we're giving it to them."

"What the hell has happened to you down there?"

"I'm just doing what we should have done all along."

"Emory, you give them an inch, they'll take a mile," he said. *"You say you want to give them a rebuild, and they'll keep asking for more specializations. Give them what they deserve."*

I know what Honeywood deserves. This will be better. I just know it.

"I took a look at the official blueprints for The Grizzly this past weekend," I say. "We can do better."

Fred purses his lips.

"I'm proposing that we build a brand-new Grizzly," I continue. "Not a new track on top or added launches, but a fresh rebuild that fits with Honeywood. Ensures confidence in the locals."

Fred leans back in his creaking chair, arms crossed over his chest, resting on his belly that stretches the body of his already-tight Honeywood-branded polo. He twists his mustache to the side in consideration before clicking his pen a few times and taking a drink of his honey cider.

I proposed we have breakfast in the park inside their signature eatery, The Bee-fast Stop. The all-wood restaurant is accentuated by the sounds of clacking plates, sizzling bacon, and '70s music echoing from a jukebox in the corner.

I wanted to be among the guests for opening day, fanny packs and all, scattered around us, also ordering Honeywood's classic over easy eggs, thick sausage links, and bumblebee-shaped pancakes. I'm trying to surround myself with Honeywood's unique eccentricities. I should have come here sooner because the pancakes are making it hard to be professional when all I want to do is shove them in my face.

I have to be on my best behavior because not only is Fred here, but also, right beside him, with an untouched fruit bowl, is Lorelei.

I resist the urge to look over at her. I know we'll be working together longer if Fred approves my pitch, but the less I look at that dreamy, doe-eyed gaze, the less I'll try to get her to kiss me again.

I remember a lot of things from Friday. How she felt soft. How much stronger she seemed under my palms. It's obvious in her thighs alone just how much she walks the park.

Her peachy scent consumed the closet we were in, and it hasn't stopped invading my mind since.

A few seconds pass, and since they both appear stunned, I continue.

"It'll match Honeywood's current values," I say. "It'll be everything you are looking for."

They still say nothing.

I finally steal a look at Lorelei. Her lips are twisted to the side, just like Fred's. Though infinitely plumper and more attractive.

Infinitely.

"I know my work ethic. I can make a good attraction," I say. "I would like to do this for Honeywood."

I feel like I'm in the first interview of my life. Or an interrogation. What's the difference really?

"Okay," Lorelei says. "I'm curious to see what you can do."

My heart beats a little faster. My stomach does flip-flops.

Is that ... butterflies?

Oh God, pull it together, man. You're thirty-six, for Christ's sake.

Fred glances at her with one eyebrow raised.

"If Lorelei thinks you're capable, so do I," he says. "I'll need to consult the board first. They might not want this though. They liked your original, uh ..."

"Generic change?" I supply.

Fred harrumphs, and I breathe a laugh through my nose in agreement.

"Yes," he says. "Generic is right. Not a Honeywood type of change one bit."

I see the businessman in him come out. The same man who gave me a stern, downward tilt of his chin when I presented last week. He's passionate about this place, as he should be. Fiercely protective. It was that expression I saw that made me realize why he's general manager for this park.

"If I give the board something more attuned to Honeywood for the same cost, I doubt they'll turn it down."

"The same cost?" Fred asks.

"That I can guarantee," I say.

His palms slap his knees. "Can't turn that down. Are you sure?"

"It's the right thing to do," I say.

His face is swallowed by a grin.

I look over to Lorelei. Her small hands are covering her notebook, but just underneath, I see sketches. Tons of them. Half-words, half–misshapen lines, forming vague ideas.

They're roller coasters.

I tip my chin toward the notebook. "If you could have a perfect coaster, what would it be?" I ask.

Lorelei opens her mouth, shifting in her chair, letting out a breath that's between a scoff and an exhalation. "You're the engineer," she says. "How would I know?"

"Yes, but you're sketching," I say. "What is that?"

She looks down at her notebook, hand splaying over it, as if to cover the drawings.

"Why are you looking at my sketchbook?" she asks defensively.

"Why won't you show me?" I counter.

Fred's elbow knocks against hers, making those deer-in-headlights eyes dart over to him. Fred smiles.

"Lore, share your ideas," he says. "It's why we're here."

"I can't," she says with a small shrug. "I'm not qualified."

"Well, clearly, you love coasters," I say.

"That doesn't mean anything."

"It does."

Her lips part in disbelief. "I wouldn't ride it anyway," she says.

"Maybe. Maybe not."

She scoffs out a small laugh.

I like the little bit of fire in her that comes out when we argue—no, *challenge* each other. I imagine most people don't push her. They do exactly what she accused me of doing. They pity her. Nobody wants to hurt her feelings.

I call bullshit.

She's got thick skin. She just needs the right passion project to talk about, and for her, it's these coasters.

"Fine," she says with a bit of a bite to it. It spurs a small smile from me. "Perfect coaster for me? Multiple launches."

"We had that in my first draft."

"No, you had two," she indicates. "We need more. Incremental throughout. Different speeds. Keeps the rider guessing."

"All right. And?"

"Maybe one big drop hill. Nothing too high though. Families should want to ride."

"Okay, and what's this?" I ask, reaching across the table to trace along the edge of her sketch with crudely drawn trees. The outside of my pinkie swipes against her fingertips. My whole hand twitches in response, like a flame melting my cold heart.

"It ... it needs to be more themed," she says, stammering out the words. "We're a fun park set in the mountains. We could use more trees and terrain decoration. People come here for the nature. For an exciting day with family."

"The current iteration isn't exciting?" I coax.

She stares at me, tilting her head to the side slightly.

"I'm not testing you, Lorelei," I say. "I'm getting expertise. You know Honeywood more than me."

"I don't want to lose some of our core audience," she says. "Families. We need to make it more approachable."

A tiny twitch forms at the edge of my mouth. I can feel it. She knows this park, this town, and these guests better than I do.

So, before I can stop myself, I say, "I want to see all your ideas."

"All?"

"Every one."

"That's a wonderful thought," Fred says.

I raise my eyebrows, as if to say, *See?*

I know I need to look away, but the best I can do is maintain eye contact. If I glance down at her biting her lip, I might reach across the table and bite it myself.

"Can you have rough ideas prepped by Friday?" Fred asks.

"By Friday?" Lorelei gapes.

Lorelei looks at Fred, who is beaming, as if the sun had started shining right through his pores, and I think I can see the wheels turning.

"I'll need *something* to pitch to the board of directors."

"Of ... of course we can," she says.

"I'll set up a meeting schedule," I say.

Lorelei's gaze cuts to me. "I might be busy with my regular work."

"I'll work it around whatever you have going on then."

Her brown eyes dance over my face. She gives her head a small, almost-imperceptible shake, as if wordlessly asking me, *Why?*

I also wish I knew why the gentle small-town girl capti-vates me so.

Sometimes, you see a tall ride peaking toward the sky, and you know you shouldn't get on. Your stomach will fall. Maybe you'll get motion sickness. But the potential excite-ment is too deliciously intriguing to walk away.

21

Lorelei

"What would you say if I told you I'm in trouble?"

"Where are we burying the body?"

"Quinn, I'm serious."

"And I have a shovel."

I lean back on our couch, covering my face with my hand as I hear Quinn take a victorious bite from her pizza slice.

When I told her about my permanent involvement in the full rebuild of The Grizzly, she instantly ordered the greasiest of greasy pizzas, too many sparkling waters, and a movie we've seen twenty times over.

For her, it's a celebration. For me, I wanna know what I did to deserve my life getting turned upside down. Maybe it was that time I didn't donate to the Sarah McLachlan dog commercial at three in the morning. Yes, surely, the universe is giving me karmic retribution for that.

"Okay, I'm sorry, what's up?" Quinn asks. "I assume you murdered Mr. Roller Coaster, and this is why you're getting to contribute your ideas. Yeah, *your ideas*, lady!"

I smile when she punches my shoulder but deflate not even a moment later.

"I kissed him."

Her pizza slice drops to her lap, tiny bits of mozzarella splattering her yoga pants.

"Freaking-what?" It comes out as one word.

"He kissed me first," I rush in, like a child begging someone not to tell their parents. Which, I guess, I kind of am.

It was irresponsible. My mama raised me better than that. She would murder me if she found out I'd kissed the guy I was suing. First degree. Premeditated. She'd be smiling in her mug shot, all while my dad said, *I brought you flowers for jail, honey.*

"You ... kissed ... ohmigod."

Quinn is an expert at those multi-word mashups.

She shakes her head, flopping her pizza slice back into the box. "Landon is gonna kill you."

Landon. I didn't consider my brother.

My stomach flips at even the thought of him knowing.

I bet he knows. A twin always knows.

"Nobody can know!" I say, waving my hands around and scooting closer to her on the couch. "Don't you dare snitch to anyone."

I can feel the panic tugging at me, coursing through my body in waves.

Quinn sighs, placing a hand on my knee, which I cover with my own.

"I won't. I promise. But, Lore, that was a bad idea."

"Horrible."

"Like, the worst."

"One hundred percent."

"So, how was it?"

"Wonderful."

I don't realize what I said until it's all out in the open. I cup my palm to my mouth, as if I could shove the words back in.

But the words are there.

Emory Dawson is an excellent kisser.

He's the type of man who kisses with his whole weight and all his passion.

I wonder if he's won awards in that too.

"Figured," Quinn says, leaning back on the couch with her lips curled up in a smile. "Not surprising. He's gorgeous."

"Quinn!" I whine. "You're not helping!"

"Wait, but I thought we liked good kissers?"

"Not the ones I'm in a massive *lawsuit* with!"

"Bit of a complication."

"Or the ones that we hate."

Quinn's mouth tilts down in mock disappointment. "You don't really hate him, do you?" she says. "Plus, we shouldn't hate good kissers. Remember Daniel from tenth grade? Slobbered all over me. The worst. And then Lewis? Ugh, he was all teeth. I think good kissers get a pass on things."

Part of me wants to agree. It's that same part of me that wonders how he would kiss me the second time. Would it be as exciting if we weren't in a closet, but instead under moonlight? At some romantic dinner?

I'm sick in the head.

"He admitted that his last presentation was generic too," I say.

Quinn, mid-sip, sputters out her drink.

"Good Lord, let me keep my food down!" she says, placing the can next to her discarded pizza. "How is this getting crazier with each passing second? You got Mr. Roller Coaster to admit he was *wrong*?"

I sigh, grabbing the nearest pillow and shoving my face into it with a groan.

My voice muffled, I yell, "Oh my God, I kissed *Mr. Roller Coaster!*"

Quinn slurps her drink. "Good kisser though."

I throw the pillow on the ground and loll my head to the side, blinking at her.

"And," she continues, "I bet he's good at oral too. Most good kissers are."

"Quinn! Jesus!"

That didn't help my nerves.

Because now, I can't stop thinking of his head buried between my thighs.

Well, if my thighs could open that wide ...

I've had my fair share of partners throughout my twenties, but nothing serious. I dated a Games supervisor for a few seasons at Honeywood; there were a few online dates in Atlanta that led to so-so nights. But after my accident, there has only been one man. I regretted it. Due to my injury, my legs hurt when they're forced apart. He thought I was just being a prude and left.

I wonder how Emory would react.

No. No, no, no.

"Can we go back to when I said I was helping with design?" I ask.

"You're thinking about him in bed, aren't you?"

My face heats in seconds.

"You're blinded by the fact that this super-genius beef-cake might just wanna screw your brains out," she continues.

"Oh my God, Quinn!"

"Just saying." Quinn smirks again, and then her face falls. "But ... you probably can't kiss him again. You know that, right? I mean, good kissing aside, you're in a lawsuit with him, Lore."

"I'm suing his company," I correct. "Big difference."

"You've got to tell your lawyer."

"Quinn, come on. No."

"You've got to stop being so nice too," she says, her eyebrows rising. She's in lecture mode. "What if he's ... I don't know ... manipulating you? Getting you to drop the lawsuit?"

"I don't ... I don't think he would do that."

But why not?

Who is to say he's not twisting my rubber arm to get me to like him?

What if he's playing the long con?

But my gut tells me that's not the case. I just feel it.

It's the fact that he's barely charging us for this reconstruction. The fact that he's doing even more work for no increase. That he tries to catch me when I fall. Every single time.

"Can you trust me?" I ask Quinn.

She looks at me with furrowed eyebrows. I can tell she's considering a snarky comeback, but she can see the optimism in me. It's what makes us work—my incessant positivity contrasted with her realistic pessimism.

I don't expect to win this unspoken discussion, but she finally licks her lips and nods.

"Fine," she says. "Okay. Yes. I'll trust your judgment. Just be careful."

Normally, my nerves lessen when I feel like I've made the right call, but I am weighed down even more.

22

Lorelei

It's *blue sky* phase again. This is the time when all practicality is thrown out the window, and every possibility, want, and dream is presented for the idea of a new coaster.

I get to Honeywood early, writing down ideas of my own. I should be on the phone with our ad agency, telling them the news. That we've got a huge campaign—bigger than expected—coming our way. But I'm too busy, doodling out the twists of a new coaster track and a messy loop. It looks like a kindergartner drew it, but at least it's not in crayon.

I hear a knock on my doorframe. My hand covers my drawings on instinct.

I look up and see him.

Him.

Just looking at him sends me on edge. I've seen his usual heather-gray T-shirt too many times to count at this point. But today, he fills it out well.

Don't you dare swoon, Lorelei.

"Hi," Emory says.

"Hey. Uh ... can I help you?" I ask.

"Right. Yes," he says, shaking out his hand.

Oh my God, is he *nervous*?

"Would you like to join me? With the other engineers?"

My heart pounds faster. "Seriously?"

"Yeah. Would you like to see how it goes?"

I don't even hesitate or ask why he's inviting me. I grab my notebook and roll back my chair to rush toward the door. I practically stumble out, like a kid being told it's snack time or that they get an extra recess.

I think I see a twitch at the edge of his mouth as I pass.

In the conference room, it's just me, him, and the projector screen, showing tiny windows of other engineers on the virtual conference call. Emory types fast on a new document as they all jump in with ideas. They call out roller coaster terms that make no sense—*Lagoon roll, in-line twist*, and something called a *Drachen fire dive drop* that they all laugh at, even Emory.

Emory. Who I've never seen truly laugh before. When I hear the laugh, it makes my neck jerk back in reaction to how loud, genuine, and booming it is. How white his capped teeth are. How lines form at the edge of his mouth, making it seem like he carries no weight on his soul.

It's beautiful.

Even the team seems apprehensive about this new development in Emory's personality. But after a while, their hesitant smiles relax, and then they're laughing too. Everyone is throwing out new ideas, thoughts, and jokes. It's a freaking joy-fest in here.

I'm so out of my wheelhouse, which is why I drop my pen on the floor when Emory asks, "Thoughts, Lorelei?"

Thoughts? What thoughts?

What ideas could I possibly have in a room full of

people who have created so many attractions throughout their careers? All I've done is create a gingerbread house. And the cookies came precut with instructions.

"I ... it all sounds ..." I huff out a laugh. "I don't even know what stuff is called, to be honest. What's the dragon ... roll ... California sushi thing?"

Emory turns to his laptop.

Great. I blew it. I look like a fool. I clam my mouth shut, looking back down to my notes.

"The Drachen fire dive drop," he starts, "has only been on one coaster, and it was shut down. Just some silly coaster humor. But that is a good point. You might not know lingo, so try showing us what you want for The Grizzly."

I look back up, and on the projector, all the tiny windows of faces have been minimized and replaced by diagrams and sketches of different roller coaster elements. They're all labeled.

It's like an encyclopedia just for me.

"Well," I say, trying to spur up confidence again, "I like that one. The heartline roll. And ... I actually kinda like the Lagoon roll too."

When I turn to him, he's smiling.

Emory Dawson is smiling.

My face heats.

"Nervous?" he whispers with a chuckle.

A chuckle. Oh my heart.

"Never," I say, smiling back at him. This only makes him smile wider.

"I think that one"—I point toward one in the corner—"wouldn't go over well with our younger crowd."

"Oh, of course," a voice says from the speaker. "It's Honeywood. Apologies, ma'am. We can get rid of that. Hang on."

"Yeah, I was thinking too ..." another voice chimes in.

And then, suddenly, they're alternating sharing their laptop screens with on-the-spot sketches of a roller coaster, surrounded by trees and smaller drops. They're taking the one sentence I said and reading my mind.

These are true professionals.

I look to Emory.

He's nodding along with their ideas, and I see the twitch at the side of his mouth, as if a smile is begging to come out once more. I wonder how often it does appear or what brings it to the surface. And I wonder if I can figure out the secret.

23

Emory

I t's a rush to the finish line before Friday's presentation.

We get on a call with Honeywood's contracted ad agency and talk promotional ideas and timing. I pitch a few concepts, but marketing has never been my forte. Their creative director, Grace, is the first to tell me that. After too many embarrassing ideas, I finally shut up and let them do their jobs.

Lorelei tosses me a smirk, and they dive back in, sans my crappy Comic Sans opinions.

She's smiling around me more, and my heart stumbles like a teenage boy every time.

It's fun, seeing Lorelei in her element. Her relationship with the creative director is quippy yet professional. Grace knows which of Lorelei's buttons to push to get her to open up and bloom.

I'd be lying if I said I wasn't jealous of that skill.

On Thursday, we pull in guests from the park throughout the day, giving them vouchers for a free drink if they vote on which marketing image appeals to them most.

Almost all votes go to Lorelei's idea instead of Grace's.

I didn't need park guests to tell me that though.

Lorelei Arden knows Honeywood.

We stand there, me with my arms crossed and her with a finger tracing her bottom lip as she clutches a clipboard to her chest.

My stomach clenches as I watch her dazed stare fall over every line on the poster.

I tell myself that I cannot, under any circumstances, kiss her again.

No matter how bad I want to.

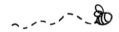

I try something new.

I decide to run through the park in the morning rather than on the musty hotel treadmill. The employee key fob Fred gave me lets me in.

I didn't sleep well—worse than usual anyway—knowing today was the second presentation to the board. I also couldn't stop imagining Lorelei under me, on top of me, and curled next to me. So, my feet hit the pavement hard and fast to relieve the tension.

It's not perfect; my form never is. I've been too banged up by testing new trains and barreling down half-finished pipes for water parks to be a fully functioning human body at this point. But with each step pounding the ground, I can feel the nerves float away.

I made sure to get here before Lorelei normally walks the midway. At least, I hope I do. The last thing I need is to be a nuisance to her. This is her quiet place, not mine.

But I can't ignore the tinier thought that mocks, *Don't you want to run into her, Emory?*

I ignore that voice. I ignore it until the end of my run

when I'm walking out to leave and I finally see her, creaking open one of the entrance gates.

Yes. Yes, I do want to run into her.

"Oh. Hi," is all she says when she sees me. She looks like a classic animated princess in that moment with her paused hand hovering over those full lips, the hesitation in her step, and the way her soft cheeks pink.

Her initial shock passes, and her eyebrows furrow in the middle.

That's my feisty girl.

"You do know the park is mine before hours, right?" she says, smirking.

Smirking. At me. Like we're friends.

Or ... is she ... flirting with me?

No. That's not possible.

"I can stay out of your way," I offer.

All she does is smile, and I'm lost in the mixed signals again.

I walk toward the gate when she suddenly says, "Thank you, by the way."

Her mouth is twisted to the side, as if she's fighting her own words. Or maybe concerned how I'll react to them.

"For what?" I ask.

"Don't make me say it," she says with a breathy laugh and a smile. "You know what."

"For staying?"

"For redoing the coaster."

"Right," I say. "Yes. You're welcome."

Why do I sound like a robot?

I shift to my other foot, stretching out my calf and trying to look nonchalant. I don't think I could look relaxed even if I tried.

But I want to stay. I want to talk to Lorelei more and get

to know the woman who won't leave my thoughts. But at what point am I crossing a line?

No, I should leave.

"Well, I'll just ..."

"Do you want to join me?" she asks.

"I ... well, this is your time, isn't it?" I say. "You walk here in the mornings."

She huffs out a laugh. "Are you stalking me, Mr. Dawson?"

My body stiffens, and I clear my throat.

Busted.

"I'm a morning person," I say. "I notice things."

She scrunches up her face, pulling her lips in, as if holding back another laugh.

I cringe and run a hand through my hair. "Yeah, okay, that still sounded bad."

"Come on, stalker," she says. "Walk with me. But only if you promise to be nice."

"I can try," I joke.

I fall in line beside her, one cautious footstep after another.

We walk together, our footfalls in sync. It's going to be a sunny day. Her hip must not be hurting because she's able to walk in step with me.

"Do you like walking?" I ask.

It's stupid small talk, and I feel ridiculous the second it comes out.

Lorelei peers at me from the corner of her eye. She can tell.

"Yeah," she says. "I actually used to run the park every morning. I guess old habits die hard."

"If you ever want to join me on my run, I'll try not to leave you too far in the dust," I say, trying to be playful.

"I can't," she says.

"And here I promised to be nice too."

"No, I ... physically can't," she says, heaving out a breath.

"Oh ... I ..."

I'm a piece of shit.

"It's fine," she says. "I've grown to like walking. It helps ease the pain. Keeps the blood flowing."

Her leg and hip. Of course. How could I be so dumb?

And here I was, about to apologize when she probably gets that from everyone.

We pass The Grizzly. I think back to my first conversation with Bennett and the knowledge that she's scared of coasters now. I look over, and her gaze softens. She has that same dreamy look, like she's zoning out just by being near it.

"I understand what it's like to be scared of it," I say.

She scoffs. "I'm not—"

"I know you won't ride any coasters. Bennett told me."

"Freaking Bennett," she says with a playful roll of her eyes. "It's only because it hurts."

I narrow my eyes. "Is that really the only reason?"

She pauses, placing a hand on the queue line railing, tracing a finger along the path.

"No," she admits. "But it's hard to explain the fear."

"Is it kind of like ... you can't get any breath in?" I ask. "Like when you're on the lift hill, it's like you're floating up to the clouds? Wondering if maybe they'll just swallow you whole before dropping you down to nowhere?"

Her eyes cut to me, and she breathes out a small, "Yes. How did you know?"

"You test rides enough as a kid, you get a fear yourself."

"And how'd you stop feeling that way?"

I shrug. "Had to run a business. Without my mom, it's

just me making it thrive. I promised I'd take care of it no matter what it took. If I got hurt, I got hurt. I had to pick myself up and go again."

Her lips tug into a weak smile. "That easy, huh?"

I toss my head to the side. "Well, my physical therapist, Wesley, would say it took years of that, plenty of exercise, yoga ..."

I think I catch her eyes roaming my chest for a split second before snapping back up to me. It's the same look she gave me at Yogi Bare. She was checking me out. My pulse picks up.

"How long have you been practicing yoga?" she asks.

"*Practicing* is a loose term."

"No, you looked like a natural."

She was watching me.

Hold it together.

I laugh. It immediately sounds awkward. *Does it sound awkward?*

"I go because it helps my aching bones," I say.

"Okay, old man," she jokes with a smirk. It's playful and lovely. Only Lorelei can seem to capture that sly type of balance. When I don't answer, she says, "I'm kidding. It helps me too. Plus, it's the next best thing to running, I guess."

"Did you run in high school?" I ask. "Track star?"

"*Star* is a loose term," she says, echoing my sentiments about yoga with a slight smile.

She's being modest. I can tell.

"What about you?" she asks. "Track and field?"

"Nah, I was homeschooled," I say, waving my hand around. "Yeah, yeah, make your jokes."

"I would never," she says, blinking at me. "Lots of people homeschool. We only have one high school in Cedar

Cliff, so if you don't like it, you figure out other options. Did you like being homeschooled?"

"It was ... fine," I say. "Lots of construction."

"Who'd you hang out with?"

"Other homeschooled kids in the area," I say. "My mom had a whole gang going."

"A *gang* of homeschooled kids?" Lorelei says with a laugh. "Y'all do graffiti?"

"Oh yeah, we were tough as nails," I joke.

Her eyebrows rise.

I shrug. "We mostly just watched movies."

"What was your favorite?"

"You're gonna laugh."

She puts her hand to her heart. "I promise I won't."

"*Indiana Jones.*"

"Which one?"

"*Temple of Doom.*"

"Oh, that's a good one. The part where he ripped out the heart of that guy gave me nightmares."

I laugh. "I honestly think that's the core reason why I can't sleep now."

"You have trouble sleeping?"

"It's ... yeah," I say with a shrug.

"Oh, I get it. You stay up too late still, watching *Indiana Jones.*"

"Hey now," I say, pointing my finger. "And you call *me* the ass."

"Hmm ... no, Emory, you're like a cat."

I can't help but let out a laugh. "A cat? Normally, I get Eeyore. Fits the whole 'ass' thing I have going for me."

"Ha-ha," she says, exaggerating the word. "I guess what I mean is that cats have no emotions on their faces."

"Still offensive, weirdly enough."

She laughs. "Well, hang on. Let me finish. I've read studies that say cats actually feel a lot. That they get more attached to their owners than newborns do to their parents."

"Is that true?"

"I don't know," she says. "But I think deep inside, you really are a softy."

My heart swells, and I realize we've been talking for a while now. And she's been smiling most of that time too.

"Since when are you nice to me?" I ask.

"Since you promised to be nice to me."

We continue to walk around the perimeter of The Grizzly's entrance, making our way through the queue line. When we reach the bottom of the lift hill, next to the operator booth, she sighs.

"Wanna know something weird?" she asks.

"Always," I answer.

It causes her to pause before she huffs out a laugh and continues. "In a messed up way, I kinda love him."

I follow her line of sight to the track.

"The Grizzly?" I ask.

"Yeah," she muses. "We both went through something very unique together."

I don't know what to think. All I know is that Lorelei is unlike anyone I've ever met. There's a kindness about her that seeps from her body over to mine, like a whiff of perfume floating into my system and giving me life. Or maybe hope.

"The Grizzly didn't mean to hurt me," she says.

"It's the ones we love that sometimes hurt us the most."

She barks out a laugh, severing our moment. I let out a laugh too.

"What?" I ask.

"That is *so* cheesy, Emory."

I suck in a breath, trying to ease the nerves flowing through me at the sound of my name on her lips. The fact that we're standing here, laughing and talking without fighting, is enchanting. I'm absorbed in it all. I'm absorbed by her.

"We'll build him back up to be better," I say. "I promise, The Grizzly will be good as new."

She tilts her head to the side with a smile at the edge of her lips. "I hope so," she says.

I can't stop looking at her—at the way the light breeze ruffles her wavy chestnut hair, at how she's almost wistful with her words. Soft and gentle but passionate.

I feel my eyebrows pinch in.

When she looks over at me, her head instantly rolls back as she groans. "No, please, I beg you. No more pitying eyebrows, please."

I step back, hands raised in the air.

I didn't even realize I was looking at her a certain way.

"But I'm not pitying you. I promise."

"Then, what's with the whole eyebrow thing, huh?" Her finger waves at my face. It's cute. I can feel my eyebrow inch inward more. "See?!"

"I guess you surprise me. That's all it is," I say. "I can't control these guys. They do what they want."

She giggles and echoes quietly, *"These guys.* You're funny. I should have known when you told that fish pun on The Beesting."

All I can do is let out a low hum. I feel more peaceful here with her than I've ever felt in yoga. I've laughed more than I have in years.

We're standing so close, and I know we shouldn't. I want to reach out and touch her, but the last time, I took without asking. I stole a kiss without a second thought. It's not my place to do it again. But when she's looking at me through hooded eyes with a smile that could power a thousand theme parks, I wonder if maybe I could.

She sighs. "You want to kiss me so bad, don't you?"

Cue the record scratch.

Suddenly, everything comes back into view. My schoolboy-crush rose-colored glasses are ripped off. The birds chirp loud. There's a hedge trimmer roaring in the distance. It's not just me and her.

I'm so stupid.

"Wh-what?" I ask with a forced laugh.

A bigger smile creeps over her lips.

"What?" I repeat. "No."

"Then, your gym shorts should know better than to give you away."

I suck in a sharp breath. I don't dare look down. But, God, I can feel myself harden more under her gaze.

She looks down—*bold woman*—and then she grins back up with a lifted eyebrow.

"Is this harassment?" I ask.

"I could ask the same."

"I didn't do anything. You did."

She nods to my shorts. "Hey, your friend there started it."

"He'd beg to differ, I'm sure."

"How so?"

"Well, there's a reason it's like that ... and it sure isn't The Grizzly."

She curls her lips in, and I shake my head, running my hand through my damp hair.

I wonder if I should take it back, but before I can, she asks, "Want to walk to the top with me?"

I don't know the last time I felt both anxious and excited

all at once. At this point, it feels like it's all bursting out of me.

"Is that a smile, Mr. Dawson?" Lorelei asks.

My stomach flips and my chest flutters.

Only if you call me Mr. Dawson again.

When I don't respond, she shakes her head.

Is it adoration? Annoyance? I can't tell.

"Come on, Eeyore," she says with a laugh.

A laugh.

With me.

I follow her up the stairwell, trying hard not to look at her ass the whole time.

I fail.

My phone rings on my running armband. I ignore it.

24

Lorelei

I have a new obsession with watching Emory Dawson in a boardroom.

I like the way he laughs with his colleagues, but even better, I love the way he fights with them. And with today being presentation day for the board, he's fighting hard.

"No, no, the force from that turn will give the guests ..."

How about the force between my thighs, making me clench my knees closer together?

Emory just interrupted this man. His tone was authoritative and stern. He's intelligent, and he knows what he's talking about.

And it is freaking *hot*.

I squirm in my seat, glancing over his outfit. That dang heather-gray shirt. Not to mention, his worn denim, which is dirty at the knees, where he crouched under a ride this morning to pick up a fallen cell phone from the day prior. (Guests will never learn.) But when he rose from the crouch to his full height, it was intoxicating. I could feel the heat rush in my chest and the need flow down my stomach to my lower abdomen.

I think a snarky comment at that moment would have helped me relax. It would have broken the tension. But I have a feeling Emory knew that because he didn't say a word. He just smirked, and then he went on his way, his boots scratching on the crumbled gravel and shifting sand.

"No, Mark, there wouldn't be enough clearance to ..."

I fold my paper in half—literally anything to distract myself while he says someone's name out loud with such a commanding and passionate voice. Part of me—the part that still feels his grip in my hair—knows passion is his greatest strength.

"I want the final sketches in an hour," he says. "We've had a rough week, so once they're turned in, take next week off. We'll pay for your hours."

The call ends, and he closes his laptop.

I'm still breathing heavy, and I am not hiding it well.

He looks at me, eyes trailing over my parted lips and heaving chest. "What?" he asks.

I shake my head. "You just know what you're doing, is all."

"I hope I do."

It's such an innocent response from him, so at odds with the intense call, where he was demanding and confident.

Emory's face softens the longer he looks at me, and my already-pounding heart speeds up once more.

"Lorelei?"

"Yes?" My lips part to let out a breath.

"Ask me if I wanna kiss you," he says.

And with that, he steals the breath right out of me.

I blink at him. He dips his chin, coaxing a response.

I shake my head. "No."

A slow but gentle smile rises on his face. "Good."

We both know that's a bad idea, but we can't stop looking at each other.

He finally breaks the spell, gathering his laptop and walking away so I'm left practically panting in his wake.

I wait five minutes, letting myself recover from the lust pulsing through my veins.

Get it together, girl. You cannot hook up with him.

I need a distraction.

I text Theo, asking if she's busy.

She texts back a quick, *Sorry, honeybees got out of the greenhouse. Can't.*

I then text Bennett.

I receive, *Can't talk. Honeybees are everywhere.*

I'm not surprised to get a text from Quinn that says, *Girl, the bees are attacking guests!*

This whole park is reflecting the mess inside my soul.

I decide to go help—or honestly do anything. As long as it takes my mind off of Emory and our presentation, I'm on board. But that's when I bump into someone else. Literally.

I run headfirst into a giant man. His protruding stomach bounces me back into the doorjamb.

"Oh, I'm sorry. I ..."

I finally get a good look at the wrestler-looking man in front of me.

His suit is immaculate. His cologne smells like bourbon. He has a beet-red face and veins trailing over his bald head. There's a deep-set crease between his eyebrows that looks permanent, like he's never smiled a day in his life.

But I'd recognize those thick eyebrows anywhere.

This is Thomas Dawson.

CEO of Dawson Manufacturing.

Emory's father.

25

Emory

Honeywood partially shut down after a swarm of honeybees escaped their greenhouse and surrounded the right quadrant of the park.

It was my ass of a father who caused this mess.

Go figure.

He had been getting a tour with Fred, left the door open, and swatted at the swarm. They angrily flew out, closing down half the park.

I clench my jaw when my dad runs into Lorelei. I would have assumed she had left the conference room by now.

Watching him stare her down makes me bury my hands in my pockets to try and still my nerves. He towers over her, tilting his chin up further so he looks down at her.

The prick.

He's trying to force the same power dynamic he has over everyone else in his life. I'll be damned if he says anything demeaning to her.

Then, his face contorts.

He holds up a finger before saying, "Wait, I feel like I know you ..."

I shake my head, running a hand through my hair.

Don't say anything, Lorelei. Don't do it.

Her hand shoots out. "I'm Lorelei Arden," she says. "Nice to meet you."

Oh hell.

All my dad can mutter out is, "Oh."

By the way she's white-knuckling her notebook, I know she's not comfortable. But a guy has to admire the confidence in which she tries.

They shake hands, hers getting dwarfed by his beefy mitt.

"I'll be seeing you." Her voice wavers, and she hurries down the hall, faster than usual, even for her normal sunshine-energy level.

Thomas Dawson's face twists toward me.

"After you," I say, gesturing to the conference room.

We enter, and he doesn't hesitate to bark out his thoughts the moment the door clicks shut.

"How long have you been friendly with the Arden girl?" he asks.

I scrunch my nose at the smell of his bourbon breath. His eyes are red. The idiot has already started imbibing, and it's only ten o'clock in the morning.

"She's the marketing manager," I say. "Maybe a bit more respect should be had."

"She's our biggest lawsuit that is ravaging our clientele, Emory."

"And our best chance at also reviving said customers."

He plops into a leather chair, leaning back in it, allowing it to creak under his weight.

Thomas Dawson is a large man. Hard jaw, thick neck,

broad arms, and hands the size of frying pans. He's always a different shade of red or purple, and veins exist as tattoos beneath his skin. I might be intimidated if I didn't know how stupid he was.

He's a meathead in every sense of the word. He might know construction, but outside of knowing the difference between a right angle and an acute angle, he's just an angry alcoholic who's grown bitter throughout the years from sickness and divorce.

"Friends close, enemies closer?" he asks.

I tsk. "This isn't a soap opera."

"I'll get the lawyer to call you tonight," he says before adding for emphasis, "*Tonight*. You need to tell him everything."

I clench my jaw. "I'm capable of making the call myself."

He grunts, like a snort from a hog.

"Get your head out of your ass," he snaps. "I can't believe Lorelei—"

"We're making coasters with the person *we* potentially injured," I interrupt, leaning forward with my palms on the table. I don't like the sound of her name in his mouth. "In fact, think of it like a PR haven. We're collaborating. How can that look much better?"

"She's trying to get money out of us."

"No, she's not."

His jaw slackens. I wonder if I've said too much.

"You're to stop talking to her," he says.

"You can't tell me what to do."

"I'm your CEO. I damn well can."

There's no *I'm your father* because we're past that. He's my boss. He likes that power structure more.

Personally, I don't like either.

"And I make your coasters," I say, "So, maybe watch who you're commanding."

"That's an empty threat, Emory. You'd never leave your mother's pride and joy."

My gut clenches.

Because he's not wrong. I wouldn't leave the company my mother once loved in the hands of this man.

And he knows it.

"Why are you even here?" I ask.

"You weren't answering my calls."

"Yes, but you never come to client meetings."

"Shouldn't I see what we're basically giving away for free?" he asks. "I want to see what fabulous thing you're promising them."

I inhale.

In, out.

Think of yoga.

Think of Lorelei.

"You give them an inch, they'll take a mile," he says. "You never overpromise a board of directors. You know that. And yet here you are. What the hell has gotten into you?"

"It'll be fine," I say. "It's going to be fine."

26

Lorelei

This was not the surprise we needed on presentation day, and I can tell Thomas's presence has shaken Emory.

Thomas Dawson is not impressed with our little slice of home. It's his sneer at the statue of Buzzy, the sniff when he sees the wild bees, and the squint while the sun beams over his well-fitted suit, a bead of sweat rolling down his bald head.

Something about the way Emory's jaw is set in place also makes me anxious. The way he's mechanical again. It's the man I met a month ago, rearing his stoic head back to the forefront. Smiles are gone.

They are two giants walking side by side, rolling by in a stormy cloud, passing the happy—yet fearful-of-the-bees —guests.

I can see the resemblance, like stress was built into their DNA. But where Thomas's tall presence is overpowering and domineering, Emory's carries a natural confidence to him. Less like a fist and more like a stern, hard palm.

No, don't think about Emory's hard palm, you freak.

An hour later, I'm bustling into the mini theater at the back of our offices, where we occasionally host private events. Emory and I thought it would be perfect to make this one a bit more of a wine-and-dine affair—to get the taste of the old boardroom and the old pitch out of their mouths. It's designed in a similar Western-style like the rest of our office space, complete with creaky floors and the scent of old wood. I wheel in a cart of brewed coffee and an assortment of snacks.

I try to catch Emory's eye. He doesn't meet mine. He's in his suit again. He must have changed in his hotel room during our break.

He looks sharp. Prepared.

I sit in the back with empty rows between me and the board members, who are back to their loud and jaunty voices. Them, I can handle; I just wish we didn't also have to impress the veiny, bald man up front. From back here, Thomas Dawson looks like a gross, engorged mushroom. That gives me a little solace, for whatever it's worth.

"Hey, lady."

I practically jump five feet in the air at the sound of Quinn's whisper in my ear.

She rounds the aisle and sits next to me, sliding down so that she isn't visible to anyone else.

"What are you doing?" I whisper.

"I'm on break," she says with a shrug. "Can't do much with guests when they're scared of bees."

Her face is still caked in Queen Bee makeup, but she's in a loose Honeywood button-up and small running shorts that accentuate her curvy figure.

"Plus, Jaymee is outside. Probably thinking she can get a scoop on the coaster, and I want nothing to do with her, thanks."

Jaymee Johnson, columnist for the *Cedar Cliff Chatter*, is always on the lookout for gossip. That magazine is a scourge upon our town, but it's not like you can hit them with defamation or slander. Everything they print is accurate; it's just the parts of our town we all want hidden.

Jaymee always lurks around Honeywood when she knows something is going on. After all, when your dad is the nicest general manager in Honeywood's history, you always know the inside scoop. And Fred is too sweet to tell his daughter no.

When I look back up to the stage, Emory is at the podium, already staring at me.

He holds out a finger and rolls it toward him.

That motion alone sends a hook around my gut, coaxing me to my feet and up to the stage, taking the steps one at a time.

His scent overwhelms me instantly. The woodsy-candle goodness.

I try not to look like a creep when I take a big whiff. His freshly applied cologne is intoxicating.

He grins. "Did you just sniff me?"

"No. What's up?"

He looks from side to side, red blushing his cheeks, and then leans in to whisper, "I can't get the video in the presentation to work."

His hot breath tickles the shell of my ear, rushing down to my chest and lower stomach. I didn't realize Emory whispering would set me on edge so much.

"Jeez, give you a program for 3D design, and you're a wizard, but presentation software is your downfall."

He snorts with a half-smile. "Watch it."

I click around, but my attention is split as his hand hangs by his side behind the podium, a single finger reaching out to trace circles along my thigh, pinching the fabric of my pants between his index finger and thumb.

I thankfully get the video to work before my knees give out.

"Thank you," he says, and it might as well have been said against my clit, given the amount of throbbing that ensues.

I nod and quip a small, "Learn the program, old man," and his eyebrows rise with a small twitch at the edge of his mouth.

I go back to my seat, where Quinn is looking up at me from her slouched position.

"Oh boy," she mutters, so low that even I almost don't hear it.

"What?"

"Mr. Roller Coaster has it *bad*."

I watch him at the podium, straightening his stack of papers and clearing his throat.

"All right, everyone," he says, his low tone reverberating through the microphone and commanding the room. "Let's get started, shall we? Let me introduce ... the new Grizzly."

His eyes find mine, and it doesn't feel scary or nerve-racking. It feels right. It feels like we're a team.

"Just be careful," Quinn whispers. "Don't let his storm cloud rain on your flower garden."

But I don't tell her that, sometimes, plants need a little water to thrive.

27

Emory

"**G**ive them an inch, they'll take a mile."
　　The board of directors loves our idea, but they want *more*. Something special. Something that I did not pitch.

And when I look over at my dad, he's grinning from ear to ear, mouthing, *I told you so*.

Son of a bitch.

I'm practically kicking myself when I walk out of the office's double doors, the sun beaming into my face. I rip off my jacket and hang it over the railing to Buzzy's statue.

My stomach rolls when I hear him beside me.

"What did I tell you?" my dad says.

"Now isn't a great time," I mutter.

Fred bursts through the swinging doors. "I loved it, team!"

Team. A concept my father knows nothing about.

A team member would say, *Let's keep working, and we'll get it at the quality it needs to be*, or, *It's going to be fine, son.*

Thomas Dawson can't fathom the idea of teamwork.

"They didn't like it," I mutter.

"Oh, they loved it!" Fred says with a swat of his hand. "Just a couple changes here and there, but it's fine!"

I inhale sharply.

It's fine.

I feel a moment of relief, but my father shoots it down like a man wielding a crossbow right at Buzzy the Bear himself.

"We need to discuss price, of course," he says.

"Price?" Fred asks, furrowing his brow. "I thought we had a set deal."

"This is more customized than we agreed."

I can feel my world crashing down around me. I had ideas of doing the right thing, but our reputation of good business practices is crumbling down around us with this gauche approach from my father.

"We'll talk about that later," I say through clenched teeth.

"No, we'll talk now," my dad says.

I close my eyes, pinching my nose with my thumb and forefinger.

He's going to lose Fred's trust altogether if he doesn't shut his mouth. He's going to lose this contract.

But my father doesn't care. He never has.

"We'll think of more things," I say. "We'll brainstorm. We'll make this happen with our originally set price, Mr. Louder."

My father shakes his head. "Not if we can't afford it."

"We've got more than enough resources."

"This is a massive project."

"And it's worth it."

We stare at each other, and I only distantly see Fred

edge out of the frame and back into the offices, leaving us to stare each other down in two defiant forces.

Screw it.

This coaster is happening the right way even if it kills me.

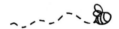

I'm sitting at the fountain bench when Lorelei finds me. My dad left for the airport with threats about calling the company accountant, and I haven't moved an inch since.

"Hey." Her voice is soft, like a fresh, cool breeze.

"Hey," I echo back.

She sits next to me, placing her hands on her thighs. "Your dad seems like a peach."

I huff out a half-hearted laugh, nodding as I grab the knot in my tie and loosen it.

"That's a nice way to put it," I mutter.

"Okay then, he's an ass."

I laugh more. "Last I checked, you were calling *me* that."

"Oh, no," she says. "Y'all are very different."

"Yeah?"

"Well, first of all, you don't have veins popping out of your head."

I laugh more.

"At least I have that," I say.

"And you look much better in a suit."

"Is that right?"

She shrugs. The gesture is so innocent and cute. I can't stop the smile on my face.

"Anyway," she says, "I need you."

"What?" I ask.

She instantly shakes her head, throwing a thumb over her shoulder. "The, uh ... the tunnel ride," she says. "The bees got to it."

"And how can I help?"

"I can't figure out the control panel. They messed it up."

"The bees?" I ask, blinking. "Do they have opposable thumbs?"

"I think they've learned over the years," she says.

I can't tell if she's serious or not.

"Anyway, can you help? Our mechanics are pretty much all over the place right now. As an engineer, you might have more expertise than me."

"Engineer, not an electrician."

"Same thing to me."

I sigh. Maybe I need the distraction from the wrath that was my father today.

"Come onnn," she says, nudging my elbow with hers.

It's such a small gesture, but it warms me even more than the humidity surrounding us on this hot Georgia day.

I chuckle. "Of course. I'll take a look."

"Of course," she mimics. "Who even are you? Agreeing to me so quickly?"

"Someone who had a hard day and would rather work with his hands than in a boardroom."

She smiles. "I can get behind that."

We walk to the entrance of The Romping Meadow, bypassing the empty queue line, where guests evacuated earlier. A bundle of bees hangs along the railing, as if staking their claim. Two people in beekeeping suits stand off to the side, eating sandwiches.

Hard work, wrangling bees.

Lorelei turns the handle on a hidden door, painted like a tree. We enter, and the sunlight disappears behind us.

When the door clicks shut, we are enveloped in darkness. The only things I can see are what's illuminated from the spotlights over the shifting animatronics.

It's hard to think Lorelei and I were here just a couple weeks ago. We were still at each other's throats, coming to an impasse that lasted only a couple days. It was before my dad called, making me second-guess my designs and morals.

I should have never agreed to add the top track in the first place.

I follow Lorelei to the control board. She's glowing in the lighting's purples and blues, looking like an angel drifting through the swamplands of the ride. We might be surrounded by the stench of mold and chlorine, but it's hard not to be at peace with the sound of gently lapping water in the canal and the vision of beauty in front of me.

When did I become such a sap?

"The panel is over here," Lorelei says, stepping over foam rocks and disappearing behind a booth disguised as a log. "Hopefully, it makes sense to you."

After she keys into the cabinet, I pull it back. A sticky line of goo stretches with it.

"God, how did honey get here?" I ask.

"I'm telling you, it's a mystery that we no longer question."

I squat down and rustle through the wires, a bee zipping out and into the darkness.

Honeywood is indeed an odd, odd place.

The only sounds for a few moments are my handiwork and the whirring of the animatronics. I find the switch that controls them and turn it off.

"Those things freak me out," I mutter.

Lorelei giggles.

"So," she finally says, "your dad."

"I'd rather not," I say with an exhale, trying to keep a lighter tone even though the thought of discussing him makes me want to rip the cords right out of this panel. "He's ... got problems."

"Your mom then?" Lorelei offers.

"Wonderful," I say without skipping a beat. I don't need to think about that question. "Didn't deserve him."

"They're not still together?"

"No."

"Why?"

I adjust the wire in my hand, and the music of the ride starts once more.

"Oh, wow," she says, peering around the brightly lit room.

"Fixed it."

Satisfied, I flip the switch to cut it off again.

"So ... they're not ..." she continues.

I was hoping she'd dropped it.

I stand up again. Lorelei's head is dipped down, hands clasped behind her back, legs crossed at the ankles as she leans against the wall. She looks ashamed she even asked.

"Why are you poking into my personal life, Lorelei?"

She shrugs. "You're interesting."

"Not a lot of people would say that."

"How would they describe you?"

"Quiet. Mean. Scary."

She shakes her head. "You're not as intimidating as you think."

"You're not intimidated by much, are you? The look on my dad's face when you shook his hand ..." We both laugh, the sound echoing through the empty cavern. "You're fearless when you try."

The moment I say it, I want to take it back. Her eyebrows rise to the top of her forehead, and I swallow.

Fearless with everything but the coaster that hurt her.

"I didn't mean it that way," I say.

She nods. "It's fine."

But I can see the wavering in her eyes, the way she's slowly drifting away. I wonder if she relives the accident in her head every time it's brought up. I wonder how much I'm contributing to her pain.

I take a step forward. She doesn't move, but her eyes dart up to mine. I extend my hand, grazing it over her cheek. She leans into it, and my breath hitches. Her cheek is so smooth against my rough palm.

"I wish I knew what happened with your accident," I say, moving a strand of hair behind her ear. "I wish I knew why the wheels fell off the track that day. I want ... I want so much."

Admitting it out loud lightens my soul. If only I could do the same for her. I would do anything to fix her pain.

Her eyes move to my lips, my neck, my shoulders, like she's analyzing me as a person. Or maybe even deciding if I'm a man worthy of being next to her.

I already know she deserves better than me.

"What do you want, Emory?" she asks.

But at the end of the day, I'm a selfish bastard.

"You."

28

Lorelei

"Y ou."
Me.

I've successfully melted the heart of the giant.

I take a step closer, my hand landing on his chest, feeling the expanse of it.

It's a motion I've wanted to do for days. I've wanted to stroke across the creases in his shirt, drag down the length of his loosened tie, twirl my finger through the two layers, and look up to see his eyes completely dilated.

Turned on.

By me.

His index finger meets my chin, tipping it up.

I tug him forward by the fabric of his tie right as he leans in to kiss me as well.

I couldn't have imagined this moment if I tried—the way his lips form so perfectly to mine, the way his tongue grazes across my bottom lip. How it pauses before dancing with mine, as if the very act of my letting him in is a gift.

His hand soothes along my jaw, cupping it in his palm and dragging me deeper into his embrace.

I wind the tie into my fist, and he takes a step forward as I take one back. His hand hits the faux rocky wall behind me right before my shoulders do.

Our touches get rushed, filled with shaky inhales and exhales, both of our hands traveling up and down fabric—his reaching down to cup my ass, giving it a gentle massage, only to turn rough within the span of a second grab.

He pulls away, instantly sending growling kisses across my neck and down to my collarbone. I'm still catching my breath, panting as each planted kiss is like fire against me, singeing and leaving circles of ash in their wake.

His thumb parts the collar of my shirt, and he nips at the top of my breast—a tattoo of him left behind.

I run my hand through his hair, mussing it up, feeling the soft locks drift through my fingers as his head tilts back to look up at me.

He smiles, and it's so genuine. So happy. So ... him. The new Emory I know.

"You should smile more," I say.

The gesture deepens into a grin, flashing those beautiful teeth in the faint light of the purple scene across from our rock enclosure.

"I will," he says. "I will if it keeps you smiling too."

I didn't realize I had been until that moment, but my cheeks hurt from it.

Have I been smiling like a fool this entire time?

My hand rises to my lips, but he reaches out to grab my wrist and pull it away.

"No. Keep smiling for me, beautiful."

Beautiful.

He leans down, nosing into the crook of my neck, and I feel his hot tongue on me, licking up to my ear, where he nips the lobe. A shiver runs through me.

195

"How do I keep this nice version of you?" I pant.

Emory's hand ghosts over my waist and stomach, settling just below the curve of my breast. He trails a line along the swell.

I take in a sharp inhale, but it's interrupted by a low whisper in my ear of, "My niceness can be here to stay if you'd like."

His thumb trails up my breast, circling the peak, teasing, twirling, as my head falls back against the wall.

I don't know what's making this more erotic—the fact that I'm in the biggest dry spell of my life or that I'm in the deft hands of Emory.

"Oh, don't tell me that," he grunts.

He nips my ear again, and I gasp.

I halt, my body temperature rising. "Did I say that out loud?"

"This is erotic due to my hands alone, Lorelei. Dry spell or not."

His thumb brushes over my nipple, flicking it, running the roughness of the fabric over it, and without thinking, I let out a small moan.

It feels like forever since I've been touched. I forgot how sensitive my nipples were, how they respond to every single touch.

"You like that?" he mutters against my cheek as his thumb rolls circle after circle over me.

It's magic. I shouldn't be this turned on by something so simple, but my back bows into him, increasing the pressure of his touches against me. He reacts in kind, rotating slower but firmer.

I groan again, tilting my head to the side, trying to get any type of fresh air.

I'm drowning in him, surrounded by the glorious woodsy scent and the heat of his breath.

"Moan louder for me," he says and, God, if that doesn't send my nerves alight. Right down between my thighs, which I clench tighter, rubbing them together.

His thumb whips across my nipple.

Rough, possessive, and domineering.

"Come on, beautiful," he coaxes.

So, I do it.

I do exactly as Emory asked, and I moan.

I moan my little heart out, and the porn-like echo bounces off the walls of the tunnel.

I'm so turned on. I don't know the last time I was this wet—or if I ever have been.

Yet here he is, elevating me to new heights, moving his knee to rest between my thighs, rubbing against my core as I desperately grind myself against him.

"There you go," he murmurs, the heat warming my ear. "Use me, Lorelei."

The words stir my stomach. My heart is pulsing in my chest, all the way down to my clit. He presses his thigh higher between my legs.

His leg is large between me, and my legs spread farther than I know they should.

I wince from the pressure, but I don't even care.

I'm slick against him as I grind faster and more wanton. The low exhalations of Emory's warm breath against my ear build the pressure in my lower stomach.

The thing that almost does me in is when Emory takes my nipple between his thumb and finger and pinches.

I moan so loud that I would be embarrassed if he wasn't also growling, "That's right, Lorelei. Let me hear you."

No, the final blow that brings my orgasm crashing down

is when he demands, deep and low against the shell of my ear, "Come for me, beautiful."

I'm absolutely lost.

My legs clench together one final time before all the pressure in my lower stomach releases.

My mind is reeling through space or some other worldly dimension who knows where as my mouth falls open to obey his commands, to moan through my orgasm.

It's a free fall down a steep track.

It's relief. It's joy. It's exhilaration.

When I open my eyes, Emory is grinning down at me, and he places one last kiss against my lips before saying, "Attagirl."

29

Lorelei

I lost reality TV bingo night.
I think.

All I see are my friends—particularly Bennett and Ruby
—dancing in the living room, arm in arm, swinging each
other back and forth as they celebrate their completed bingo
board, all the way down to the option of *Bachelor Admits to
Bodily Functions*, which we all hoped wouldn't be the case.

I don't care.

I'm still daydreaming.

My head is in the clouds with Emory Dawson and his
large hands teasing me, his knee at the apex of my thighs, his
lips against my neck.

And those words.

God, those words.

"Use me, Lorelei."

"Let me hear you."

"Attagirl."

I loved every sentence. Every syllable. Every breath.
Every wink of desire that pulsed from his mouth into mine
and lapped over my skin like water after a hot day.

Quinn's hand waves over my face.

I blink back to reality. "What?"

"While Tweedledum and Tweedledee are celebrating, you seem less pissed about it than I am."

"Maybe I'm less competitive."

"Bullshit," she whispers. "It's Mr. Roller Coaster."

"Oh my God, is there new drama?" Ruby asks with a giggle. "Tell me there's new drama."

She's in a great mood after winning. Who can blame her? Bennett's arm is on her waist, and he is laughing one of the biggest laughs I've ever seen. He only ever laughs like that with her.

But when they both see my eyes linger on his hand touching her waist, they pull apart.

I didn't mean to make them feel uncomfortable. I even shake my head slightly, like I can somehow communicate that I wasn't judging their closeness. I know he has a girlfriend. I know it meant nothing. He loves Jolene.

But Ruby gulps and walks to the kitchen with her hands wringing together.

I look away, nobody else the wiser to their shame, except me and the two best friends with something to hide.

Curious.

Theo rolls on her side, over the ottoman, and down the length of the couch toward me and Quinn. She's drunk as a skunk.

"You want Mr. Roller Coaster's penis, don't you?" she says.

I shove her arm, trying to hide my reddening face. "Ew, come on."

Theo blows out a raspberry. "If you don't like him, at least try to play it up less. *Ew* should never apply to that man."

I scrunch my lips to the side. "Nothing's happened," I mutter.

Quinn, adhering to her best-friend promise of keeping it a secret, nods with me. "Lorelei would tell us if something did. Let's talk about you instead. Any new dudes in your life, Theodora?"

Theo scrunches her nose and then boops mine. "Nope!" She pops the *P*.

"I hear Meghan is with Orson now."

Theo rolls her eyes, and it is the most dramatic eye roll I've ever seen. Quinn is smart. She knew that would do the trick to distract a nosy, drunk Theo. She loves the other yoga instructors, but they also all brag about their sexcapades—especially if it involves local bar owner Orson.

I don't think he gets around as much as people say he does. In fact, I've only ever seen him be sweet with women. But I guess that doesn't exactly mean he isn't doing other stuff too.

"I know Meghan's with him!" Theo says too loudly. "She won't shut up about it."

Bennett laughs from the other sofa. Ruby sits on the opposite side. They're noticeably far apart now.

"I think Meghan is good for him," Ruby says. "She's sweet."

Theo groans. "Okay, yes, she is a total sweetheart, but I hear about his penis *too much*."

"Is that what you guys talk about when I'm not here?" Bennett asks. "Penises?"

"We talk about that when you *are* here," Theo slurs out. "Oh my God. Wait, don't best friends view other best friends' genitals? Bennett, have you seen Orson's penis too?"

"Okay, this conversation is over," he says with a chuckle,

clapping his hands together in the universal sign of *we're stopping* here.

"Wait, wait, but he's your best friend!" Theo says, rushing over to him. "I need to know if Meghan is lying about his big weiner! Wait, Bennett!"

She chases him to the spare bedroom, and he shuts himself in while the rest of us laugh.

Quinn crosses her arms. "Hmm. Now that I think about it, I guess I *have* seen everyone's genitals here. That is weird."

I tilt my head to the side. "I haven't seen Ruby's."

"No," Quinn says with her finger raised. "We all did. Florida trip three years ago."

Ruby's face flushes a deep red that makes her ginger hair seem blonde by comparison.

"Oh my God," Theo breathes, walking back into the room. "That's right! You were *so* high."

"First and only time, guys. Come on." Ruby pulls her lap pillow up to her cheeks with a giggle.

I see Bennett in the doorway of the room with a smirk on his face.

"Bennett, I don't know what you're smiling about," Quinn says. "We all saw your thing when you streaked across the football field in high school."

His smile disappears in a split second, and the group falls into a fit of laughter.

Shortly after, we call it a night. We clean up our beer, chip, and dip mess in Ruby's living room. Theo helps Ruby grab bedding for the foldout couch since she's clearly in no sober state to drive.

It isn't until we get in the car that Quinn says, "Well?"

"Well what?"

"Theo had a good point. How's the Mr. Roller Coaster penis endeavor?"

"Quinn!"

My car's Bluetooth interrupts our conversation with ringing from my phone. I recognize the number immediately.

Quinn gasps. "Oh shit, is that—"

"My lawyer."

I press the button to answer, and the charming voice of my lawyer, Ian Chambers, carries through the speakers.

"Evening, Miss Arden. How are you?"

If I were into older men—specifically men over ten years my senior as opposed to the engineer who is almost that amount—I might be attracted to the man on the other end of the line. Tall, handsome, sarcastic, and all with a smooth voice that instantly cools a room.

Ian is my attorney for the Dawson Manufacturing case. Normally, he warns me before calling or starts the call with some jokey one-liner. He knows lawsuit calls make me nervous. He's considerate like that.

So, a random call like this is odd. I'm on edge.

"Hi, Ian," I answer. "I'm fine."

"Fine, you say?" Ian barks out a hearty laugh. "That's funny. I just had a wonderful conversation with a friend who says otherwise."

"A friend?" I ask.

"That's a lie," Ian says. "It was Dawson's lawyer, who now claims that you and his client are working together."

Quinn winces, cringing at the statement. I grip the wheel tighter.

"Are you working with Emory Dawson?" Ian asks.

I do not respond.

"Every day?"

I'm quiet as a mouse.

"For upward of eight hours or more?"

I open my mouth, then close it.

Quinn coughs.

"Your silence, aside from your friend—hello, Quinn— says more than I need to know."

"We're working on the new coaster," I say. "We just pitched it to the board of directors for Honeywood. It's all work-related."

He sighs. "Lorelei, that doesn't matter."

"Nothing is happening," I repeat for what feels like the fiftieth time.

"Hey, you're not on trial," Ian says. "Well, sort of."

He chuckles. The sound is low and rumbly over the phone. He really could be a sex operator, if he wanted to.

"I'm sorry, too far?" he says. "My wife says I need to work on that."

"Oh, you have a wife?" Quinn asks.

I slap her thigh.

"That's beside the point, ladies," he says.

"Well, I can't stop working with him," I blurt out. Then, I pull a line from Emory's book. "It's my job. It's his job. I'm suing his company, not him. Correct?"

The line goes silent as Ian sighs.

"Do you want my advice, Miss Arden?" he asks. "I mean, I'm mostly being nice here. I'm your lawyer. You pay me for my advice, so I'm going to give it."

"Okay ..."

"You should stop working with him," Ian says. "That's my advice. In fact, that would be my demand. But you are an adult, and I can't exactly monitor you."

"That's good advice though," Quinn chimes in.

I glare at her.

"Thanks," I say. "But I can't. We have a coaster to make."

"Right. Why would you pay me and follow my advice anyway?" Ian asks. "Sounds ridiculous to me."

"I'm sorry."

"Don't apologize. Just listen. Don't say anything I wouldn't," Ian says. "Keep a record of literally everything. Don't delete texts or emails."

I gulp. Well, at least we haven't sent anything through text.

"Will do," I say.

"Great. Well, I'll let you go. Good evening, ladies."

"Bye, Ian," we chime together like two-thirds of the freaking Charlie's Angels.

Two beeps indicate the call has ended, and I look over at Quinn.

"Ruh-roh," she says through a sputter of laughter.

"Very funny, Scoob," I say, shaking my head.

My phone dings again, and I look down to see an email from Emory.

The subject line reads, *Current mock-ups*.

Quinn must read it, too, because she says, "Well, as long as you're only exchanging work emails, that's all that matters, right?"

I nod. "Yes, absolutely."

Except then my phone dings once more and it's a text.

Emory: What time do you get off work tomorrow?

"Never mind," Quinn says. "Just don't get caught on camera or something."

"That's it. I'm moving out," I say, tossing a pen from my center console over to her.

She bats it away with a grin. "You'd be lost without me."

"I know," I say, looking down at the text.

I don't answer him.

But I'd be lying if I said my heart didn't feel wrong for doing so.

30

Emory

Memorial Day at Honeywood is a doozy.

As with all theme parks, holiday weekends are a mix of excitement and slight terror.

And I'm terrified.

Lorelei's friend Quinn has her Queen Bee makeup slowly bleeding off her face in the humid Georgia summer. One member of the security team is walking with her to ensure she doesn't pass out while the others are running around, trying to put out fifty different fires. I'd be surprised if none of them quit by the end of today. They're over-whelmed.

The issues range from Honeywood's wild bumblebees landing on guests' sugary Push Pops shaped like Buzzy, to kids trying to play in the midway's fountain, all the way to the real problem—long lines.

Since The Grizzly is out of commission, Honeywood's second-largest coaster, Bumblebee's Flight, has an astronomically long queue. So, when the ride breaks down, it's mass chaos.

A part-time teen operator has to tell the bad news to the

next woman in line with a backward haircut. In retaliation, she can't exactly punch the teen—because Southern hospitality, I guess?—so instead, she twists on her heel and punches some other guy square in the eye, sending him over the ropes like some pay-per-view wrestling show.

I can practically hear the dinging bells.

Security drags her off and bans her from the park, but the ride is unfortunately still down, and Lorelei is now playing the fun game of marketing manager maintenance. I could be working on our project, but the last thing I want is someone punching her, too, so I stand by for crowd control.

She placates the guests with free fast passes to any ride.

I give anyone who looks like they want to argue a glare that says, *Keep walking, buddy*.

"You look like a bouncer," the teen operator says.

"Who says I'm not?" I counter.

Lorelei, in the middle of a conversation with a guest, overhears and smiles to herself.

After another thirty minutes, Bennett finally shows up, huffing his way through the crowd with a yellow Honeywood *Staff* tee that looks so at odds with his burly frame and long black hair. He finds the issue in seconds, and the ride is operating once more after a couple test runs.

Lorelei and I hang out near the front of the queue, leaning over the railing and waving as the now-happy guests—aside from the guy with a black eye, who has pocketed a free season pass for his troubles—start the slow lift hill with beaming smiles.

"So, what if there were bunny hops?" Lorelei asks.

"Hmm?"

"On the new version of The Grizzly."

"You're back to talking business after that fiasco?" I ask, tossing a thumb over my shoulder.

"We probably should," she says. "We haven't come up with any new ideas in the past week."

"Okay," I say, dragging out the word.

While I know we have a job to do, I also know we haven't addressed the elephant in the room where she had an orgasm under the watchful eye of Buzzy the animatronic nightmare. "We can add bunny hops then. But first ... how about dinner?"

"I don't know ..."

"Lorelei," I say, reaching out my hand to trail a line from her forearm to her wrist before relaxing it back against the railing.

Her eyes meet mine.

"I wasn't joking when I said nice Emory can be here to stay," I say.

"I didn't know you could tell jokes," she says with a smile.

I exhale. "I want to take you out."

"And what are we supposed to do about"—she waves her hands in the air—"literally everything?"

"We'll figure it out," I say. "First, we go on a date, where I eat you out."

"Emory! Oh my God."

"Second, we make a great coaster. Third, we worry about the lawsuit."

She toys with her ID badge at her hip, tugging it out and letting it zip back in.

"My lawyer called me," she says. "He knows we're working together. He found out from your lawyer."

"And how much money does he think he can demand from the company now?" I joke.

Her eyes dart to me, and she shakes her head. "That's

not funny," Lorelei says. "He said we need to keep our relationship work-related only."

"Okay. Then, why are we talking about the lawsuit? Let's talk about work. We'll have a date in Honeywood," I say. "That's still work-related, isn't it?"

"Should I worry about how easy you find loopholes?"

"Beautiful, my job is creating loops."

"Ha-ha, very funny."

"I'm a riot once you get to know me. Let me take you on a date."

"Emory ..." she says, soft and slow.

It makes me grin a little—the shyness of it all. Because I know Lorelei Arden and she isn't as shy as she seems. But somehow, I like that her moans are our little secret. Well, me, her, and Buzzy.

"Lorelei," I echo back.

The corner of her mouth tilts up at me.

"I like it when you say my name," she says.

"I could potentially say it a lot in a restaurant with food."

"No," she insists, pushing away from the railing and walking down the stairs next to the maintenance entrance.

I exhale, following in her steps.

"You make it difficult to be a gentleman, you know," I say.

"Shush your mouth until we get away from where people can hear us."

I grind my jaw as she scans a key card over a box. A small beep unlocks the door, and I reach around her to pull it open.

She rolls her eyes.

"I think you forget that I'm suing you," Lorelei says.

"Suing the company," I clarify. "Not me."

"I tried that clever little line too," she whispers with a small laugh. "And my lawyer still advised me against you."

The door clicks shut behind us.

The roaring of the coaster's track echoes through the maintenance tunnel, vibrating the walls as the long train whooshes past. I walk closer to her. She takes a few steps backward before her back hits the wall. My hands gravitate to her hips as I lean down to bury my nose in her hair. The smell of peaches is a comfort; I could get lost in her all day long.

"Emory, we're playing with fire."

"Good," I mutter against her neck. "I prefer the heat."

Her hands grab my shirt, curling the fabric in her fists before pushing me away. I back up, continuing to walk backward until I land against the opposite wall.

There's nothing else but the sounds of the park around us.

I bend my foot to rest behind me. The sound carries throughout the tunnel.

And then—

Her eyes widen. "Oh my God, I know how we can make the ride better."

31

Lorelei

"We can make the ride double back."

I look like a mad detective with sketches and colored pencils spread all over my office desk. There are smears of an eraser. I hold a red colored pencil, poised and sharpened, like I'm about to stab the paper rather than write on it.

"The echo from my foot made you think of this?" Emory asks with a chuckle.

His laugh is cute, but that's beside the point. No time to address it now.

"Shh. It runs underneath itself, see?" I say, sketching another loop that goes under the existing track. "In tunnels with launches. And dark areas—"

I take a dark blue pencil and shade underneath. It looks like a five-year-old sketched it, but it gets the point across—I hope.

"With sudden launches and bunny hops, there will be massive airtime ..."

Emory's eyebrows are furrowed together, and it's hard to tell what he's thinking.

It might be concern for my mental health.

"Well?" I step back from the mess of art supplies and paper.

He takes a step forward, picks up a pencil, chews on the end, then starts sketching.

I lean over his shoulder to watch.

"What are you doing?" I ask.

"I'm doing a mock-up," he says. "Can you pass me that pink eraser? These ideas are great. I wanna make more notes."

He holds out his hand, and I glance at it, then back to him.

He thinks my ideas are great.

"Pink eraser?" he asks again.

He wants to use my ideas.

I blink.

"What did you say?" I stammer out.

A smile tugs at the edge of his mouth when he says, "Eraser?"

My stomach drops, and I practically run to the eraser, tossing it in his palm.

He goes to town, reworking, adjusting, taking my idea but making it beautiful—more technical. Watching him buried in his work is like watching Michelangelo paint the Sistine Chapel, da Vinci create the *Mona Lisa*, van Gogh imagine *Starry Night*—minus the prior ear removal.

"Thoughts?" he finally asks.

He steps aside, but I don't have to look closer to know it's a masterpiece.

"Let's do it," I say.

He grins, taking a step toward me. For a moment, I wonder if he's going to kiss me, but he walks right past. My bottom lip pouts at the rejection. He's in work mode.

"Print the existing plot of The Grizzly," he says. "I'll be back with my laptop."

"Yes, sir."

Emory lifts an eyebrow and walks out with a smirk.

By the time the layout of the current coaster spits out of my printer, he's sitting at the corner of my desk with his laptop open and our sketches beside him.

Like the wizard that he is—the coaster genius who earned the title of the youngest CEO in the business—he translates our work into a 3D digital rendering within two hours. I give suggestions, pointing to where things might work better, and if it's a possibility, he adds it.

Each time he makes a change based on my suggestions, my heart soars.

By the time it's done, the new Grizzly is gorgeous.

It's his magnum opus.

It's my baby.

It's the combination of our two minds—a dream coaster.

It's not a record-breaker on height or speed. But it's unique. And it's very Honeywood—with carefully placed trees, rocky terrain, and the tunnel that started it all. Yes, it is very, very Honeywood.

The queue line will steal a good chunk of real estate from the honeybee exhibit, but God knows we need to downsize that anyway. The honeybees might have something to say about that, but the guests certainly won't. The board of directors will love it.

Emory's face tilts up to me, and I'm beaming from ear to ear.

He finally says what we've both been thinking.

"There's no way they can say no."

He's right.

It's perfect.

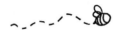

Grace, the creative director from our ad agency, is our first test subject, and she immediately starts gushing about it.

"Oh, this is so good," she says. "I'll get a few new promo ideas running to my team, then get back to you. But let's get the coaster approved first this time, okay?"

I look at Emory, who cringes like a boy getting caught with his hand in the cookie jar.

"We can try," he says.

"Seriously though," Grace continues, "this should be one fun ride. Great job, Emory."

"It was a team effort," he says, glancing over at me.

My breath hitches.

"Then, you're a natural, Lorelei," she says. "You really understand parks."

I loved the whole process. The design. The integration into Honeywood. The placement. All of it.

I forgot how much I love coasters. How much I adore the functionality behind them, the process, the purchasing ...

And in that moment, I realize what I truly want.

I want to be general manager.

I want to be in Honeywood, working on projects like this with manufacturers. Making the park better.

It hits me that I need this project to go well, not just to keep my current role, but to also prove I can do more for this park. I need the board to know that I am leadership material.

When we hang up with Grace, Emory raises an eyebrow, as if he can sense something is not sitting right with me. What he doesn't know is, I'm having an epiphany on an astronomical level.

"How do you feel?" he asks, his eyes trailing over me, jaw twitching in anticipation.

"I want to do more of this."

The side of his mouth twitches up, the small lines starting to form along his beautiful mouth. He gives me a crooked smile, and I feel ... right.

I feel whole inside for the first time in two years.

"Kiss me," I demand.

Emory Dawson doesn't hesitate.

He steps forward, taking the back of my neck in his palm and exhaling in—is it relief? Happiness? Desire? Then, his mouth smashes against mine. His hand rushes through my hair, letting my strands fill his palm before fisting it in a grip.

My heart hammers against my chest.

Kissing Emory is like when you've been waiting for ten seconds to ascend a roller coaster's hill, and now that you're at the top, you realize there's no going back. No matter how loud you scream, you're not getting off this ride. You're diving deep into the other side—into the wild unknown.

I used to love that feeling before everything went wrong. Before the car tore off the track. Before Dawson Manufacturing became a consistent force of nature in my life.

But kissing Emory Dawson has brought it back.

The fervor with which he nips my bottom lip and curls an arm around my waist in possession ... I want it all. I want to feel every bit of him he can offer.

His hand grabs my thigh, hiking it up his leg. A shot of pain drives into my hip, and I wince.

Dang it, come on!

216

My hip doesn't want to negotiate like I do. But I don't tell Emory. You try telling someone you can't spread your legs for them.

I try to distract myself by running my own hands through his hair. It only coaxes him further, gripping my legs rough and backing me against the desk so that I'm hoisted on top, his body resting between mine.

My legs are spread too wide. I can feel the ache radiating up my hip.

But I can do this. I want him.

A phone buzzes in the distance.

Emory breaks away, lowering me back down, sliding my chest over his on the descent.

"Maybe not here, huh?" he says with a shaky exhalation and grin.

I look at the ringing phone on my desk. It's Emory's device with the name *Dad* shining in bold.

And reality comes crashing back in.

"It's Thomas," I point out to Emory.

"I don't care." He doesn't skip a beat, but my heart does.

"You should."

Emory runs a hand up my throat and to my chin, raising it to look at him.

Shivers course through me at the motion. His eyes are lit by fire.

"I'll tell him about the new coaster. And he'll tell me no," he says. "So, I don't care to answer his call."

"You don't like to be told no, do you?"

"Not without good reason behind it."

My stomach drops as his hand drives up the side of my leg once more, drifting inward to graze the inside of my thigh before splaying across my hip and up my side.

I close my eyes, letting out a wisp of air.

There's so much more to this than just us.

It's far too complicated.

"We can't do this," I say. "I'm in a lawsuit with your company."

"Oh, so we're finally changing it to my company and not me?"

Cheeky man.

I smile with a dreamy sigh that I didn't intend to let out. I can't help that he makes me swoon.

"Okay, what if I said I was scared of losing my job?" I ask.

His hand pauses, only his thumb continuing to caress my skin in languid circles.

"You're running this project," he says. "Nothing will happen to you."

"What if I said I was scared of *you*?"

His stroking stops. He looks down at me, eyebrows furrowed. And whether he's doing it consciously or not, his hand starts to withdraw.

"Me?" he asks.

"Yes," I answer. "You're an intimidating man sometimes. What if I was scared of you?"

"I'd never hurt you," he says, the words strained.

Wait, strained?

I step closer, letting his arms curl around me.

Where did he just go?

"I know you wouldn't hurt me," I say quickly. "I meant, us. This."

"Good," he says, setting his cheek against mine. "I'm not scared of us."

"You're not scared of anything."

Emory rests his large palms on my hips. His head bows down, hair falling forward a little. Strands are loose and slightly ragged, but only in the best of ways. A man after a hard day's work. A rugged cowboy.

His head tilts back, and he looks at me, dark brown eyes darting between mine.

"What if I told you I was scared of The Grizzly?" he asks. "Would you believe me?"

"No," I say with an unconvinced laugh.

He shakes his head, the tip of his mouth twitching into a smile before frowning again.

"It hurt someone, and I thought I had done everything to prevent it. But it still did. It scares me to ride it. To face my failure."

It hits me that he might actually be serious.

Well, dang.

He leans in again, knocking his forehead against mine, letting it rest there in so intimate a way.

"We all have our fears," he says. "I've been injured a lot. Banged up from test run to test run throughout my whole life. Not much stops me from continuing. But that ride is the only one that scares me now."

I place a kiss on his lips, but he doesn't continue. He just holds me.

Emory looks so vulnerable, curled around me, as if shrouding me from the pain of the world. He's my guardian in this moment, whether he notices or not. But he's a guardian with more to him than he lets on. How could I have not seen that before?

"What else scares you?" I ask.

"Saying something wrong and messing this up."

"What is this anyway?" I ask.

"Something, I hope."

Hope. Like a little kid on Christmas, staring in a storefront window at the present he wants so badly.

"You're a nicer person than you give yourself credit for," I say.

He chuckles, low and sweet.

"Don't tell anyone I have a heart," he says. "It'll ruin the illusion."

I run a single finger along his forearm, watching as goose bumps rise from my invisible path.

"Come with me to Employee Night tonight," I say.

His mouth ticks up into a sly smile. "Are you asking me on a date, Lorelei?"

"Oh, definitely not," I say. "What would our lawyers think?"

He chuckles, and my stomach clenches.

This is temporary between us. I know that. And it should be, given how we're connected. We have an unresolved lawsuit. He doesn't even live in Cedar Cliff.

We have separate lives that would be impossible to intertwine.

But I can't resist keeping him for the little time we might have.

He's so different from other men I've met. He's motivated and confident. But he doesn't boast about it.

It's inspiring.

If Emory can be bold and stay in Honeywood for the summer despite what his dad—his CEO—tells him to do, then I can be bold too. If he is doing what feels right, then so can I.

"I ... I think I want to ride something tonight," I say. "Maybe start with a small coaster, then go up from there. Baby steps toward The Grizzly. I want to ride it again when it opens."

He kisses my cheek. It's sweet and gentle, but some-

thing about it—the way he lingers for just a second longer—
is empowering.

"Okay," he agrees. "Then, I'm with you."

As long as I have him by my side, I think I'll be fine.

Hope is all I need.

32

Lorelei

We always close one hour early on Memorial Day for Employee Night. It gives the part-time college kids a night to enjoy the park with no crowds. Us full-time employees also get a kick out of it by watching all the teens stumble into flirting. We try to guess who has been on The Canoodler with whom. It's an easy game because these kids are ravenous and horny.

But who am I to judge?

I went back to the apartment to freshen up for a not-date date with Mr. Roller Coaster.

I curled my hair in the *I just went to the beach, and this is totally natural* kind of way. I changed into my bright yellow miniskirt, complete with bumblebees trailing around the hem. It is, without a doubt, the shortest skirt I own while still keeping me respectable if I run into Fred or other colleagues.

I look in the mirror, eyeing my scar along my thigh, tugging down the skirt to ensure it covers it. Just barely, but good enough.

I go outside to drive back to the park, but there's already

a car idling at the end of our driveway. Leaning against it, hands in his denim pockets, is Emory.

"Stalker," I breathe out.

"Felt weird, having you meet me at my place," he says. "For our date."

The smirk that ensues almost turns my knees to jelly. I could flop over right here.

Be cool.

"Not a date," I correct. "Also, you're staying at the park's hotel. It would have made more sense for me to meet you there."

He shrugs with a smile. "Still."

I'll never get tired of that smile.

"Wait, how'd you find out where I lived?"

"Fred told me. I said I needed to drop off maps."

"That's wrong."

"Sue me."

I try to fight the grin that overtakes me, but it pulls at my lips all the same.

Emory opens the car door for me. I don't know a thing about vehicles, but if I had to guess, this is a nice one. The interior is leather. The dashboard is lit up in blues. The engine is barely audible.

Fancy-schmancy, says my non-mechanic brain.

Emory comes around the other side, the leather squeaking beneath him as he settles in.

In such a small, sporty car, Emory looks even larger than life. His long hands grip the wheel. His stupid, wonderful woodsy-candle scent fills the space.

When his brown eyes meet mine, he lets in a sharp breath, followed by a strained chuckle.

"What?" I ask.

"Nothing."

"No, what?"

His hand trails along the hem of my skirt, tracing over the bumblebee stitch. Emory exhales and swallows, spreading out the hand over my bare knee. His palm covers it completely.

I don't know if I've been more attracted to a single sight in my life.

"I like you," he says. "And I like your little bumblebees." He flicks the patch.

"Going soft on me, Mr. Dawson?"

He pauses at my statement.

"Maybe. I can't help it if you're the silver lining in my day."

"You'll make a girl blush if you keep those words up."

"I have plenty of words to give," he says. "And I like to see you blush. Win-win."

Emory throws me a wink, and I melt into my seat like ice cream on a hot day.

He presses the car's clutch and shifts gears, and off we go.

We drive through Cedar Cliff's downtown on our way to Honeywood. Though to call it a downtown area in the sense of a metro city would be inaccurate. It's a beautiful collage of red brick, second-floor cast-iron balconies, bookstores, antique shops, cafés, and even the white-steepled church my parents were married in.

It is the beating heart of our small town.

It'll be busy tonight. Since you can see Honeywood's fireworks from the grassy center in downtown, there will soon be lawn chairs scattered throughout and Frisbees thrown as families pass the time until sundown.

"Fun fact: we had prom there," I say, pointing out the

small white gazebo beside a slew of picnic blankets. "My date was Andy Griffith."

"Andy—"

"Not the real Andy Griffith," I say, laughing. "His parents had a horrible sense of humor in naming him, I guess. He was shorter than me, but that didn't stop him from asking me out. Then again, most guys are shorter than me."

Except for Emory.

As if he could read my mind, his eyebrows pump once.

I smile. He smiles back.

I look out the window. We stop at a red light on the edge of the city's square, and on the opposite side is—

"Oh God," I say. I slide down in the seat, slippery as a penguin on ice.

"What?" Emory's eyes follow my movement with a chuckle.

Now is not the time to be cute.

"Jaymee," I hiss-whisper.

His face contorts as he spits out, "Who?"

The bright pink Volkswagen belonging to our resident gossip columnist is idling on the other side of the intersection.

"*Cedar Cliff Chatter* reporter," I say. "Gossip columnist. I don't trust her as far as I can throw her. The apple falls very far from the tree."

"What tree?"

"She's Fred's daughter. And nothing like him."

He barks out a laugh. "No kidding?"

"You think it's funny now. It's not as laughable when she gets dirt on you," I say. "And last I checked, you and I are a freaking landfill."

He straightens up at that. "Fair point."

The light must turn green again because we drive forward as he mutters under his breath, "Small towns, I swear. Gotta know everyone."

I swallow down my nerves, but they're unable to rest until his thumb starts to stroke mine in circles.

"She's gone."

I sit up, biting back my shame from my freak-out before looking out the window again.

"Is she really that bad?" he asks.

"Just hope you never find out."

He pats my leg. "Tell me more about this crazy place."

I swear, that hand is going to be the death of me.

"Well, I used to run this path," I say, gesturing along the tree-shaded sidewalk. "My brother and I would race to see who could get to the bakery first."

"You've never mentioned a brother."

"Twin actually. I always beat him, but never mention that to his face. He still gets worked up about it."

Emory chuckles. "Noted."

I lean my head on the cool window. I can picture running down the street like it was yesterday.

"I kept running into my twenties, and I still always stopped at that bakery," I say. "They've got this sugar bread that is perfect during the summer."

"Do you miss it?" he asks. "Running?"

I curl my lip in, nodding. "Every day."

His hand squeezes my knee, and something in me feels that much lighter.

"I think my mom would love Cedar Cliff," he says. "She's from a small town too, you know."

"Tell me about your mom."

"She's much cooler than me. Lives on her motorbike essentially. Nomad."

226

"Really?!"

"Yeah, really," he says, pulling into The Hibernation's parking lot. "Turned into a biker babe after the divorce. Her words, not mine. I think she wanted to feel the open air on her face, you know? Wind in her hair. Freedom."

He turns off the car, and we sit in silence.

I meet his gaze and swallow. "Can I ask what happened? Why she left?"

He looks from me to the floorboard, then back up. "My father ... he pushed her. And it was one time too many. Or maybe not. I honestly don't know how long it went on. She'll probably never tell me."

My heart wants to shatter in that moment, but I grip his hand tighter to be strong for him instead of myself.

"How old were you?" I ask.

"Already an adult," he says. "No worries—no childhood trauma." He laughs sardonically. "I tried to leave the company. I wanted to quit. But she didn't want me to. Wanted me to help run the business with my father since he couldn't be trusted. Our family always puts the business first, even then."

I think about my parents' floral business. They never pressured me or Landon to carry on the legacy. But I'm willing to bet we had very different childhoods than Emory.

"I'm sorry," I say.

"Don't be," he says with a weak smile. "He's a man with his own demons to work out. He tries to drink them away."

Then, it hits me.

Emory only drank water on trivia night.

I'm not sure if I should ask why or tell him I noticed. Is it even my place?

"Is that why ..." I start, immediately feeling wrong about asking. But when I look at him, his eyebrows are raised, inviting me to continue. "Well, I've never seen you drink."

He nods. "I don't have any issues with it. But ... that's one less thing I can have in common with him, you know?"

"I'm sorry."

He chuckles. "You keep saying that."

"Well, I am."

Emory reaches out his hand, tracing a line over my forearm and down to my elbow. It sparks goose bumps over my skin. He exhales. I want to ask what he's thinking, but part of me wonders if I've already asked too much of him tonight.

He tilts his head toward the park. "Enough of that. Ready for Employee Night?"

"Only if you are."

"With you? Always."

I can't resist the smile that spreads across my face. My heart flutters when he returns the gesture.

"Then, let's go make fun of teenagers."

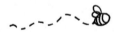

"Blondie has definitely been with McPumps over there," Quinn says.

"Give her more credit," Theo croons. "Look! She's touching Emo Kid's arm. Maybe she likes personality more than gym rats."

"Oh my God, that would be adorable."

Emory and I found Quinn and Theo sitting in chairs outside of The Bee-fast Stop, iced sugary drinks in hand. They were already mid-evaluation of the teenage horniness when we showed up.

"I bet he gives good oral," Theo says, sucking on her straw.

"Who?" Quinn asks. "The guy with the skinny arms?"

"Oh yeah," she says. "He's got something to prove, and I bet he figured that out early on in life."

Emory lifts an eyebrow in my direction, and when we both see Quinn staring at us, we look away.

"Did you have something to prove, Mr. Roller Coaster?" Quinn asks.

"Mr. who?" Emory asks, lifting an eyebrow.

"Ignore that," I stumble in. "She means you."

My heart pounds at being outed as a total weirdo, but he still grins at me like the sun shines out from every fiber of my being.

I didn't know someone could look at me that way.

"Why would I have something to prove?" Emory continues.

"I dunno," Quinn says. "You seem like you were an awkward kid."

"Says the girl still wearing thick eyeliner," I chime in.

She snorts. "Rude, Lore."

"I didn't have a ton of friends, if you must know," Emory says.

I try not to meet his eyes, so he won't know I'm internally squealing at the thought of an adorable, awkward, younger Emory. To think he was not infallible at some point in his life is humbling.

However, I also don't need to know if Emory has *proven himself* over the years.

My mind doesn't need the distraction of knowing whether Emory is a pussy-pleaser.

"Oh, oh, oh, look!" Theo says.

We glance at the teenagers re-riding the kiddie coaster.

"They're up to no good on that ride," she says. "Fifth time riding alone. God, am I gonna have to step into my supervisor shoes? I really don't want to."

"Will it help if we kick them out?" Emory asks.

"We?" I ask.

All three sets of eyes land on him.

He keeps his gaze on me, and I feel hot all over.

"You and me, Lorelei," he says. "You want to ride it, don't you?"

Theo gasps. "Wow, good for you! You're riding coasters again? You should."

Well, now that he's made a spectacle of it, it's not like I can say no.

"Baby steps, right?" Emory says. He extends his hand out to me. "Come on, Lorelei."

I look to my friends. Theo, with eyes as wide as saucers, and Quinn, giving the slyest, most knowing grin I've ever seen.

She's going to dog me about this later; I just know it.

I take his hand and am whisked away to the ride.

When we get to the front of the queue line, Emory throws a thumb over his shoulder at the two teens, who practically slink out of the seats.

I settle into the train's car, buckling the seat belt over us and pulling down the lap bar.

My knee starts to jitter. Emory's eyes scan over me.

"You all right there?" he asks.

I tilt my head to the side in an *are you serious, of course I'm not* way.

He tilts his head too, mimicking me with a smile growing on his face.

Emory looks so boyish for once. Endearing. Innocent.

230

No, not innocent—not the man who whispered dirty things to me while pinching my nipples.

They stiffen at the thought. And my shirt is thin.

Emory's eyes flick down to my chest, then back up.

"What are you thinking about, beautiful?" he asks, his voice husky, almost a low rumble in his chest.

"Could you be more obvious checking me out?"

"How can I resist when you're wearing this?" he asks, his finger reaching out to trace the edge of where the skirt meets my thigh.

Thankfully, my scar is on the opposite side.

I shake my head with a grin, but it disappears the second the train jolts forward and we start moving up the tiny lift hill.

Rationally, I know it's only a kiddie coaster. The drop won't be more than twenty feet at most.

And yet my hands white-knuckle the lap bar.

"Relax, Lore," Emory says from beside me.

"I can't."

"At least don't break the lap bar."

My head jerks toward him. "Emory, please, I'm not in the mood for jokes anymore."

My forearms shake. My palms ache with the tight grip I have on the bar. Emory's face goes from boyish laughter to a deep frown and pinched eyebrows.

"I'm sorry," I whisper. "I'm just ... nervous."

The clicking of the lift hill grows louder, beating heavy in my ears. My heart pumps faster. I wonder for a moment if it'll explode.

Emory leans in, lips close to the shell of my ear as he whispers, "Can I help you relax?"

His hand ghosts over my knee. It trails up the interior of my thigh, leaving fiery embers along my veins.

"Y-yes," I stammer out.

He knocks the hem of my skirt aside and slides underneath. A finger traces along the outside of my underwear, ghosting over my fabric-covered slit, rising and falling along my lips.

"This all right?" His thumb nudges my panties aside and slides along my wet center. "Is this?"

"Keep going," I whisper.

My ride anxiety twists to excitement with every rub of his fingers over me.

"Does it feel good when I touch you?"

The pad of his thumb spreads me apart, and his middle finger grazes my entrance. I feel light-headed with need.

"Are you nervous now?" he asks.

"No."

"Good."

My stomach clenches tighter when we crest the hill, but I don't even notice the descent because in the moment that we plunge, his large finger enters me.

I exhale—my breath whooshing out with the dip of the fall, my sigh coordinating with his finger pumping inside me, rolling against the soft spot he found so easily.

He matches his rhythm to each curve of the ride and every bounce over the small hills. His palm presses into my clit as we curl around the corner.

"I did have something to prove, by the way." He inserts a second finger, adding pressure, sending my head flying back against the seat.

My hips try to buck up, but the lap bar holds me.

"And I can't wait to feel you on my tongue."

I gasp, gripping the bar harder. My wetness slicks his fingers, making a mess on my inner thighs.

He pumps faster. I can feel the pressure building in my

stomach. Right as we enter the final brake run, I suck in a breath. I can feel it coming on—

But then he stops. He removes his fingers, and my body already begs for them to return. I feel empty and hungry for his touch.

He adjusts my panties back into place and tugs down my skirt right as we come into view of the operators.

Emory pats the fabric. "Sorry. Ride's over, beautiful."

I exhale. The tension in my pelvis is coiled so tight. My heart is pounding hard with no release to be had.

"Oh, you son of a ..."

"You know, I think I'm a bad influence," he says.

"You're the worst."

He gestures to my skirt, wrinkled and haphazard from his touch.

"You've got a real conundrum here, huh?" His leg extends out, rubbing the outside of it against mine. "Hmm," he muses. "Wonder what you'll do."

I swallow, letting my head fall back against the seat once more.

He chuckles.

If I wasn't so stressed, I might have loved it.

I could do this forever with him. This push-and-pull. The teasing.

But it's not in the cards for us.

The most we can do for now is have fun.

And Emory is one heck of a ride that I fully intend on exploring further.

33

Emory

Our night was initially coaxed forward by small touches—her hand grazing my leg, my palm on the small of her back—but I might have crossed a line to something much more when I decided to christen that car with her sex.

Once we exit the train, Lorelei storms forward. And it's straight to Honeywood's exit.

I'm not stupid. I follow without a second thought.

The sun has mostly set, but the park is still roaring. I can hear various attractions' strained wood with each passing train, the screams of employees conducting a symphony of thrills. And yet I'm laser-focused on watching Lorelei's long, slender legs march us out of the park.

To think I could have ever considered her as the true villain in our lawsuit seems baffling to me now. I was delusional, as I have been with so many things for much too long. And watching her shift from confident manager to nervous rider was humbling. She was vulnerable, and it only made me admire her more as she faced such an incredible fear.

Lorelei is gorgeous when she walks with determination. She floats on air, even when her ass tempts me through that cute skirt.

The blood flow rushes down to my cock, and I walk faster, trying to hide it from view.

We're still working together after all. At least to any onlookers. Hell, we're still in a freaking lawsuit.

But that doesn't change the fact that we both know where we're headed.

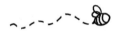

My keys rattle on the side table when I toss them down. I close my hotel room door behind us.

She sighs. "You know, for some reason, I thought we'd end up on The Canoodler or something."

I chuckle. "The boat ride?"

I don't tell her that I wouldn't want to have our first time in the park, on a ride, or anywhere public. Maybe someday, because I'd do anything for this woman—who I'm slowly realizing might be an exhibitionist—but that's an adventure for another time.

Not tonight. Not for the first time with this woman who makes my heart beat three times as fast as any woman before her. The woman who assists in the park when it's not even her job. The woman who had the guts to tell me off without fear.

She deserves so much more than a quickie in a theme park.

"Lorelei, do you ever think that maybe I'm a traditionalist?" I ask, running both my hands over her shoulders. "That I like a bed to ..." I don't want to say *be with you for the first time* because what the hell are we? Teenagers? No, I'm a mid-thirties man, and she's a grown woman. I can say what I want, and what I want isn't romantic.

"To what?" she asks.

I tip her chin up. "To have you."

She swallows, her eyes dilating.

It's a weird thing—this possession us Dawson men feel about things, businesses, and even people. But she has me wrapped around her finger. And not only do I want her, but I would also give myself to her in a second if she asked.

I can feel my hand shaking, so I pocket it.

Lorelei smiles, and it's beyond her usual kindness. It's sly. She's a temptress. I should have known she had this layer to her. She walks to the balcony. I toe off my shoes, trying to shake out my hand as I do so.

Pull it together, Emory.

She opens the French doors and leans against the railing.

The setting sun beams in from the outside. Normally, it'd bother me. I shut the curtains every night to keep out the rays of light. But with Lorelei standing there, an angelic silhouette against the golds and peaches of the sky, I realize she's the sunshine I want to let in.

I move behind her, letting my hands rest on her hips, spanning the width of her waist.

"This doesn't feel real," she says.

"What do you mean?" My thumbs run circles on her lower back.

She leans back against me, her head falling against my shoulder. I wonder if she can hear my heart pounding.

"Me and you."

"You mean, you and Mr. Roller Coaster?"

She covers her face with her hands. "Oh God. I'm so sorry. It's just a silly nickname my friends made for you."

"It's a new one for me," I say, kissing the column of her neck. "But why do I feel bullied when Quinn says it?"

She laughs. I can feel it vibrate through me. I want to make her laugh more.

"I think it was her idea too," she says.

"I'm not surprised."

"It's weird though. For the longest time, you felt ... untouchable because of it. Like some mythical person that had all the power over me."

I kiss her neck again, my palm covering it for a second before trailing down to her collarbone. I savor her small gasps.

"I'm not"—another kiss—"untouchable"—I kiss her shoulder—"now."

She exhales, arching her back. Her ass rolls against my groin, and I'm already there, hard as a rock. She lets out another shaky exhale, sending goose bumps over my skin.

Her hand reaches around her back, falling between us, running along the length of me.

I can barely breathe.

I grip her shoulders again, turning her on the spot and taking her jaw into my palms.

She kisses me at the same time I kiss her.

Bliss.

It's a mix of mouths, tongues, and teeth. Hard desperation in every movement. She takes a step forward, and I walk back, blindly leading us both to the bed. When the backs of my knees hit the mattress, I bend down, cupping her ass in my hands and raising one of her knees to my waist.

I wait for her to jump and wrap her legs around me.

But she doesn't.

I knead every inch of her leg, moving a hand to her hair, giving it a slight tug.

She moans. God, she moans so loud.

I grip all of her hair in my fist, letting her leg down and turning us so she falls backward on the bed.

I've imagined Lorelei in this position, but never like this. No, my mind couldn't have conjured up this image—her hand splaying out across her stomach, her fingers dipping down to lift her skirt. I didn't expect gorgeous silk panties. I watch as she parts them to the side, running a single finger over her clit.

I fall to my knees. I don't think it's even voluntary. It's like the weight of this moment, of watching her, willed me to do it. She is my goddess, and I'm poised to pray at her temple.

"Let me do that for you," I say, reaching out with my hand, running it over her fingers for a moment before she withdraws, allowing my thumb to rub where she once was.

I can't help but look at her, to watch as her head lolls to the side on the mattress.

"Emory, God," she says.

My name on her lips is like a toxin, and I want it flooding my body more.

Ruin me, Lorelei.

Her knees are still closed together—not nearly enough room for me to do what I'm desperate to do—so I place a palm against one knee. My hand looks giant on her, and the appearance of it all sends my nerves reeling once more. I kiss inside her thigh, then gently start to spread her knees apart.

"Wait."

I jerk back, seeing her as she meets my eyes. I remove my hand from her.

"I'm moving too fast," I say quickly.

"No, no," she answers, sitting up on the bed.

I tilt my head a little because I'm confused as hell, and she laughs.

Okay, so that's a good sign.

"I ... my hips hurt when my legs are too far apart. The, uh ... the injury makes spreading them not feel great."

My stomach rolls over in guilt.

My ride did this.

Me.

"Emory?" she asks.

I'm quiet for too long.

I can apologize. I can make this better.

"All I want is the taste of you," I say. "And I'm a creative man."

I think for a moment, savoring her smile in response, letting it wash over me before nodding. "All right. Turn around. I want to see you on all fours. Think you can do that, beautiful?"

She nods in response, turning on the spot, hoisting herself onto her hands and knees and obediently pushing her ass out to me.

Good God, seeing her presented like a gift is almost too much.

"Attagirl," I say.

Her small moan is the only approval I need to dive in.

I push her underwear to the side and roll my desperate tongue along her slick center.

I've heard men say their women taste like candy. Or fruits. Or something else ridiculous.

Why mask it with such flowery language?

Lorelei tastes like pussy. And I fucking love it.

I devour her, cherishing the taste, dipping my tongue

239

inside to get every bit of her wetness. And when she whimpers, I add a finger, rolling it against her soft spot. Her reaction gets better when I add a second one.

She's bucking against my face, and I place a hand to steady her, kneading her ass cheek in my palm. When she pushes against it, I take that as my cue to slap it.

"Oh God, Emory," she groans.

She could kill a man with that voice, so I do it again—smacking her behind, working my fingers inside her, rubbing against the place that makes her say my name again, licking her to high heaven until I feel her walls clench around me.

She shivers against my touch before releasing with a loud, "Oh God."

I would die a happy man if that was the last experience I had.

I rub my palm over her ass cheeks, soothing the redness from my slaps.

I don't get time to admire her before she's flipping over on the mattress, sitting on just her knees. I'm still on my own knees on the ground, my face now at her stomach. I wrap my arms around her waist and hold her against my cheek, the cotton of her flipped-up skirt soft against my hard stubble.

My body is practically shaking with nerves.

I feel like a teenager again, completely enraptured by this woman and unable to keep my anxiety in check.

A hand strokes through my hair, and I look up at her. Lorelei's eyes are hooded, filled with the lust of sex, and I could stay on my knees for her forever.

"Your turn, *Mr. Roller Coaster*."

I growl. "You're gonna pay for that."

"I sure hope so."

I stand, holding her face in my hands. I know my face is slick with her wetness.

"Just let me go wash ..." I start, but she reaches up and pulls me down for a kiss.

"You're going nowhere," she whispers against my mouth.

Her hands grab my belt. I hear the metal clank against fine leather, followed by my zipper hissing down. She doesn't break eye contact even once. Those brown eyes stay on me, as she runs a palm over the outside of my boxers. She removes me from beneath my waistband.

I suck in air, the whole sight so unbelievable and wonderful.

"Tell me what you want," she says.

"You like it when I talk to you, don't you?" I ask, running a hand through her hair.

"Yes," she admits.

Her tongue whips out over the head of my cock, and I let out a hiss. It twitches under her slender hands that barely cover even half of me. The juxtaposition drives me wild.

"What do you like?" I ask. "You like being told when it feels good?"

She gives a long, languid stroke against me with her tongue.

Christ.

"Anything good," she says. "Just talk."

Ah, so she likes praise. I'm more than happy to give it to her.

"Be a good girl and suck me off, beautiful."

She groans in response, taking me whole. And, God, she takes more than I thought she could. My head jerks back in response, and I let out an involuntary groan. I can't help it.

241

The sounds she's making are too sexy to be true. Slurping and sucking and just absolutely obscene in the best ways.

"You're doing so great," I say, petting her hair as I hit the back of her throat.

But even with her gorgeous mouth, it's not enough. I want all of her.

I tug her away from me, watching as she falls back, a crude line of drool following with her.

"Oh my God," I moan. "Off with the clothes."

I step out of my pants and underwear and walk over to the side drawer, pulling out a condom I bought at the local convenience store yesterday.

I roll the condom over me, looking back at her just in time to see her clothes thrown to the opposite end of the bed. She's sprawled out like a dream. Breasts on display, the line between her ribs leading down to her flat stomach, and the area between her thighs practically calling me home. And trailing up her leg, stopping right at her hip, is a scar. Thick, curved, and dotted on either side, like metal has been infused within.

She swallows when she sees me looking.

I walk over to her, my eyes roaming the length of it. I run a hand over the tough skin. But it's not the scar I notice when I touch her. It's her muscles. Her strength.

She opens her mouth to speak, and I shake my head.

"Don't," I say. "You're beautiful. Don't say anything."

I did this to her. She deserves so much better.

I lean down and kiss her skin, letting my lips linger along the puckered line. I can hear her barely there sighs before rising back up.

She looks at me. Her brows are stitched together. Her eyes dart between mine.

"You didn't have to do that," she whispers.

"Did it bother you?" I ask.

Lorelei lets out a small, breathy, "No."

"Good."

She tips her chin toward me. "Are you ... taking off your shirt too?" she asks, a smile crossing over her face once more.

I can feel the energy slipping us back into where we were before.

I chuckle, pulling my shirt over my head before tossing it over the chair at the desk. "Better?"

She sits up to run a hand over my chest and down to my stomach. "You hide all of this too well," she says, dipping her fingers between the boxes of my abs.

"I'm not always in a boardroom. I mostly work with my hands. I prefer it."

"God, I prefer it, too, if it gets you like this," she says with a smile.

I lean down, kissing her, then bend at the waist to take one of her breasts in my mouth, removing it with a pop before pushing her shoulders back down on the bed. The sight sends my nerves alight. My body shakes again. I stretch out my hand to soothe the nerves.

Her eyes dart to it, then back to me.

"Are you shaking?" she asks.

"I like you," I say with a chuckle that comes out timider than I'd like. "And you're ..." I run a hand across her stomach, gripping the side of her hip. "God, you're ..."

"Emory Dawson. At a loss for words."

I run a thumb over her plump bottom lip, the one she can't stop biting.

"Lie back."

She falls back on the bed with a grin, and I walk forward right as her eyes dart to her hip.

"Oh, don't you worry," I say with a wink. "I'm a quick learner."

I bend down, gripping both her ankles in one fist. I lift them up to rest on my shoulder, keeping her knees together so as not to hurt her. The height of the bed is almost perfect, but not quite.

"Hand me a pillow?" I ask, pointing to the head of the bed.

She reaches her long arm out, grabbing one and throwing it at my chest.

I catch it midair. "Problem-solving, see?"

I lift her off the bed by gripping her ankles. I slide the pillow beneath her hips so that she's angled exactly at my waist, then lower her back down.

"Is that all right?" I ask.

She's grinning from ear to ear, and I think I see a wink of something in her eye.

"I knew there had to be a reason you were an engineer, Mr. Dawson."

"Say that again."

"*Mr. Dawson.*"

"Good girl. Eyes on me."

34

Lorelei

Emory Dawson should never wear shirts.

He's bulky, but only in the way a man of his height could be. Broad-shouldered, a prominent collarbone protruding above his lightly furred chest and toned stomach. He's rugged. Massive. And mine.

My feet are on his shoulder, gripped together by a large hand as the other fists his cock.

He didn't go running out the door when I couldn't move my legs to a certain position. In fact, he put me in one that felt even better. I should have known Emory would be careful with me.

I can feel him at my entrance, rubbing against my clit, driving the already-sensitive bud from my first orgasm wilder.

Then, he presses in. It's only a bit. We can both feel that I'm tighter than I should be for a man of his size.

He pulls out, then pushes back in. It's slow. Agonizing.

I know he's trying to be accommodating. I'm realizing Emory is kind in more ways than I've ever given him credit for. I adore him for it.

Julie Olivia

God, I *adore* Emory Dawson. I never imagined those words could be true, but here they are. I adore his looks, his touch, his stupid little eyebrows … I can't get enough of him. I can't get enough of how gentle he is.

Except I don't need gentle right now.

"Please," I say, searching his eyes. I don't want another person tiptoeing around me. The free passes. The pity. "Please, Emory."

I can see the moment he has the realization of what I'm asking. I see the moment his eyes light on fire.

"You want this cock?" he asks, low and husky.

That mouth of his will be the death of me.

I nod, my cheeks burning with heat.

"You gonna take it as good as you did in your mouth?"

"Yes."

"Yes what?"

I wonder for a second what he wants, but then I remember, and I can't help the smile that spreads across my face. It makes it even better when he smiles back. The smile reserved for me.

"Yes, *Mr. Dawson*."

And he enters me with a growl.

My head falls back as I close my eyes with a wince. The feeling of his entire cock inside me has a tinge of pain to it, but not nearly enough to overpower the sting of pleasure.

His large hand grips my jaw and directs me to look at him again.

Emory's eyes are intense. Like he's the man in the boardroom. Powerful. Domineering.

My chest constricts, a coil winding tighter and tighter.

With our eyes locked, he pulls out and thrusts right back in. I let out a heavy sigh, feeling him hit exactly where he needs to. And with each subsequent push, it

246

transforms into something more powerful. When he jerks into me faster, I can't help the continued moans that escape.

And suddenly—there's a whiz and a *BANG!*

We halt, looking out the open French doors to see fireworks exploding into the sky above Honeywood.

Something feels different in that moment. The colors dance in Emory's eyes. The bright pinks and greens illuminate half of him while creating contrasts of shadows along his toned body.

His thumb drags down my bottom lip.

My chest feels tight. Tighter than ever, bound up in nerves and *him.*

Whiz, BANG!

"I want to hear you over the fireworks," he says. "Understand?"

I nod. Emory smiles, and it is beautifully devious.

He removes his hand from my ankles, and keeping them balanced on his shoulder, he grips the sides of my hips.

Then, he goes absolutely wild.

Whiz, BANG!

I'm panting with need as he growls with each thrust, moaning each time he hits that spot, every time I hear the obscene sound of our bodies slapping together.

"Emory!" I moan it louder for him, just as he likes.

Emory takes my nipple between his fingers, rolling it, pinching it.

My stomach pulls tighter. Sparks ignite in my chest.

Another pinch and a groan from him sends my second orgasm boiling over.

My nerves shoot outward to every extremity, and I can't help the loud, "Emory!" that whines out of me.

Whiz, BANG!

Emory moans, moving his hand to my ass, kneading it as he pumps faster.

Whiz, BANG!

He drives inside me, faster, faster, sending me over the edge again right as he lets out a low roar and releases.

BANG!

Emory slumps down, his shaking hand reaching up to steady my ankles on his shoulder.

I run a hand through his hair as his eyes meet mine.

His eyebrows are stitched in the middle, his pupils dilated as he searches mine. For what, I don't know.

"You've ruined other women for me," he says. "You must know that."

Emory traces my jaw with his large hand, stroking down to my chin.

"Don't worry. No other man can compare."

"No, beautiful," he mutters. "No other men will ever get the chance."

BANG!

My stomach drops.

I accept his comment without words, tonguing his thumb into my mouth and sucking on it as he hisses in air.

When it pops out, he whispers, "Mine."

And without even a second thought, I find myself saying, "Yours."

Whiz, BANG!

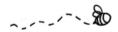

I wake up to the sound of waves.

The smell of a freshly laundered pillowcase.

The feel of a large arm slung over my waist with knees bent into mine.

Am I spooning?

I roll to the side, and there he is.

Emory.

Gorgeous, surly Emory with his brow furrowed in the center.

I press my thumb into the crease, and he blinks awake. He looks almost innocent, if I didn't know any better.

He sees me and smiles, kissing my nose and nuzzling his face into the crook of my neck, his light stubble scratching against me.

"You look grumpy, even in your sleep," I say.

He chuckles. His drowsy morning voice is rough and husky.

"You gonna turn off that alarm, beautiful?" he asks.

"Oh, right."

I reach out to the side table and fumble to slide the phone screen off.

The beach sounds from my alarm end, and then it's quiet. Just the two of us in his hotel room, still darkened by the anticipation of a rising sun in the next couple hours, only a small sliver of light peeking through the balcony outside.

At the end of the bed, I see a giant mural of Buzzy, giving me a thumbs-up, as if congratulating me on a job well done.

"Holy—"

"Oh yeah," Emory says. "Say hi to my roommate."

"Why would we paint that there?"

"Talking to him about personal space has been on my to-do list for a while."

I whisper, "He saw what we did."

"Want me to beat him up? Ain't no pervs looking at my woman."

My woman.

I can't contain the swoon at his faux Southern twang when he says it.

The soft comforter shifts as Emory's hand spreads over my stomach, sliding me closer to his chest.

"Let's not work today," he whispers against me, lazily pursing his lips against the nape of my neck.

I shiver, letting out a satisfied sigh.

I usually never have trouble getting out of bed. But I've also never woken up with a burly man's arms hugging me close.

"I have to leave in five minutes," I say.

Emory's unintelligible mumbles resemble a puppy's grumbles. He's adorable. I would put him in my little pocket if he fit.

"Talk to me," he says.

"About what?"

"Anything. I love your voice."

Love.

I swallow down my nerves and let out a small laugh.

"Okay, well, it's the day after Memorial Day."

"Yes."

"And on the day after Memorial Day, we open a little later since we stayed open so late the night before."

"Makes sense."

"So, I normally get more time to walk the park when a man isn't keeping me captive."

"That guy sounds like a dick."

I laugh. He holds me tighter.

I think of all the years I've participated in my annual post–Memorial Day tradition of traipsing through the park on my own terms. It's just me, the maintenance team, and sometimes Fred.

I remember jogging past him as a teen, giving a small thumbs-up with each subsequent circuit around the park. It hurts to think about those moments now. I took running for granted.

I don't realize I've stiffened up until Emory pulls his hand from my stomach to rub over my shoulder.

"What's wrong?"

"Nothing. Just thinking," I say. "I used to run in the mornings after Memorial Day. I'd have the whole midway to myself. It was nice."

He doesn't speak, almost as if inviting me to keep talking.

"The wind is always good the day after," I continue. "I can't explain it. I wouldn't even put my hair up in a ponytail those days. I wanted to feel it everywhere."

Emory tugs at my waist. I roll over to see he's rested his head in the palm of his hand.

"What exactly is stopping you from running?" he asks. "Medically?"

"My hip is missing pieces of bone. I can walk, but too much strained movement on my hip ... that pounding of feet on pavement ... it's just not good for me. They said there's experimental surgeries that they could look into or an adjustment or something, but ... it's fine. It just seems like too much trouble. It's fine. I still have my life. It's not the end of the world."

But when I say it, my words hitch in my throat.

Not being able to run *isn't* the end of the world; it's just a giant chunk, taken out from the happiest parts of it.

Emory wraps his arms around me, tugging me closer to his chest. He exhales before letting out a small, "I'm sorry, Lorelei."

My heart melts into his.

I don't know what he's apologizing for. The accident? His potential involvement? The fact that it affected me so much?

I realize it doesn't matter. I love that he said it at all.

"How much longer do we have together?" he asks.

We know this peaceful bliss we've found in the bedroom of Honeywood's hotel—aside from Buzzy's knowing gaze—can't last. We've got a lawsuit and an injury between us, and that might always create a divide.

"We have fifteen minutes," I say.

"Wow, last time, you said five minutes."

"I'm feeling generous."

He smiles. "You know what that means then?"

"What?"

"That sounds like fifteen minutes of a slow dessert. Lucky me."

I laugh out another, "What?" right as he twists me onto my back and disappears under the covers.

My ankles lift onto his shoulder once more, and his face disappears beneath me.

35

Lorelei

I try not to let the front door squeak when I get home. For someone who never snuck out of the house as a kid, I am actually impressed by my ninja-like tiptoes down the foyer.

If I'm lucky, I can brew coffee and take some to Quinn's bedroom as a *wow, I woke up early and am totally not coming from another person's hotel room, so look what I made!* type of moment with no suspicions attached.

But when I step into the kitchen and see both Quinn and Bennett at the breakfast table, sipping coffee, I pause mid-step.

Her lips curl in on an inhale, and Bennett leans back in his chair, crossing his arms. They look like disappointed parents—cups of prepared black coffee between them and a newspaper splayed out.

Well, there goes my coffee plan.

"Good morning," I whisper, but it comes out strained, so I clear my throat. "Good morning, friends."

They both sip their coffee in silence.

"Bennett, funny seeing you here," I say.

He doesn't answer.

"Okay, silent man. We'll have to charge a small fee for coffee if you're planning to drop by more often."

I walk to the coffeemaker, picking up the premade pot and pouring myself a mug. Unlike the two soulless people next to me, I fill up the remaining quarter of my mug with creamer.

"Bennett is here because we've got a situation," Quinn says.

"Okay ..." I pull the mug up to my lips.

"So, I don't know if you were at this staff meeting," he says, "but ... the cameras now work in The Romping Meadow."

I spit out my coffee, spraying the cabinets. I twist and drool the rest into the sink before wiping my mouth off and setting the soaked mug onto the counter.

Because the last time I visited The Romping Meadow, it was with Emory.

Very explicitly with Emory.

"Since when?" I ask.

"Since March."

Oh God, I'm gonna throw up.

"Yeahhh," Bennett says, droning out the word on another sigh. "Remember when the ride went down about a month ago?"

Don't say anything.

Why incriminate myself for a crime they don't know I committed?

Is it a crime?

I grip the corner of the sink.

"Sure, yeah, the bees did that," I say, letting out an awkward, forced laugh. "Pesky bees."

"Well," Bennett says, "we noticed the ride was fixed.

And, hey, you shut down a park, and you cover your bases, right? I hadn't hit that area yet, so I wanted to know which of my guys did and ..."

My head swims, flounders, and drowns in misery as I realize what I'm about to hear.

"Ohmigod," I say, my back hitting the sink counter as I slowly slide down to the tiled floor. "Ohmigod, ohmigod."

All I can hear is Emory's heady words. *"Moan louder for me. Come on, beautiful."*

All I can see is the memory of me panting like a dog in heat as his leg pressed between my thighs.

Oh my *God*.

Quinn gets up from our small breakfast nook and sits on the floor next to me, wrapping an arm around my shoulders.

Bennett leans back in his chair as Quinn moves my hair to the side.

"Yeah," he says, taking another sip, "we checked the camera footage."

"What did you see?" I ask.

"Do you really want me to say it out loud?"

My stomach feels like it's going to empty every meal from my lifetime all over this kitchen floor.

"Looked like you had a blast, Lore," he says.

Oh my God.

"Bennett!" Quinn yells. She tosses invisible tomatoes at him. "Boooo!"

He laughs, that low, booming sound that fills his whole chest. "Lore, I just didn't know you were so ... vocal ..."

"Bennett, please," I say, burying my head in my hands with a groan. "This is like if my brother saw me ..."

The silence that ensues is not reassuring. In fact, something about it sends goose bumps over my arms and down to

255

my ankles. Like a ghost just shivered its way through my body. I look back up.

"What aren't you telling me?" I ask.

Bennett and Quinn exchange a look, and I repeat myself, "What aren't you telling me?"

"We tried to hide the footage."

If you ever get stuck on camera while someone flicks your nipple to orgasm, *we tried to hide the footage* is not the thing you want to hear.

"Who ..." I stammer. "Who else ..."

The words cannot come out, but Quinn answers for me anyway.

"Fred."

I run a hand over my face. "Oh my God."

Bennett half-says and half-coughs, "And Jaymee."

"Jaymee?!" I squeak.

After last night, I thought I could see the light at the end of the tunnel with me and Emory. But I realize now, it was just the headlights of a train barreling down the tracks to collide right into us.

Bennett grabs the newspaper on the counter and tosses it to me.

It lands at my feet, and right on the front page is the headline, *CEDAR CLIFF'S LUSTY LAWSUIT?*

My stomach drops. My vision blurs.

There's a picture of my work headshot, taken when I was twenty. Beside it is a photo of Emory, looking far too debonair for the girl in the picture next to him, wearing invisible braces and bangs.

"Personally, I think the worst crime is using that picture of you," Quinn says.

"The alliteration of the headline isn't half bad though," Bennett throws in.

But I'm not laughing.

Jaymee is a menace.

"How did she find out?" I ask.

"She came to see her dad, remember?" Quinn says. "Couldn't get in because she's press?"

"But why ... how ... the camera room?" I ask. I'm stumbling. My sentences no longer make sense.

"She was badgering Fred. How else?" Bennett says. "Followed him in right as he was trying to get away from her. And, well ... kinda walked in at the wrong time."

There's a knock at the front door, and all of our heads jerk toward it.

"It's the paparazzi," I breathe.

Bennett snorts.

Right. Who am I kidding? This is Cedar Cliff. There won't be paparazzi, but I can guarantee we'll start to get people walking their dogs past our house more often. The people who have known me since I was a kid will likely drop off a pie on our porch. After my accident, I started to dream about the cherry cobblers lining our fridge.

The doorbell buzzes.

"I don't want to answer it," I say.

But the voice on the other side is the boyish tone of my brother saying, "I took time off for this, Lore. Open the door."

Quinn rolls her eyes. "Oh, great. Your security detail has arrived."

I get off the floor, rush to the door, and swing it open.

My twin stares back at me. He looks ragged with his ruffled hair and beard. His hands are on his hips, and one look at my smeared makeup and walk-of-shame outfit makes his face slacken to disappointment.

"You didn't answer my texts, so I got worried," he says. "That twin feeling, you know?"

"Landon ..."

"I saw the paper. What the heck, Lore?"

"It's complicated," Quinn says from behind me. She's staring down my brother like she's ready to rumble if he insinuates even one thing about me.

Not that he would anyway. She always assumes the worst of him.

Landon takes in a sharp inhale before throwing his hands in the air. "This is nuts, Lore," he says with a dry laugh. "NUTS!"

"It's ... not what it seems."

"Listen, I trust your judgment," Landon says. "Maybe he's not an asshole. Who knows?" His shoulders hike up to his ears as he laughs again. I wonder if those laughs are the only thing keeping him sane. "I don't know! But unfortunately, this is some serious gray area. And the caravan doesn't stop with me either."

Quinn and I lean to the side, looking behind Landon.

Oh no.

On the opposite side of the street is a parked red pickup truck. My dad steps out of the driver's side. My mom barrels through our yard with a newspaper extended into the air.

Landon raises his eyebrows. "Have fun."

36

Emory

Something about today feels new. Hopeful. Inspiring.
When I say it out loud in front of the mirror, I feel
like a doof. But maybe that's a good thing for once.

"Silver linings," I mutter, lacing my running shoes
before walking out of Honeywood's hotel.

I want to run through the park, but it's much too early.
Lorelei won't be there yet, and I'd love to walk with her
instead. Side by side. Hand in hand. But I'm too wired—too
excited—to not let this energy out. Maybe I'll run that
downtown path she suggested last night.

My feet hit the pavement, and I take in the sights of
Cedar Cliff as I head toward downtown.

There's the video rental store somehow still in business,
a relic of a decade before. Billboard signs look both old and
new, chipped yet repainted, signaling Honeywood Fun
Park's entrance with Buzzy smiling down.

Hello again, friend.

I run by the gas station with only one pump and a man
outside in a rocking chair reading the paper. I wave to him
as I pass.

He calls out, "Good morning!"

I say, "Morning!" with a smile.

It's a great day.

I get to Cedar Cliff's historic downtown, where I pass by the little gazebo featured in Lorelei's prom story.

I didn't go to prom. But I would have if it had been with her. I wish I could redo a lot of things with Lorelei. First kisses, first dates, first coaster design ...

I run faster.

It irritates me that I couldn't prevent her injury. I calculated The Grizzly ten times over. Even my father double-checked my math and documentation. Nothing odd popped up in construction, and testing was a breeze. It ran perfectly for twenty years.

What changed?

I break into a sprint.

I understand wear and tear happens, but this is different. The team members at Honeywood are attentive to safety. Bennett's maintenance team has passed inspections year after year.

I take a deep breath, slowing my sprint to a run, then a jog.

I need to relax.

I don't want to be that guy anymore, engulfed in my anger and irritation. I refuse to be my dad.

I need to just think. Focus. Find a solution.

There's always a solution.

I look around, hands on my hips, gathering my breath.

I spot the bakery at the end of the street. A smile breaks out on my face.

The sugar bread. Lorelei's sworn favorite after each run.

My grin is probably goofy as hell, given that I'm smiling to myself at seven in the morning in an empty town.

But this is the feeling I want. The feeling of Lorelei coursing through my veins, making me a better person, a happier person, a person who likes to experience the small things in life.

I stroll down the sidewalk. My phone starts buzzing against my arm strap.

I look to see that it's my dad calling.

No. Not today. You're not ruining this perfect morning.

I mute the incoming call, breathing in the fresh air as I reach the bakery's storefront.

A large floor-to-ceiling glass window opens to the checkered linoleum floor, the pastel wall paint, and the small, cozy booths lining the walls. It's empty, except for one table in the back, packed with a group of people. A single chair is pulled up at the end, where a tall man with lanky legs and black hair sits.

When I walk in, a bell chimes above me, and the woman kneading bread behind the counter says, "Just a moment, dear!"

The sweet aroma of freshly baked bread is potent. The burned sugar smell practically breathes into me.

All of it is wonderful.

That is, until I hear, "Oh my goodness, is that him?"

I turn my head around to face the booth.

Staring back at me from the full table is the one woman I've been thinking about all morning. She's just as gorgeous as she was last night. But my chest feels lighter for only a moment before an anvil drops on it.

Lorelei might be there, but she isn't smiling. Her doe eyes are wide. She looks shocked to see me.

The three people sitting at the booth look like varying shades of her. They are equally as surprised.

This must be Lorelei's family.

There's an older man—I assume her father—who has her deep brown eyes and walnut-colored hair, peppered with gray. He looks tired, staring back at me, his glasses edged to the end of his nose. He removes them to rub the lenses with the sleeve of his green polo shirt.

A woman sits next to him with wild red hair locked into heavy curls. She wears a flowing green kimono top. I would find it funny that she matches her husband's color palette, but she stares, slack-jawed, at me. I can see the faint laugh lines embedded into her. This woman has had a good life, but I'm guessing I was not the catalyst for those happier times.

The man beside Lorelei must be her brother. If she hadn't told me they were twins, I wouldn't have known. He has chestnut hair with tints of red from his mother. He's broad-shouldered, leaning against the wall, arms splayed over the back of the seat as if the booth can barely contain him in it. He has a lopsided smile, accentuated by an indented dimple in his thick beard. He looks far less stressed than the rest of the table.

"Mr. Dawson. It's nice to meet you."

The voice comes from beside me.

That's when I finally recognize who the tall man is, sitting in the single chair at the end—Ian Chambers. Lorelei's lawyer.

Shit.

The woman at the counter behind me breaks the awkwardness. "Sir, can I get you anything?"

I turn and try to say, "Yes, sugar bread, please," with as much composure as I can. It still sounds awkward among the dull silence, which is only broken by the whirring fans overhead and the low tunes of the '80s pop band Wham! singing "Wake Me Up Before You Go-Go."

No worries. I'm wide awake now.

Ian clears his throat. "I recommend your lawyer be present if you'll be joining us, Mr. Dawson."

His sharp blue eyes stare back at me, but I'm not perturbed. I've come this far in Cedar Cliff without my lawyer. I can navigate this minefield unscathed.

"I'm fine," I say. "I can watch my tongue."

"Something tells me not," Lorelei's brother says through a choked laugh.

Lorelei's mom smacks his arm. "Landon James!"

My heart pounds in my chest, and suddenly, sugar bread sounds like it might destroy my stomach.

They know about me and Lorelei.

How and why doesn't matter right now, I guess.

I look to Lorelei, whose eyebrows are pinched in.

I want to reach down and take her chin, kiss her on those lips, reassure her that I won't be a jerk to her family. That I can be a nice guy. That, lawsuit or not, I'm still in it with her.

Were this happening under different circumstances, I'd want to meet her family properly. I'd want to be the man she was proud to bring home. I'd buy flowers for her mom. I'd try to talk sports with her dad, if that was his thing. I'd bring a bottle of wine for the whole family—assuming that wasn't a problem for them, like it is my father.

But our reality is that I'm meeting her family after a long run in the Georgia heat, still sticky with sweat and smelling like shit, all with their lawyer present.

Not ideal, but we work with what we have.

"Sorry I didn't introduce myself. I'm Emory Dawson," I say, leaning forward to reach out my hand, hoping I don't smell too bad. "It's a pleasure to meet you all."

Lorelei's mother tilts her head away from me, like a

small dog at the vet, apprehensive on whether to trust the veterinarian. That's fair.

Eventually, her small hand reaches out to shake mine. It's so tiny in my grasp. Lorelei's father follows suit without fear—firm and confident—and then her brother does the same, except with a grin of humor that his parents lack.

"I'm Landon," her brother says.

"Yeah, I hear you used to lose races to get to this bakery."

He shifts uncomfortably.

Okay, so humor isn't appropriate right now. Fantastic.

Lorelei clears her throat, announcing her presence once more. She didn't have to; my eyes have barely left her since I got here.

"Things are complicated," she says.

Ian sighs. "Understatement, but that's fine," he responds.

"Complicated has never been foreign to me," I say, crossing my arms, then instantly uncrossing them.

Right. Not surly. Friendly. Approachable.

Lorelei notices, and her mouth twitches into a small smile.

I can't help but return the gesture.

That's enough to give me hope that things might be okay.

My phone buzzes against my arm again. I glance down. It's my mom. I don't want to ignore her, but I'll need to call her back. I don't want to seem rude when I'm meeting Lorelei's family.

I mute the call.

"Well," Ian says, "if you can tell me that *this* is untrue, then we're all good."

Ian holds up a newspaper, which I take.

264

Staring back at me is the cutest picture of Lorelei and the worst, angriest picture of myself. We look to be twenty years apart in these pictures, and the article claims ... well ... the unfortunate truth of our relationship.

Damn.

"It's also my understanding," Ian continues, "that you increased the pricing for the new coaster construction."

My eyes flash to him right as Lorelei's jaw drops.

"You increased the pricing?" she asks.

This is getting worse with every second.

My father must have called our lawyer. He must have then talked to Ian.

I open my mouth to speak, but he interrupts me.

"Everything about this situation is now a conflict of interest," he says. His tone is sharp, commanding.

He's in lawyer mode, and I can't fault him for that. But my stomach curls in on itself.

"Were you hoping she'd fall for you? Drop the lawsuit?"

I can feel my blood pressure rising and my fists curling into the newspaper. I set it down before I rip it in half.

"You're not giving Lorelei enough credit," I say. "I couldn't manipulate her if I tried."

That at least gets a snort out of her brother.

Ian continues, "Maybe when your father—"

"My father is an ass and doesn't know how to run a business properly."

Ian's eyebrows rise.

Something tells me I shouldn't have said that.

"I'd like to talk to Mr. Dawson alone," Lorelei says.

There's a fire in her eyes. And it's not the type of fire that uses *Mr. Dawson* as a pet name in my hotel room. She's saying it to be professional. I feel uneasy.

265

Lorelei rises from the booth, sidestepping Ian's lanky legs and walking out the front door.

I follow her without a word.

"Be honest with me," she says when I catch up to her.

We walk across the street to the grassy area in the middle of the shops. The white gazebo is only a few paces away.

This is definitely not the type of conversation I would have imagined at our prom.

"I'll always be honest with you," I say.

"Are you charging Honeywood more for The Grizzly?"

I swallow. "I remember my dad talking about it, yes. I didn't know he went through with it."

"And do you want me to drop the lawsuit?"

"That's a separate conversation."

"Emory."

I sigh, looking away, then back to her. My nerves feel like they're itching inside me.

"It's complicated."

She crosses her arms over her chest, and I hold out my hand.

"Wait, don't get defensive yet." I can hear my voice grow stern. "We're just discussing the obvious right now. Sure, the lawsuit is damaging our company. I'm not gonna sugarcoat that. But that doesn't change anything I said last night. I'm with you regardless."

"What about after this season?" she asks. "After we rebuild The Grizzly, you go back to your company, and we only see each other in court?"

"No. I want you," I say. "I thought I'd made that clear. I'm yours; you're mine."

"Jesus, you can't claim people, Emory." Her arms fly to the air, then fall to her sides. "You want to have control over everything around you, but have you considered that maybe you can't?"

It's like being slapped in the face.

I heard similar words said from my mom when she left my dad.

"You can't control me."

"I'm not yours to own."

I am just like my father.

"This is too messy, and you know it," Lorelei continues. "There's no way I'm not going to lose my job at this point. I'll ... I'll have to leave Honeywood." It's like the words pain her.

I step forward and try to wrap her in my arms. She resists for a moment before softening into me. Her arms wrap behind me in a hug. I nuzzle my face in the crook of her neck, holding as tight as I can.

She exhales a shaky breath.

"I'll be the talk of the town forever," she says. "This is eventually going to grow past just local news, and then what?"

"Then, people will think I'm a dick. I'm used to it."

"No," she says, pulling away.

I don't want to let her leave my arms, but she does. She even walks a few paces to create more distance, which adds insult to injury. The sudden loss of warmth is startling.

"They'll think I'm pathetic," she says. "They'll continue to think I'm weak. That I gave in to the guy who'd ruined my life."

Ruined my life.

There it is.

Something is about to happen. I can feel it like a buzz of electricity in the air after a crack of lightning. I'm anticipating the last rumble of thunder.

But that doesn't mean I can't try to salvage my sunshine before it's shrouded in the storm.

"I will spend forever apologizing and making this right, if you'll let me."

And Lorelei simply says, "No."

37

Lorelei

It takes everything in me to say that one word, and it rips my heart apart. But we can't be together. The combination of the lawsuit and the fact that I'll likely lose my job over this is too much. There's no way we can continue. It's not a solid foundation for any relationship.

He must know that.

I must know that.

So, why does my heart want to erase the *no* I put out in the world?

I see the damage already.

Emory's eyebrows are strained together. A line is creased down the middle. His posture is lacking. He no longer appears like a large, unbreakable man. His heart looks broken, and mine—as if intertwined—echoes the same pain.

"Lore." His voice cracks.

I have to look away.

His hand brushes over my crossed arms. Even now, I get goose bumps at his touch.

"What did we expect, Emory?" I ask. "Some happy ending, where this all magically resolves itself?"

"Let me fix it," he mutters.

"Fix it? How in the world can this be fixed?"

We stand there in silence, his hand slowly trailing its way down my arm. It settles into my palm. Our fingers entwine.

"Look at me," he whispers.

I do, and his eyebrows are no longer worried. They're determined.

"Tell me what to do," Emory says. "You say I need to control things? Well, I won't control this. I'm yours, Lorelei Arden. Control me. I want you to tell me what to do to make this better. Want me to apologize to your family? I'll get on my knees. Want me to go public, saying our relationship was all a lie? I'll stand behind some dumb podium and tell them I was the asshole who seduced you. That I made promises. That I lied about everything. That I manipulated you. I'll clear your name. Just say the word. Just tell me what I need to do."

A breath catches in my throat, and I shake my head. "Emory ..."

"Please."

Emory Dawson is not a man that begs. He does not whimper. He does not plead. And right now, he's pleading for me to change my mind, and it's breaking my heart.

"Let. Me. Fix. This." He accentuates every word, and I shake my head.

"You can't fix everything," I say. "This isn't a project you can weld together piece by piece."

Emory doesn't look away, but I see the tic in his jaw. The hurt in his eyes.

I can't stay here. There's no reason to. This isn't going to be our happily ever after, and we both know it. We've known it from the start.

I lower my hand from his, our fingers slipping apart one last time.

"I'm running late for work as it is," I say. "I've got to go. Let me go say bye to my family."

"Lore."

"Emory, this is it," I say. "It was never going to work out. We knew that. So, let's just call it now. Let's drop it while we're still intact."

But even as I say it, I know that *intact* is what I will never be again.

I walk away from Emory, and I leave a piece of my heart behind.

38

Emory

I stand in the cold hotel shower. The drain swallows my happiness from the past couple months. Honeywood and Cedar Cliff were a reprieve from my life of grinding work—a break from beating my head against the brick wall that is my father.

But it's all gone now.

Lorelei was right; I don't like being out of control, and right now, I feel like I'm spiraling.

My dad had increased the pricing for The Grizzly's rebuild. I called him when I got back to the hotel.

"Are you fucking kidding me?" I yelled. I was sure Honeywood patrons could hear me from the open balcony.

All he said was, "I'm not talking to you while you're like this. Not while you're giving us a second scandal to deal with."

That was it. That was all the time he gave me. Then, he hung up.

I called him three more times.

He never answered.

I could feel the steam of anger rising off me in waves. I

threw the phone onto the mattress. A hot shower only made my mood worse, so I've been standing under an ice-cold downpour ever since.

I finally towel off, my body shaking from the chill. I don't truly feel it. It's like my skin is separated from me, like I'm just floating in a dream, hoping this isn't real.

There's a knock on my door, and some distant hope wonders if it could be Lorelei. But I should know better; optimism has never been my friend.

I swing open the door, and before me is a woman in an oversize leather jacket. Her black hair is rooted in gray. The strands are wild and windswept. She is poised with a fist on her hip that clutches a newspaper and a motorcycle helmet tucked under her arm.

"Hey, Emmy."

"Mom," I say. "What are you doing here?"

Willa Dawson raises the familiar newspaper with me and Lorelei on the front page up in the air.

"Answer me truthfully this time," she says, the hard country drawl of her voice carrying to me. "How are ya liking Georgia?"

I sniff, looking away right as she steps past me, drops her helmet on the dresser, and pulls me into a hug.

"What are you doing here?" I ask.

"Being a guardian angel."

I exhale and wrap my arms around her, leaning my chin on the top of her head.

"Come on, kiddo," she says. "Let's go for a walk."

"I have to work," I say stubbornly.

She barks out a laugh like a witch's cackle.

"You make your own schedule," she says, slapping my chest. "You can take some time for your mom."

I rub the heels of my palms in my eyes and nod. Mom

273

waits while I throw on a plain shirt and shorts. I put on my sneakers.

As we pass through the hotel lobby, she picks up two complimentary cups of coffee from the guest counter. We cross over the automatic glass doors and emerge outside. The sun is already brutal this time of day. The humidity could be a swimming pool.

We pass her motorcycle, leaning on its kickstand. The body glimmers in the bright sun. I keep following her until we reach the concrete sidewalk, strolling in tune to each other's steps.

Her black boots clomp on the ground, chains from her jacket dangling around as she removes it and slings it over her shoulder. I take it from her, inspecting the back with all its patches, ranging from skulls to cartoon corgis and an inspirational *Lord of the Rings* quote. It's eclectic. It's very her.

"You know, I think some of those patches lessen your rebel look, Mom."

"I'm getting a new patch soon," she says.

"Oh yeah?"

"Yeah. I'm joining a club."

I toss the jacket over my shoulder with a laugh. "You're joining a motorcycle club? To do what?"

"Wouldn't you like to know?"

"Jesus Christ, Mom."

"Okay, this isn't about me though," she says with a wave of her hands. Her nails are long and dipped in glittery black nail polish. "Orson sent me that paper this morning."

"Judas."

"I realized I knew nothing about your summer here," she says. "You've been so quiet. I want to know everything."

I don't know where to start. All I know is that, while my

mom is tough as nails, I feel weak. And the last thing I want is her bad opinion of me or for her to compare me to my father. I'm not him.

"You don't wanna hear it," I say. "It's ... bad."

Her head leans back to bark out a laugh. "You're not The Hulk." She cackles. "I'm not scared you're gonna destroy New York with your fists. Just vent. We've got miles of road to talk."

I look ahead. There's nothing but road and trees. We're walking away from Cedar Cliff and down the mountain.

There's got to be something metaphorical in this.

I take a sip of my coffee and shake my head.

"Go on, son," she says.

"Well ..." I exhale. "Dad hiked the prices up for our coaster build even though I'd guaranteed we wouldn't. Some reporter publicized my personal life. And I just lost a woman who deserves way better than me. And that's just this morning."

"You can never say you're bored."

"Is that my silver lining for today?"

"No. It's probably that you get to leave soon," she says with a laugh. "Bet you're excited to go home."

Right when her words come out, I can feel in my bones that it isn't true. And I know that's exactly why she said it.

"No," I admit. "I like Honeywood. I like Cedar Cliff."

"Have you been hanging out with Orson?"

"Yeah," I say. "I like him. He talks enough for the both of us, which is nice."

"It's fun, talking to people who aren't your dad, huh?"

She at least has the decency to look like she's joking.

"Yeah, it is," I say.

"You know, maybe Cedar Cliff is what you've been

275

missing. A place that's yours. Friendships that aren't just me."

I know what I've been truly missing. The soul of Cedar Cliff. The heart of Honeywood.

As if reading my mind, she says, "So, tell me about the girl."

The girl. The woman. Lorelei. The owner of my heart.

"She's ... different," I say.

"I'll be honest. I was surprised when I saw the paper," my mom says. "You were always so stubborn. Leave it to you to fall for the wrong girl."

"She's not though." A huff of weak air comes out, almost a laugh. "She doesn't put up with my shit. She's funny. She's confident. She shook Dad's hand the first time she met him, as if he were just another guest at the park."

"A woman after my own heart. Did his forehead vein explode?"

I laugh. "She did it all while wearing a bright yellow shirt. I think her happiness was kryptonite for him."

She smiles at me, patting my back. "You look happy when you talk about her."

"Wanna know something funny?" I ask. "I think I fell for her the first time I saw her. Before I even knew who she was. She was halfway across the midway, picking up trash, and I still thought, *Wow, that is the most beautiful woman I have ever seen.*"

"You're such a softy, son."

I laugh. "Maybe I am."

I breathe in the refreshing mountain breeze. It's the only relief on such a hot day. But it's not enough to cool the fire burning in my chest for Lorelei.

"I want to fix this, but I don't know how," I admit.

"Tell me the silver lining."

"I'm not sure there is one this time."

"Every situation contains two sides of the same coin," she says. "If you find a penny on the ground, it only appears to be lucky or unlucky based on which side shows its face. But it's all about perspective. It's all about what you believe. Are you going to let the other side of the coin make your day unlucky? Turn this situation over. Find the other side."

I sigh. "Okay, well, on one side, I have Lorelei. On the other is the lawsuit. Which"—I click my tongue—"doesn't feel right anymore."

"What do you mean?"

"The more time I spend here, the more I'm not so sure we're innocent in this." Saying the words out loud feels both wrong and right at the same time. "Something doesn't make sense with The Grizzly. It's like a feeling in my gut that won't go away."

"You think you made a miscalculation?" she asks.

"No," I say, "I don't."

"Emmy, you're only human—"

"I know, but I tested The Grizzly into the ground," I say. And I did. I poured blood, sweat, and tears into that ride. My hard work coats the lining of those wooden boards. "It was my first coaster. I was terrified there *would* be issues, so I overprepared for the worst. I think there's more to this."

She stops, and I halt beside her.

"Emory."

"Are you going to give me motherly advice?"

She purses her lips. I button mine shut.

"Are you or aren't you the man who fixes things?" she asks.

"Depends on who you ask."

"Well, ask me."

"Am I?"

"You are," she says. "So, go figure out what happened to your coaster, then go get your girl."

"My girl," I say with a weak laugh. "Yeah, I'm not so sure."

"That's how you feel about her though, right?"

Lorelei doesn't belong to me. It's my heart that's owned by her.

"Yes," I say. "She makes me happy. I'm tired of being angry. I'm tired of being like Dad."

"You're not like Thomas," she says. "Your dad's never had the drive you do. You're a better man than him."

I swallow, running a hand through my hair and looking off to nowhere. It takes me a second before I can look at her and nod. "Thank you."

"It's not a compliment," she says, placing a hand on my forearm. "It's a fact, son."

I nod, biting back the sting in my eyes before laying an arm over her shoulders.

"I'm gonna figure this out, Mom," I say. "I'm gonna figure this out."

39

Lorelei

When I get to my office, Fred is already waiting for me, his hip perched halfway on my desk and hands folded together.

I don't even try to force a smile. I shut the door behind me and press my back against it.

Fred looks stern, and that's what makes this frightening.

"Lore, do I even need to tell you what I saw?"

"No," I say.

My heart feels heavier with each passing second.

"Are you okay?"

I nod. "I'm fine."

"If you're not, tell me now, Lorelei," he says. "I saw a woman I view as a daughter involved with a man who holds all the cards. That power dynamic feels wrong. And yet I still can't figure out if it was."

"It wasn't like that," I say. "It was mutual. He's ... he's not who you think he is. He's kind. He's generous. He would never take advantage of me."

We're silent once more. I want to say something,

anything, but I'm not sure what I could say to make things different.

"Fred—"

"Involving yourself with Mr. Dawson is a clear conflict of interest regardless of your personal lawsuit," he says. "Misconduct on company grounds. Harassment, if I had to make a stretch. Lore, I'm not mad at you. I'm just disappointed."

How is that always worse?

Fred is a passionate man, an honest man, and a man whose trust I broke. I can't blame him for growing cold.

"Fred, this ... this isn't a reflection on my work ethic or my integrity. Or on my dedication to Honeywood."

"I'm not concerned about your dedication," he says, waving his hand. "You're the most dedicated person we have here. But this is serious."

"It was a lapse of judgment," I say. "It won't happen again."

"I know it won't," he says. "But ... the board might think differently if it gets to them. And it likely will."

I've never been involved with the board of directors before. Not outside of assisting with annual meetings. They're all from Atlanta, which is two hours away. Not exactly locals.

"I just always assumed I wasn't on their radar," I say.

"You're my retirement plan," Fred says with a sardonic laugh. "Of course you are."

My heart halts in place. Screeches.

I open my mouth, then close it.

"You want me for the general manager role?" I ask.

"Of course I do, Lore. You're the best fit. You know this place better than anyone," he says.

I only just realized this was what I wanted. But Fred

knew the entire time. He knows me better than I know myself, which makes me feel that much worse.

"Why do you think I dragged you into The Grizzly's build?" he asks. "For all intents and purposes, it was irresponsible of me to do that. You're in a lawsuit with him. But I wanted you involved. I thought you could handle it."

"I could," I say, the words rushing out of me. "I did. I ..."

I don't know what to say.

The truth is, I couldn't handle Emory.

Quinn was right; he was my storm. And sometimes, rainy days and sunshine create beautiful skies afterward. But instead, some clouds come with lightning. We tried to harness that spark ourselves but failed. The electricity struck down parts of our lives, all while we hoped a rainbow might be on the other side.

We were wrong.

"It was irresponsible, I know," I say. "The media can have their field day. But it is absolutely no reflection on my job or my work. They have to see that. Jaymee has to."

He clenches his fist.

"Jaymee ... was irresponsible in reporting this," he says. His face is red. I don't think I've ever seen him this stressed. "She should have known better."

I wonder what it's like, having your own daughter make a mess of things in your park. Though I can't blame her too much. She only did her job. I was the irresponsible one who didn't do mine.

"This is a media nightmare," he says, rubbing his temples. "I just ... I can't find another way around this."

This.

I fire the shot before Fred has the opportunity, and I try to tackle it with as much of my dignity as I can.

"Am I fired?" I ask.

His eyes flicker up to mine.

"No," he says. "Suspended temporarily while we look into the situation."

I roll my bottom lip into my mouth. It's the only thing I can do to keep from crying in front of a man who has been like a second father to me for most of my adult life.

"Suspended?"

"For now."

"This feels ... wrong. I mean, Fred, How many of our summer employees mess around in The Romping Meadow?" I ask. "There are babies conceived in this park. I think Tyler in ticket sales even named his firstborn Honey."

"I know," he says. "But this is different. You're upper management."

"But, Fred—"

"Just let me work with PR to settle this. I'll be in touch when we find out more. We still need to talk with Emory."

My gut clenches at the sound of his name. It's like one hit after another.

I curl in on myself, trying not to appear weak, but I feel like my life is falling apart piece by piece.

Fred sucks in air, clutching the edge of the desk more. I can tell he wants to reach out to me. He doesn't.

He sighs. "We can always break the contract with Dawson Manufacturing."

I blink up at him. "What?"

"We don't have to suspend you," he says. "We can nip this in the bud right now. I will always take your side, Lorelei. We can close The Grizzly forever and hire another manufacturer to tear it down."

So many things rush through my head at once.

This would solve Honeywood's problems. We'd still get a different ride. We'd move on and be fine. But Emory wouldn't. His company's reputation would suffer even more. Not only would he have not fixed the ride, but he'd have also tried, gotten caught with the woman in the accident, then bailed.

I fell for a man I shouldn't have. It might not have been purposely, but it was my decision. He doesn't deserve to be punished for this.

If I must leave Honeywood to ensure he will be fine, then I will.

"No," I say. "Suspend me. I'll go home."

"Lore—"

"It's fine. I understand. Keep his contract. He needs it just as much as we do."

I sniff back tears, trying to appear strong. But I feel helpless.

Over the past two years, the people of Cedar Cliff knew I was weak, and now, so do I.

40

Emory

I scour blueprints at The Honeycomb. I'm hunched over my laptop, searching through every trial and test I have on file for The Grizzly. My mom sits on the other side of the table, sipping her cup of coffee Orson made. As Cedar Cliff locals walk past the locked doors, she gives a small wave.

"Any luck?" Orson asks, leaning against the bar top.

I run my hand through my hair. "Not at all."

The Honeycomb isn't open yet, as it's still only mid-morning. My mom wanted to see her nephew before she rode off. He let me set up my research camp here. The two of them have been catching up while I remain deep in my notes.

I keep asking myself the same questions. *Were there any bumps in the road with The Grizzly's construction? Were there any red flags we overlooked?*

But I find nothing.

It was perfect. We tested every fail-safe. An alarm activated every time, as intended. Reading through our notes, I'm remembering the exhilaration of those moments. I remember the buzz of knowing I created something flawless. That same thrill has only been replicated in the tunnel with Lorelei.

But with a perfectly operating coaster and perfect inspection records, what went wrong?

What calculation am I missing here?

There's nothing.

I groan, clicking through more files.

Mom puts a hand on my shoulder. "You'll get this, Emmy."

"Yeah, *Emmy*," Orson echoes with a grin.

Orson is like the teasing brother I never had. I've always been averse to the subtle jabs, but it's grown on me the past couple months. Everything in this town has.

"Orson, are you seeing someone nowadays?" my mom asks.

I lift an eyebrow at him. He clears his throat.

"Just running this bar and getting through each day, Aunt Willa."

I guess we're not discussing the yoga instructors.

"Aren't we all just trying to survive?" she says.

She kicks her steel-toed boots up onto the table, and he laughs.

"Hey, feet off the table," Orson says, swatting at them. "Jeez, you're an animal now."

She laughs, pointing at the folders on my computer. "Is that where you keep your porn?"

Now, it's my turn to swat her away.

"Good Lord, stop it," I say with a chuckle.

I click open more folders—notably the one she pointed at to prove that, no, I do not have porn saved—and find The Grizzly's original operation manual.

"Wow, been forever since I've seen that thing," she says.

My mom wrote this guide. It's hard not to admire her

work. She was always a ballet dancer with copy. Elegant yet exact.

"Dang, my writing wasn't half bad," she muses.

I laugh. "You could write a book on vacuum cleaners, and I would read it, Mom."

I squint, peering over a few sections that don't flow as well. These must be the contributions my father made. The sentence structure is less concise.

I grumble to myself.

He always insists on making final edits to these manuals. He calls it the CEO's final sign-off.

Ridiculous.

I flip to the employee operating section.

It also has been edited from my mom's original, succinct verbiage.

But then my heart stops.

Because that's when I see it.

Right there, in the footnotes.

It states that the max operating speed for the coaster is forty-five miles per hour.

But I know my coaster. I could rebuild The Grizzly from scratch with my eyes closed. And I know how it is meant to operate.

I only configured it for a max of forty miles per hour.

Oh my God.

They've been pushing it beyond its capabilities, like a small drip of water against a rock.

That's the thing about engineering—one simple calculation gone wrong is enough to break apart any system. One transposed number—or a purposely adjusted one in this case—is enough to grind down that track. It's enough to cause the wheels to dislodge over time.

I scramble to my feet, my chair falling back in the process, and head to the front door.

"Hey!" Orson says.

My mom clicks her tongue. "What's going on?"

"I need to call Dad," I say.

I burst out into the morning sun, standing on the sidewalk with my phone to my ear. My hand is shaking as it rings. My heart is pounding out of my chest with anger.

He finally answers. "Done moping?"

The fact that he picks up with such a stunning opener sets my blood on fire.

"I don't even know where to start with you," I say.

He grumbles, "What are you talking about?"

It's still mid-morning, and he is a time zone behind. Yet he's already drunk. I can hear it in his slurred words.

"I've been looking over the operation manual for The Grizzly," I say. "I noticed something interesting with the top speed. Forty-five. Does that ring a bell?"

"That's correct."

"No," I say. "No, it's not. I engineered that ride to hit forty miles per hour. Max. The track can't handle more than that over time."

He's silent, and the quiet is much too loud.

It angers me more.

He knew.

This whole time, and *he knew*. He let everything pan out as if nothing were wrong—as if Lorelei or Honeywood were the enemy.

He's still not speaking, so I do it for him.

The coward.

"The safety wheels were bound to give out after twenty years," I say.

My mom's and Orson's heads poke out of the front door.

"You didn't do your due diligence. You're the reason the ride broke."

They both mouth, *What?!*

"Emory—" he starts.

I don't let him finish.

"I didn't hurt Lorelei," I bite out. "You did."

The words feel almost cathartic, leaving my mouth. Cleansing.

My father clears his throat.

"We always do what is required in the industry," he says.

It amazes me how quickly he can turn on the business persona when he needs to even if it is sloppy.

"The other manufacturers were getting bigger than us. Your first coaster had to be a hit. Having a higher speed looks better, Emory."

"It's all business to you," I breathe out.

"Don't pretend it isn't to you as well."

"It's not about that when it comes to safety," I say. "We must have integrity."

"Don't talk to me about integrity," he snarls. "You're sleeping with the enemy."

That sends me off the deep end.

"I don't want to hear her name or any insinuation of it leave your godforsaken mouth."

"What are you going to do, Emory? Leave the company?"

I freeze.

I could.

I should.

I look back to my mom.

Willa Dawson told me to stay at Dawson Manufacturing almost ten years ago. She wanted me to carry on her legacy of a family-run company.

But this has gone too far. This is more than even I want on my shoulders. I can't do this. And that realization hits me all at once, almost shaking me to my core.

I can't listen to my father brush off lawsuits. I can't spend the rest of my life looking over my shoulder, worried he's making last-minute changes that might jeopardize safety. What happens next time? What if someone dies on the next incident? It sickens me to think that could have been Lorelei.

My mom might be disappointed. She might ride off and never talk to me again. But for once, I want to do the right thing.

"I quit." I say the words faster than I can register them leaving my mouth.

To my surprise, my mom punches the air with a grin.

To nobody's surprise, my dad snaps.

"No, you don't." His voice is sudden, loud, and sharp. I recognize it from my childhood as something that maybe once intimidated me. But I'm no longer a scared little kid. "Don't do something you're going to regret."

"I won't regret this decision," I say.

"You can't leave," he says. "I have the contract for The Grizzly."

The words carry a jaunty weight to them, like he's found some trump card.

I laugh. I laugh because I know better.

"You also have the lawsuit for it," I say. "So, good luck with that."

I can hear his teeth grinding on the other end of the line.

Then, he hangs up on me.

I wish I had instead.

That would have felt good.

My mom runs toward me, chains from her leather cut dangling as she barrels into my chest with a hug.

My heart swells.

"I quit," I say, the words muffled against her.

"I heard."

"You aren't disappointed?" I ask.

"No. Of course not."

I exhale into her mess of graying black hair.

"But it's your company," I say.

"And you can do better."

She pulls back, keeping her hands on my shoulders. Her eyes dart between mine, and I see the intensity in them. She doesn't need to say anything else.

"I'll try," I say.

"I know you will do better," she says. "You don't need to try."

Orson is behind her, looking down at his phone. When he looks back up, his eyebrows are pinched in.

"What?" I ask.

He waves his phone in the air. "Bennett says Lorelei got suspended from Honeywood."

My stomach drops.

After everything she'd done for the park, she got suspended.

And it's my fault.

No.

I'm not messing up her life any longer.

I'm clearing the air here and now.

I finally have a way to make things right. I can envision a different future unfolding in front of me now, and I only want to share it with one person.

I want to give Lorelei the life she deserves, starting with me clearing her name and her winning this lawsuit.

As if reading my mind, Mom says, "I knew you'd figure it out."

I let out a weak laugh.

"I have a couple more calls to make," I say.

"We'll get you a muffin," Orson says. He extends his elbow out to my mom. "Want to walk with me to Slow Riser, Aunt Willa?"

"Ooh, delightful," Mom says. "We'll be back, Emmy!"

"Bye, Emmy!" Orson echoes.

They walk down the sidewalk arm in arm.

I realize in that moment just how peaceful Cedar Cliff is. Idyllic almost. Birds chirp. A truck rumbles down the road. Someone passes by on a bicycle. Across the street, Mrs. Stanley walks her dog. We wave to each other.

I like Cedar Cliff.

I walk back into The Honeycomb. My footsteps echo in the emptiness of the closed bar. With the exception of where we sat, the chairs are still stacked on the tables. The only sounds are the low background hum of fridges and neon lights.

I make the first call.

"Mr. Dawson!" our family lawyer answers with too much happiness, as if my call is the highlight of his day.

I don't know who he's trying to convince. I'm the high-light of *nobody's* day.

"How are you?" he asks.

I don't bother with the same niceties.

"I'd like Ian Chambers's phone number," I say.

"Ian ..."

"Lorelei Arden's lawyer. Yes. Thank you."

"Well, generally, we don't—"

"Is there a problem?"

He stutters for a second, but he's dealt with us Dawson men enough to know not to question. I guess that's one perk of looking as mean as we do.

"No," he says.

He's such a weasel.

"No, of course not."

After some shuffling on his end, likely playing around with his reading glasses and flipping through his classic black book, he finally reads out Ian's number on speaker-phone as I type it into my phone.

I thank him, leaving him sputtering as I hang up and make the next call. I only have so much time to act. He'll be calling my dad next, I bet.

The ringing stops, and a much less pretentious voice answers this time.

"Ian Chambers."

"Hey, Ian Chambers. This is Emory Dawson."

It's a full-name kind of day.

"Emory," he says. I can tell he's surprised. "I thought we talked about having conversations behind your lawyer's back."

"I call bearing good news," I say. "I have information on Dawson Manufacturing."

Ian pauses, but this silence isn't like the one with my father, where he's stewing with grinding teeth. No, Ian is thinking. He's considering. He's a smart man.

"That *is* good news," he finally says. "Tell me more."

"First, I'd like to talk to you about something else," I say. "Get some advice."

"Why not talk to your own lawyer?"

"He's on Dawson Manufacturing's dime, and I'm not anymore."

Another silence.

But I can hear his smile on the other end when he says, "Then, it sounds like we have a lot to discuss."

We schedule a time to meet this afternoon, and when we hang up, I make one final call.

"Emory?"

"Hey, I know this is short notice and probably impossible, but I have an idea ..."

41

Lorelei

I have three pillows surrounding my head in a circle and one by my side. I've MacGyvered them into one of those custom body pillows pregnant woman get for their bellies. I have my trusty mint-flavored off brand cookies by my hip. A bag of cheese-flavored chips is open in the crook of my arm. Occasionally, I dip my hand in there before shoving my mouth full as I watch the screen of my laptop sitting high on my chest.

A coaster barrels through a corkscrew. The riders scream. The train screeches to a halt on the final brake run, and everyone claps. I click the next recommended video.

Rinse and repeat.

I've been watching roller coaster–experience videos all day. I'm blocked from company email. I don't have the sound of a scratching walkie-talkie on my hip. I'm in my pajamas at three o'clock on a summer's day.

It all feels wrong.

But most of all, I know, in this moment, Emory is likely on his way to the airport, gone from my life forever, and I'm sitting here with chip dust and coaster-ride videos to distract myself from the heartache.

Sometimes, I scoot my phone over, glancing down at the saved pictures I have of Emory's new Grizzly blueprints.

It will be a masterpiece. I just wish I could be there to watch the construction.

There's no way Fred can mitigate this disaster with me. I know that. But I chose to step down, so Emory could keep the contract. I don't regret it.

I might as well move across the country and find another theme park that will take me. Theme parks are all I know how to manage. It's all I love.

My brother, Landon, sits on the small armchair in the corner of my room, flipping through one of the many books on my shelves.

"Maybe I can go to Tennessee with you," I mutter out. "There are parks there, right?"

His eyes shift to mine. I don't know the last time I talked, but I'm sure it's been at least an hour.

"Nah, I'm moving back here," he says.

I tilt down my laptop screen. "I'm sorry, what? When were you going to mention this?"

"Well, you're over there, moping and stuff," he says with a wave of his hand.

"Ever thought this news might have cheered me up?"

He chuckles. "I'm coming back after Labor Day," he says, leaning his elbow on the arm of the chair. "I miss Cedar Cliff too much, you know?"

A lot of people would roll their eyes at that. It's common for small-town locals to dream about other state universities, traveling abroad, or simply living as far away from their hometown as possible. To think someone would want to return is laughable.

But Cedar Cliff is different. It's a community. It's family.

Whether it's the early mornings at Slow Riser, or making the short walk from here to downtown, or even competing at trivia night at The Honeycomb, this place is special to all of us. It's like a magnet that keeps pulling you back. Why fight the pull of your home?

"Where will you work?" I ask.

"I'm coming back to Honeywood," Landon says. "Fred told me the old head of security recently left."

I gasp. "It was the bees, wasn't it?"

He laughs. "Yeah, Fred said that was Paul's final straw."

"Landon, this is fantastic!"

Quinn appears in the doorway, slowly knocking on the frame before leaning against it with her arms crossed.

A smile spreads across Landon's face, accentuating his dimples as deep as they can go.

"Already your shift?" Landon asks, looking down at his leather-bound watch.

"No, Ruby is next," Quinn says. "But she's running a bit late."

"Y'all are operating in shifts?" I ask.

Quinn shrugs. "Of course, lady."

"Don't you have to work today?"

"We all took the day off," she says. "We didn't wanna leave you alone."

I inhale sharply at the influx of gratitude in my soul. I love my friends. Sometimes, I forget just how much.

If you're lucky enough, you acquire friendships in life that are just as pure as those matching bracelets they give you at summer camp. And if all my luck in life was spent on the foundation of my close friends, I'll take every accident, suspension, or heartbreak that comes at me. They're worth it.

"I've got a long drive ahead of me, so this works out," Landon says through a yawn. "I should get going."

Quinn glances over to him, watching as he rises from the armchair, reaching up to stretch, his shirt skirting just above his boxers. Quinn's head instantly turns away.

"Good riddance," she spouts back.

He lifts an eyebrow at her with a grin.

Something tells me Quinn doesn't know he's moving back yet.

That should be fun in a couple months.

Landon leans down over the bed, giving me a half-hug and a swift good-bye before sidestepping past Quinn.

Her eyes roll their way up and then back to me.

"Talk to me," she says. "This isn't like you."

"What do you mean?"

"Wallowing in bed."

"I'm not wallowing," I say. "I took a shower. Would a wallower take a shower?"

"You only did that because Landon said you smelled."

"That's beside the point."

"You're scared," she says.

I blow out a raspberry. "I am not."

"I've been in your position before. You know I have," she says.

I stiffen. Quinn doesn't like to talk about that time in her life, so I don't push further.

"Even when I thought I'd figured things out, it was fear that kept me in my bed. It was the fear of failing again. But the good news is, you have nothing to fear. You didn't fail. You got in a mess. But messes are for cleaning up, and you'll get this one wiped up quick. I know you."

I smile. "You're really good with words, you know."

"It's the lit major," she says. "Those credits weren't for nothing."

I laugh.

"I'm sorry this is happening," she says with a sigh. "The season just isn't right without you."

It isn't. Nothing is right anymore.

I miss my job. I miss the park.

I miss Emory.

Realistically, I know we can't continue with our relationship. I shouldn't talk to him again. Not when we're locked in this lawsuit. Not when we were caught red-handed. Not when we made this more complicated than it already had been. There's no way out of this, and that only makes my heart sink further.

I pull my sheets higher on my body and curl into them. Quinn twists her lips to the side.

There's a knock on the front door.

"That's probably Ruby," Quinn says. "I'll bring her in."

When she leaves, the room feels cold. She was right; I do need my friends' company. They know me better than I know myself.

I look over at the pictures on my desk. The photos are a triptych of my life. The good old days, the family I've found, and the victories that led to unspoken tragedy.

There's one where I'm between Quinn and Landon, all three of us arm in arm our senior year of high school. Quinn's hand slightly hovers over Landon's shoulder, like even touching him would be disgusting, while his hand is firmly on her waist.

There's another photo of me with all my friends attending a pirate festival down in Florida. Bennett looks like he fits right in with his messy, long black hair; Ruby is beside him, laughing at something he must have said right before the picture was snapped; Quinn is sticking out her tongue; and Theo is grinning behind all of us, making bunny ears with her fingers.

I linger on the last photo of me at Honeywood's annual marathon two years ago, holding a round medal up to my mouth, biting it with a grin. Back when running was like breathing for me. Three months before my accident, when it was all stolen away.

Ruby's light voice carries through the house. When she finally appears in my doorway, she looks over my bedroom—the peach-scented candle burning in the corner, the empty sleeves of mint chocolate cookies on the floor, and my not-so-neat purple sheets half-strewn off the bed from my time wallowing.

"Oh, Lore ..." she starts.

I shake my head. "No, no, don't. It's not as bad as it looks."

It is.

I look like I'm in hibernation for the summer.

Ruby walks to the chair where Landon once was and sits, folding her knees to her chest.

"How are you?" she asks.

I stare down at my sheets, picking at a stray string sticking out from the hem. "Suspended."

She nods slowly. "Okay, and what's your plan?"

I let out a sardonic laugh. "Plan? I'm guilty as charged," I say. "That's it. That's all I got."

"No, come on," Ruby says. "You're smarter than that."

"Am I though?" I ask. "I had sex with the guy I'm going to court with."

"You *had sex*?" She says it in a whisper, as if the walls could overhear my admission. Her eyes widen, and she

299

looks down at her lap. "I didn't know it'd gotten that serious."

"It got something," I mutter.

Something I'd never experienced before. Not with anyone. He pushed me to be better. Stronger.

Emory Dawson is a man I'm convinced I'll never experience again.

Ruby peers up at me from beneath her ginger eyelashes, staring for a moment. Then, her mouth opens and closes, as if she wants to say something but won't. When she finally does speak, it hits me harder than I expected.

"Do you love him?" Ruby asks.

I blink at her. "What?"

"Do you love him?" she repeats. Her voice is strained.

It's in that moment that I notice she isn't exactly herself. Sure, she's wearing her usual floral shirt motif, but there's no energy in her smile. She looks almost sad. I don't know how I didn't see it before.

Looking at Ruby is like staring in a mirror. We've always had an unspoken camaraderie as the two introverts of the group. We're drawn to each other, almost as if our souls recognize a fellow friend. And she seems ... off. Just like me.

"Is he," she continues, swallowing, "someone you can't live without?"

I don't like that question.

Mostly because I know the answer.

Nobody, except Emory, has ever given me this buzz. Part of me wants to say they're butterflies, but that seems so childish in retrospect. This isn't some crush. This is passion. This is the pulling of my soul toward his.

This is love.

I love Emory Dawson.

I love his sarcasm. I love his surly, downturned frown. I

love how secretly kind he is. I love that he's left his mark on me. But I don't love that it doesn't matter at all.

"We can't be together," I say.

A second passes and her expression shifts. But it isn't sad. With how her eyebrows pinch in, it's almost angry.

It's very un-Ruby. Just like the rest of her today.

"No," Ruby says.

I laugh. "No?"

"I'm not taking that as an answer." She sticks her chin out. "You need to do this. You need a happy ending."

"I mean, I can be—"

"No," she says again. She looks down at the ground, letting out a sharp exhale. "You've found someone you love, so you can't just sit here and wallow. You need to go for it. And if not him, then Honeywood."

"Ruby ..."

"Figure out how to make this right. I know you. This isn't you. Take the same anger you felt with Emory in the beginning and channel it. You always told him where to stick it even if you didn't want to."

I laugh.

I laugh hard.

Seeing Ruby so determined feels weird, but ... maybe it's exactly what I needed to hear.

I disliked everything about Emory when I first met him, but she's right; he motivated me to stop being so nice. He made me less of a pushover.

What if I did that for all areas of my life?

What if I stopped taking no for an answer?

My heart races, and I can't help but smile to myself.

I can't keep floating by in life, waiting to be saved. I can't keep walking up the same lift hill every morning, waiting for my fear to dissipate without taking action. I need to finally ride the roller coaster of life.

I look at my messy blankets, my cookie crumbs, and my cell phone, abandoned and unanswered on the floor.

My accident two years ago was exactly that—an accident. But the rest of my life doesn't need to be left up to chance.

Emory and I are complicated. I want nothing more than to be with him, but I know our limitations. We can't bounce back from our lawsuit. But I can at least ensure the rebuild goes well for him.

I can get my job back.

I refuse to be suspended. I've proven myself before, and I'll show Fred and the board just how valuable I am once more.

I look to Ruby, who has her cheek pressed into the chair.

There's something about her that feels like it's missing, but I don't know what. And why is she suddenly pushing me? She's the opposite of a pusher. That's normally Theo's or Quinn's job in our friend group.

"Why are you telling me this?" I ask her.

Ruby shrugs and tries to smile. I can tell it's forced.

"Ruby, come on," I say.

She's silent for a moment before taking a deep breath.

"Because," she says, "I can't see someone else let life pass them by."

She toys with the pink string knotted around her wrist. Bennett has the same one. For as far back as I can remember, I've never seen either of them without it.

My gut clenches, and in that moment, I think I know what she's talking about. Or whom.

"You don't have to answer if you don't want to," I say

slowly. "But is there something going on with you and Bennett?"

Her face falls, but she says nothing. Her fingers shift over her legs. She looks to the floor.

I know that look. I made the same one when Quinn asked me about Emory.

"It's none of my business," I say. "But just know, I'm here for you."

It's quiet as she shifts the bracelet around.

"No," Ruby finally says. "No, it's not about Bennett."

She smiles, but it doesn't reach to her eyes.

I don't believe her.

"So," she says with a clap of her hands, "this is your breakdown. What do you want to do?"

"You're invited to my breakdown too. If you need to cry."

She laughs. I can see a little bit of her spirit return with it.

"Nah, let's do something more productive," she says. "Let's conquer something."

"Like what?"

"Hmm," she muses. "We'll start small, then tackle the big things. How about a shower first?"

"Done."

"Perfect. You're already on the right track. Um ... how about ... something to eat that isn't chips?"

I look down at my empty bag. "I can do that."

"And then maybe ... yoga?"

"Too far."

"Right," she says. "Baby steps."

Baby steps.

I think back to Emory and how he would be encouraging just the same. It's that thought and that one alone that prompts me to pull out my phone and call Fred.

"Who are you calling?" Ruby asks.

I tilt the phone to show her.

"Okay, that's a massive leap!"

"Massive leaps get things done."

She blows out air. "I thought we'd start with salads or something."

"I start here."

Just like Emory would if he were in my shoes.

And I don't take no for an answer.

42

Emory

I don't know what today will hold. There are too many potential outcomes, and if I try to control them all, I'll drive myself crazy.

I'm trying to do a little less of that.

I'm a man with issues to work out. I know that now. I have childhood responsibilities that might hang over my head for a while or forever. There's only so much I can do about it, but I know this is the first step.

I take the employee entrance at Honeywood, flashing my badge and opening the gate, winding through the alley beside The Grizzly's exit gift shop and moving up the ramp and down the midway.

This park feels so different from my first day here. It might be old, but the classic look of some buildings only adds to the character. The ride exteriors have design motifs from another generation, but they're kept up. Clean. It's like entering a time machine and transporting to the better days of theme parks—a time when families came to be together without the distractions of the outside world.

I can see what Lorelei loves about it.

Honeywood isn't half bad.

Fred is waiting for me in the offices. I can tell he's not exactly happy to see me though. At least, as not happy as Fred can be. It's not in his nature to hate.

"Thank you for meeting me," I say, reaching out to shake his hand.

He takes it with zero apprehension. It's a firm shake. He's in business mode. I can respect that.

"I know you called this meeting, but I do have questions as well," he says.

"Just give me five minutes of your time, and I'll answer any questions you have."

"Five minutes," he says.

I didn't mean it *literally*, but I don't blame him for wanting to move on to their investigation. Hopefully, after what I tell him, they won't have to.

"I'll keep it brief," I say.

We walk up the stairs to the conference room, and once he sits, I stand at the head of the table.

In that moment, my anxiety spikes up.

I've never felt this nervous for a presentation—not even the very first one I gave at sixteen when I pitched The Grizzly. I've always been confident in my ideas. But this feels different. This feels like a leap of faith with no safety net.

Fred clears his throat.

I've been standing at the head of the table for too long. The sound of the coasters outside roar past me, and I can feel myself tensing up.

There is so much riding on this, and if I don't approach it carefully, I could ruin a lot of things. My future, Lorelei's future, everything.

And then ...

Lorelei's head pokes in through the door.

My walls crumble.

My heart finds its footing, as if it recognized its missing piece—its brighter piece.

Lorelei is wearing a canary-yellow top. Her floral-printed shorts hit just above her thigh. I can see her scar in the daylight for the first time. It only makes her look that much stronger.

It's odd to think that only a couple months ago, I viewed her as the dreamy theme-park girl across the midway. She's so much more than that. This woman has sent my heart into loops and spirals, twisting into a well-constructed thrill that even I couldn't have imagined. She's brought me peace, even among all the wreckage we've caused together.

But that sounds like the type of love I'd eventually find —a beautiful mess.

"Oh, I ..." she starts before clearing her throat and continuing. Her chin tips upward. She exudes confidence. My chest swells with pride. "I have a meeting with Fred this afternoon."

Fred looks between us with a raised eyebrow before sighing at her with a smile.

"Am I surprised you showed up here, even when I said I was busy?"

Her lips curl in.

Sassy woman.

"I wanted to ... plead Emory's case actually," she says with a shrug. "And mine."

Fred buries his face in his hands, like a father overwhelmed by too many kids.

We're a handful, I'm sure.

He sighs. "You'll have to wait outside, Lore. I—"

"Well, hang on," I say, my hand reaching out toward her. I couldn't touch her if I tried. I'm on the other side of

307

the room. But my arm still extends to her as if it could. "You can stay. Please stay, Lorelei."

Her eyes dart between mine.

"You need to know this too," I say.

She looks to Fred, who huffs out another exasperated breath. His open palm gestures for her to sit in a *well, if you're gonna be here anyway* kind of way.

I smile as she sits.

And then it all comes naturally from there.

"I would like to purchase your rebuild contract for The Grizzly," I say.

I don't know what I expect after that, but it's quiet. Too quiet.

Fred purses his lips, moving his mustache here and there.

Lorelei stares at me.

Well, that shifted the mood real quick.

"I've stepped away from Dawson Manufacturing," I continue. "I'm choosing to start my own construction company, and I'd like to work with Honeywood first and foremost. And I know what happened with The Grizzly."

I dive into the accident—Lorelei's accident—with the new details I found yesterday and relayed to Ian. I explain how the operation manual contained a last-minute speed requirement change that slowly wore down the ride to an unnecessary degree. I also explain that, with a temporary speed reduction and some maintenance on the wood, we can run the ride safely for the remainder of the season until it's torn down for the new build.

"I'd like to ensure The Grizzly is rebuilt properly with a team of trusted engineers and crew," I say. "With the care Honeywood deserves."

Lorelei says nothing. All she does is stare, her lips parted.

I can't imagine what she's thinking with this new information. The last two years must feel like a lie. Or maybe it's a relief to know the truth. Maybe both.

Either way, she lets out an exhale and pulls out her phone.

"I've ... I ..." She stands, her fingers shooting across the phone screen. "I need to call Ian. Excuse me."

Fred touches her arm as she passes to walk through the door. "Come back once you're done, okay?"

"Yes ... yes, sir."

Her eyes dart to me, and a moment passes before she leaves.

My heart departs with her, as it always will.

"Mr. Dawson." Fred's voice pulls me back. "Why should I hire you and not your father?"

"Have you met him?"

He snorts, air pushing his mustache out like a cartoon. "I *do* like you far more."

I huff out a weak laugh.

"This took a lot of courage," Fred says. "And I think you can do a good job."

It feels good to have someone believe in me. To know I'm capable.

To know I'm not *him*.

"But I want to be serious with you for a moment," Fred says. "And this might sound silly, but just humor an old man, okay?"

"Okay."

"Do you love her?"

I want to laugh, but Fred is blank-faced. He isn't joking. That mustache is as tame as I've ever seen it.

"What?" I ask.

"Mr. Dawson, Lorelei has been in my employ since she was sixteen. I've watched her give everything to this park year after year. One guest at a time. She's a good person. The only bad thing she's done is sacrifice her personal life to Honeywood.

"Now, with everything you just said, I can find a way to get this business buttoned up. I can pass off some silly story about summer love. And regardless of whether you stay, I know she'll bounce back. She always does. But I won't work with you if you took advantage of my Lorelei. Manufacturers can come and go, and while I do like you and your work ethic, Mr. Dawson, I also love this girl like my own daughter. So, tell me, did all this mean anything to you? Because I'm not working with a man who might have taken advantage of my kid."

I let in a sharp inhale through my nose.

"It meant everything to me," I say. "*She* means everything to me. And whether you keep me on board or not, that's your prerogative. I know of other very capable contractors that I'm happy to put you in touch with if you feel our business relationship cannot continue." I swallow, looking to the floor, then back up. "Do what you feel is right for your park. And if Lorelei doesn't want to be around me, that's up to her as well. But this isn't some silly story about summer love. I'd do anything for her. I just want Lorelei to be happy, sir."

A smile tips at the edge of Fred's mouth. It's a small gesture of trust exchanged between us.

Something tells me this will all be okay.

Lorelei turns the corner into the conference room again. Her eyes look red, but overall, she seems to be all right.

Fred stands, whispering some words to her that sound vaguely like, "Are you okay?" before turning back to me.

He extends his hand across the table. I reach out and shake it.

"I look forward to working with you further, Mr. Dawson," he says. He looks between us. "Lorelei, whenever you're ready, we can talk. I'll be in my office."

He pats her shoulder on the way out, and then it's just me and her, staring at each other like two lost souls.

"How are you?" I ask.

"I don't know," she says. Her voice is quiet. She shrugs.

"Happy?"

"Confused. How did you find out about the speed adjustment?"

"I searched," I say. "I needed to make things right once and for all."

"Why did nobody else find it?"

"I'm the one who designed it," I say. "Who else would know?"

She sniffs, and her soft laugh echoes through the room. "And you couldn't have done that two years ago?"

I let out a small laugh in response. "I wish I had."

"I can't believe you quit," she says, shaking her head. "What are you going to do?"

"Start my own company. I'm working with Ian to get it sorted out. He's giving me pointers in any way he can."

"You really didn't think this through, did you?"

"I did a bit," I admit with a grin. "But I'm trying to be more spontaneous in life. And that's starting with tackling the right things that matter."

"That's a huge risk."

"Well, I took a risk with you, and you've been the best decision in my life so far."

Her face falls. There are a few beats of silence, where all we can hear is the whirring of the air conditioner and the distant hum of guests outside.

"What do I even say to that, Emory?" she asks with a huff of air.

"I don't know," I say. "I ..."

I could end this sentence in so many ways.

I miss you.

I love you.

But it doesn't feel like the right time. Not when I just turned her reality upside down.

After a moment, she says, "We're gonna win the lawsuit because of this."

"I know," I say. "I'm hoping you will."

She lets out a shaky breath, and my chest tightens.

I want everything for her. And she needs to know that—even if her future doesn't involve me.

I dig into my pocket, pulling out a small envelope.

I stayed up all night, writing this. The weight of its meaning rests in my hands, but it's up to her if she wants to read it or if it will mean anything to her in the end.

"I also have this for you," I say, extending it out.

She takes it. I pat the outside once it's in her hands.

"Don't open it now. I don't think I could stand to see your face, to be honest."

"Is it a countersuit?" she asks.

"Funny."

"Is it?" Her tone is playful.

"No," I say with a chuckle. "You've changed my life for the better. I just wish I could finally return the favor."

"You already did."

A knot bundles in my stomach.

She looks to the door and then back to me. "Fred's waiting. I should go."

"Can you meet me at The Grizzly after?" I blurt out.

Her eyebrows rise.

For a moment, I start to worry she'll say no, but she nods instead.

"Yes."

She gives me a final glance over her shoulder before walking out, leaving me with only my hopes.

43

Lorelei

I walk down the crowded midway alone.

The usual sounds of Honeywood in summer surround me—screams of guests, the roar of coasters, the pop music streaming through the speakers—but it feels so distant. Everything feels surreal.

I stroll past ride after ride until I reach the out-of-commission Grizzly. I climb the maintenance staircase and look out at the sea of trees spanning the North Georgia mountains.

It isn't until that moment that I feel peace. I feel at home.

"I'm here to stay," I mutter to the track, reaching my foot out to trace along the rail.

Fred pulled me into his office after Emory's meeting and said that I was no longer on suspension.

I breathed a sigh of relief.

I also might have cried a little.

Okay, a lot.

But Fred gave me a box of tissues and let me vent.

I told him about me and Emory, that it was never what

we'd intended and yet how he was so much more than he seemed. That, at the end of it all, Emory Dawson was a good man. That my lapse of judgment had nothing to do with my values. It was everything to do with him. And that we'd be stupid not to continue doing business with him. I said that if the board couldn't see I was a shoo-in for the general manager role after thirteen years of dedication, then maybe I was no longer a good fit for Honeywood.

That one hurt, but I wasn't being a pushover anymore.

Fred laughed.

Laughed.

He said that the board had a meeting today about Emory buying The Grizzly's renovation contract. He also said that not a single one of them knew about *Cedar Cliff Chatter*'s report until Fred told them, which means the news hasn't traveled outside of Cedar Cliff just yet. It's containable.

That just means everyone in Cedar Cliff knows.

I sat in Fred's office with that fact hanging over my head.

I imagined they'd see me as that sad girl who got duped.

They'd pity me more.

But it hit me like a defibrillator to my heart—a much-needed reawakening.

Who cares?

I'm in love with the surly man that I got caught with. I'm in love with his determination to fix what's wrong. I'm in love with the fact that he doesn't wear his heart on his sleeve, and I love that he still stitched it there just for me.

Emory Dawson is just a hard-shell candy with an ooey-gooey caramel center.

Even though I wait at the top of the lift hill, just like he asked, I still don't know where we go from here.

Can we recover from this?

He'll likely be going back home after the summer's over. He'll keep making attractions, and he'll try to figure out life and how to run his new business. I know he'll do great, like a fish taking to a stream he's already explored.

But I'll be here.

I love Honeywood. It's my home. The midway is my living room. The railings of the queue lines are my banisters. The Romping Meadow is my bedroom, I guess, given the illicit stuff I did there. And The Grizzly is my roommate.

I can never tell Quinn that I compared her to a coaster.

I want this to be my future. I want Fred's general manager role when he retires. But even so, a large part of my home is missing without Emory.

We will be living separate lives. I will still be suing his father.

There's no way this can work, can it?

I lean back on the railing, looking up at the sky, already blue and filled with puffy white clouds. The pine trees look as green as ever from here.

I dig in my purse, searching for my phone to take a picture for Landon. I want to text him, *This will be your home again in two months!*

But then I notice the letter from Emory.

I stare at the envelope. It's like the last piece of a treasure-hunt adventure I don't want to end. But all things must come to an end eventually.

I open it, unfolding the letter inside crease by crease until staring back at me is something much different than I expected—something that takes me a second to understand. But when I finally realize what I'm looking at, my heart catches in my throat.

I vaguely hear footsteps ascending the staircase, but my mind is still reeling. When I look up to see Emory paused a few steps below, I can feel tears threatening their way down my face.

Am I just in some shocked stupor, imagining the tall man with the concerned face and the eyebrows? No, that'd be one heck of a hallucination. Plus, that woodsy candle scent of his wafts to me, and I'm not sure I could imagine that. If I could, I'd bottle it forever. There're a lot of things about Emory Dawson that I want to keep forever.

"You were supposed to open that alone," he says, taking the final few steps until we're right next to each other.

I swallow, choking out the words, "Technically, I did."

He takes my cheek in his palm and mutters, "Don't cry, beautiful."

I hold out the letter. "You did this though."

"I tried."

What he attempted was something he's so beyond not qualified for, but he did it anyway. And that's what matters.

I finally muster the strength to speak without my words getting strangled in my throat. "I ... I might be able to run again?"

He nods, and that's all I need to see to have the tears finally roll down my face in waves.

It took me a second to register what the drawings were, but I realized after scouring the sketches—the arrows pointing to other chicken-scratch writing and beautifully mocked-up grids—that Emory had designed a hip adjustment.

"I had lots of help," he says. "I'm no doctor or a physical therapist, but I know a guy. This is the best approximation we could come up with without a proper evaluation of your hip. It's very much a first draft but ..."

"Why?"

"Why what?"

"Why do all this? Why … this is …"

"What's the point of being an engineer if I can't help?" he says with a small smile. "I mean, I know I mostly work with steel, but I wanted to try. Wesley said there are some experimental surgeries he's heard about too. The payout from the lawsuit should—"

"Why are you so …" My voice cracks. I don't even know what I'm saying before I say it, but when I look up and meet his deep brown eyes, the words spill out anyway. "Why are you so secretly wonderful?"

He brushes a tear from my cheek with the pad of his thumb, and I find myself leaning into his touch.

I let out a full-blown sob.

I'm too overwhelmed to care whether I've got snot bubbles.

"I've tried to hate you so much," I say. "For so many things. But I just can't."

He laughs. "Thank God because I love you, Lorelei."

The words curl around my heart, like a downward spiral wrapping around my soul. I sniff again, trying to swipe away some tears, likely just spreading my already-destroyed mascara.

I've probably got full-on raccoon eyes, but I don't even care.

"You really should let people see the best side of you," I mutter.

"I like it being just for you."

Then, I start sobbing again.

He takes my chin between his thumb and forefinger, tilting my head up so that I'm looking at him again.

"You are the first person who showed me it's okay to be

happy," he says. "To want something more than just my job. Because, Lore, I want you. I want you so bad. And unless you can tell me right now that this will never happen, that I will forever be wasting my time convincing you just how much I have absolutely fallen in love with you, then I'm not going anywhere. I will spend every waking moment trying to deserve you, if you'll let me."

"I hate you."

"No, you don't."

"No, I don't."

The side of his lips twitches up into a smile.

"Would falling in love with me be so terrible anyway?" he asks.

"It doesn't matter," I say. "I already have."

He wraps his arms around me, and I let myself fall into his chest.

We might have a lot of obstacles ahead of us, but I don't care about any of them.

He's mine.

I don't realize I said it out loud, but it doesn't matter because he simply responds with, "I'm yours."

"Stay," I whisper back. "Please stay."

He nods against my head. "Of course."

44

Emory

I take a red-eye flight back home that night and pack. I'm normally not a sentimental man, but I don't see myself coming back anytime soon, so I grab a few extra items—my *Indiana Jones* DVD, the first diagram of a coaster I made in crayon, and the framed picture of me and my parents when I was a kid. I'm hoisted up on my dad's shoulders in front of a castle in the most magical theme park on Earth.

You know the one.

I pack none of my suits because I'm running my new company how I want, and monkey suits are out.

Screw 'em.

Then, I head to my dad's house.

The house I grew up in is on a massive plot of land with no neighbors for miles. Fields span either side, and it takes ten minutes to get down the rocky driveway alone.

Dad is out in the workshop when I arrive with my duffel bag slung over my shoulder. The place is a mess with pipes, workbenches, and deconstructed parts strewn across the floor. He always lets it fall apart when I'm gone. Not that it matters anymore.

He sees me walking down the path and stops what he's doing. He looks ragged, like a reflection of the area around him. It's the first time in a while I've seen him without a suit on. For once, our dynamic doesn't feel like business partners, but instead father and son—just a family of engineers in grungy T-shirts and messed up denim in a workshop where we've spent countless hours.

With each crunch of gravel under my boots, I know my steps are leading me to a war zone.

"What are you doing here?" he asks.

I didn't tell him I was coming. I didn't want him to call his lawyer.

"I'm just packing my tools," I say.

He grunts as I walk to the workbench, not giving him as wide of a berth as maybe I would have before.

He doesn't intimidate me.

"Are you moving?" he asks.

"Yes."

"To Georgia?"

"Yes."

He scoffs.

"You can't run a business on your own," he says. I can sense the desperation in his tone. It has the same shake and threat to it that he gave Mom when she was packing her own stuff and leaving.

I now understand why she had tears in her eyes when she left. It wasn't due to sadness. It was frustration. This yard and these tools were my Legos and sandbox. And now, it's just rusted wrenches and a broken man living alone to atone for his own sins.

"I've run a business before," I say, unzipping my bag and packing my tools. "And I'll do it again."

"You're going to throw all of this away for that girl?"

"No," I say, twisting toward him. "I'm starting a company to be what we should have been. What Mom imagined us to be. And I'm starting my life so that I can prove a happy one is possible."

"Prove it to who?"

"To me."

He reaches for his beer, taking a swig, and shakes his head.

"You're gonna ruin everything for me," he says. "You're going to tear down my life's work. Your mother's life's work. You'll never forgive yourself."

"I can live with a little guilt if I know I did the right thing when I had the chance."

"Go to hell," he spits out.

I pause to look at him—at the bags under his eyes, the veins trailing over his forehead, and the permanent lines etched onto his brow. All I see is a shadow of the father who once felt like my Superman. I tried to defend him as a child, saying his tough love was simply what I needed to be a better man. And when I got older, I tried to assist him with clients, coaching him for meetings he ultimately flubbed. In the end, I had to realize that my father was only human. He didn't have a cape. He wasn't a hero.

"Do you understand why I'm leaving?" I ask. "Truly?"

"Because you're a coward."

I sigh, zipping my bag closed.

He'll never see why what he did was wrong. I can fix a lot, but I cannot fix him. Maybe not staying to help my father is the true guilt I'll have to live with. But I need to take care of my own well-being. I can't keep shouldering his.

"I'll see you later, Dad," I say. "I hope you get help."

He doesn't say anything in return.

I catch the first flight back to Cedar Cliff.
Back to her.
Back to my heart.

45

Lorelei

The thing about living in a small town is that everyone knows everyone.

Fred and I barge into the offices of *Cedar Cliff Chatter* the evening the board decides to let Emory purchase the contract. With him being out of town, we take the remaining drama into our own hands.

I slam my palm down on the receptionist's desk. I don't know about Fred, but I'm feeling like a buddy-cop duo in that moment. I even say, "Hey! We got a bone to pick!"

He shakes his head.

Okay, so I got too excited.

Standing in the newspaper office, where the town's gossip is written and distributed, I fold my arms over my chest like a woman on a mission.

Maria, the receptionist who is ten years younger than me and a regular at Honeywood, instantly picks up the phone.

"Jaymee, your daddy is at the front," she says.

Fred's wiggling, frustrated mustache is a sight to behold when Jaymee walks out.

"Jaymee," Fred says.

"Dad."

The tension rolls off the both of them. Though it's more from Fred than Jaymee, who looks terrified. I don't blame her.

All Fred says is, "Do better."

It's in such an authoritative tone that I can't help but exchange a glance with Jaymee in solidarity.

He's scary when he's mad.

Her face is red. Her haphazard, reporter-like bun flops to the side, as if deflating from the force of a father's disappointment.

I slide over our prepared envelope of new information.

"Do the right thing this time," Fred says, and then we turn to walk out, like two people with a building on fire behind them.

"We'll still see you at dinner tomorrow?" Jaymee calls after him.

Fred gives an absentminded thumbs-up.

He's still a dad after all.

As we walk back to Honeywood, I take the confidence from the moment and channel it.

"So, you'll be retiring in the next few years," I say to Fred. "And I'd like to seriously be considered for general manager again."

He simply smiles. "Consider you considered, Arden."

He wraps his arm around me, hugging me close as we continue down the sidewalk, right toward the parking lot of Honeywood.

Fred and I have always been obsessed with Honeywood to a different degree than anyone else. He once told me his wish was to be buried with his Honeywood tee. I don't think he was joking.

Who knows what will happen?

Who knows if it'll be five years or ten?

But all I know is, I'm destined for this park, and it's destined for me.

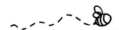

The next day, my and Emory's dark-ride deeds are nowhere to be seen in the *Cedar Cliff Chatter*. Instead, the front page boasts the news of Dawson Manufacturing's horrific mistake, the departure of Emory from the company, and finally, an announcement of The Grizzly's reopening for the remainder of the season.

Three days later, I'm leaving my house with my trusty Honeywood polo and yellow sneakers. Quinn is still inside, sipping on her coffee in anger. She found out this morning Landon will be moving back into town after the summer. I pray for the poor souls that have to endure her temper today.

When I lock the front door and turn around, I see my favorite man at the end of the driveway. Emory is posing like an off-duty model, leaning against his new black truck with his work boot kicked back on the tire.

"Hey, beautiful," he calls. "Need a ride to the park?"

"Do I look like the type?" I spin as he looks over my bright outfit and grins.

He opens my door for me, cupping my butt as I load into the truck's passenger side. Once he's in, he pulls me into a kiss, one hand tangled in my hair and the other one still gripping the steering wheel.

When he told me he was here to stay, he meant it.

He got back two days ago, secured an apartment a mile

from downtown, and went straight to work, helping Bennett adjust The Grizzly.

It was weird, watching it soar across the track, sounding different yet the same. The speed change affected the sound. When you work at a ride long enough, you get attuned to the noises. You're able to listen for the odd bits and bobs, ensuring the coaster runs at its usual cadence. I knew The Grizzly's sounds well, and I'm sure I'll get accustomed to them again.

After a day of test runs, they loaded in sandbags, and then finally, Bennett hopped in as the first rider, fearless, as always. He clapped once it completed its circuit flawlessly. He said it was better than ever.

Emory beamed at me from across the station, giving a small wink that melted my heart on the spot.

We drive to Honeywood and walk the park hand in hand, strolling down the midway, taking in the emptiness of it all. It's just us and the sound of summer birds chirping, the hum of the cicadas, and the soft breeze of the mountain air that will likely be long gone and replaced by stifling Southern humidity by mid-morning.

But for now, it's perfect.

Emory smiles. And not just at me, but as if greeting the day with happiness. It's a change for him, but a nice one. I adore that man and his smile. I wish I could tuck that expression in my pocket for whenever I get sad.

It's odd to think I hated him.

Actually, no, I take that back. It's one hundred percent plausible.

He's not the type of person to return a smile to a stranger just because it's eight a.m. and you run into them in the grocery store. He'll recall your face, but he won't be the man who asks,

Hey, Bob, how's the family? He isn't a typical small-town man, but I love that about him. He's the mystery of Cedar Cliff. My mystery. My love. My other half. And I trust him.

And that is exactly why, at the bottom of The Grizzly's lift hill, where I'd normally walk the stairs and peer out at the glow of the sunrise, I instead squeeze Emory's palm and say, "I want to ride it this morning."

"You do?" he asks.

"Yes."

The second I say it, I can feel myself shake. Realistically, I know The Grizzly is safe now. But while I know this is the case, I can still imagine the clatter of the wheels unhinging from the track, and it's enough to make me upend my breakfast.

Emory's hand tightens around mine. "I'll ride it with you," he says.

We wait for the operators to arrive at work, letting them test the train on the track as part of their morning routine. If it runs fine after a few cycles, you're clear to ride it yourself. Emory and I offer to be the guinea pigs.

We step in, lowering the lap bar and letting it click into place.

My nerves start to build as the operators double-check the restraint, pulling forward to ensure it's locked. I can feel my fingertips itching to grab anything. The lap bar doesn't feel like enough.

Emory holds my hand again. "I got you," he says.

The train jolts forward, and we're off.

We bank the first corner and start clacking up the lift hill.

I close my eyes, shifting in my seat.

Emory clutches my hand tighter. "We're fine," he whispers. "We're fine."

I nod, my eyes still squeezed shut.

"I can finger you again if you—"

I smack his hand.

He laughs.

Click, click, click, click, click ...

"What if it just stops and gets stuck?" I ask.

"The anti-rollback will catch us," he answers.

"What if we don't make the first turn?" I ask.

"It's only going to run at the proper speed."

"And what if—"

"Nothing will happen."

"But what if—"

Emory takes my face in his large palms and pulls me to him, kissing me so deep and passionate and wonderful that I can't think of anything but him.

We pull apart, and I finally look at the world around me, seeing Emory's warm brown eyes staring back at me.

"You're ready," he says.

He's right. I feel it. I can sense it in the nerves that course through me, in the fist that wraps around my heart and squeezes, only to let go, finally letting me breathe.

I settle myself into the seat, looking up at the sky that once held my fears and anxiety. I reclaim those emotions as excitement.

"I'm ready," I echo.

Our car crests the hill, and simultaneously, Emory and I raise our hands in the air and scream like banshees as we barrel down to the other side.

Epilogue
Lorelei

One Year Later

Opening day for The Grizzly's rebuild is a madhouse. It's humid, but even with the drag of summer heat, you can feel the excitement all around you.

Fred and I try to keep the long queue line satisfied with little knickknacks of promo merchandise. But we don't have to work too hard. All the guests are in good spirits. I think they're just happy the ride is back and better than ever.

Emory and I were the first two people to ride The Grizzly after it passed all the inspections. It's everything we wanted it to be. The train whips through launch after launch—slowing, speeding, faking you out in just the right places, and providing airtime when you least expect it. My favorite part is the tunnel, where, when you zoom through, the whole world goes quiet and it's just you and the ride.

It's a thrill in the best ways, all while keeping Honeywood's family-friendly charm.

Emory is great at that balance now.

He bought a few acres of land on the outskirts of Cedar

Cliff and set up shop there. The yard is scattered with tools and steel parts. The large workshop has all types of schematics strewn on the open tables. Rumor has it, he's working on the next Honeywood coaster—The Hornet. They say it was designed by an employee, but of course, that's just a rumor.

After my dad found out what had really happened with The Grizzly, he loaded up a grill in the back of his pickup and drove over to Emory's new property. He sizzled hot dogs and gave him the ol' *so, you're dating my daughter* talk. When I found them three hours later, they were out in the workshop, listening to The Rolling Stones play through the speakers and looking over Emory's latest designs.

Later, all my dad had to say about it was, "I bet he could fix our flower bed."

Thanks, Dad.

Mama took longer to warm up to Emory, but once he started smiling around her, I knew she was a goner, just like me. That smile could wrap anyone around his finger. Now, she drops by with gift baskets full of kitchen goods and family recipes. That's her way of saying, *Please make sure my daughter eats something other than Thin Mints*. I don't tell her that Emory ordered all the boxes they had on hand when the Girl Scouts came around the grocery stores this past spring.

Emory has fallen into Cedar Cliff life with ease. The town loves him. I'm not surprised. That's just how this community functions. Mrs. Stanley insists Emory help her walk her dog in the evenings down Main Street. According to Theo, the presence of his hot, shirtless chest has increased attendance at Yogi Bare. Plus, we finally got first place in trivia, much to our rival group's chagrin.

Emory has gotten close with Bennett and Orson. They

tend to spend their weekends helping with construction when needed. I think Bennett likes the distraction. His wedding planning with Jolene has been haphazard at best. I won't tell anyone—aside from Emory—my suspicions, but I think weekends at the workshop have been acting as a Band-Aid for the lack of Ruby in his life. Jolene finally put her foot down when it came to their "too close" friendship. It wasn't good.

Ruby and I have never talked about why she was upset that day in my bedroom or whether it actually concerned her best friend. But every time Bennett and Jolene's wedding is brought up, she wants to change the subject.

As of right now, Ruby seems okay. She's smiling out from her place in the queue line. Theo is dressed in a giant Buzzy the Bear outfit, bumping her big caboose around and purposely knocking into Ruby. If Theo's boyfriend were here, he'd either be laughing hard or already trying to strip her out of that outfit. Who knows? You try containing those two.

"Where's Landon when you need him?"

I look over, and Emory is fighting his way through the crowds, his grumpy little face trying to form a smile but he's annoyed all the same.

"Probably bugging Quinn," I say, kissing Emory on the cheek when he reaches me.

Fred shakes his head. "If he gets her to break character again, so help me ..."

"I'm sure we'll listen to them argue about it later," I say, looping my arm in Emory's.

He looks at me, a slow smile forming on his face.

"How's our buddy doing?" Emory asks, tipping his chin toward The Grizzly.

"He's a hit," I say. "We'll have to make sure it doesn't go to his head."

"I'm more worried about yours."

"Oh, because I helped design the best coaster in the world?"

"In the world? Come on."

"We're up for awards, Emmy."

"Let's not jinx it, beautiful."

He kisses my forehead, and I lean into it.

Some days, it feels like I'm living in a dream. I have my goofy friends and my ridiculous park.

Our schedule will change drastically come tomorrow. The money from my winning lawsuit is paying for experimental pelvic surgery—the one that might hopefully let me run again. The adjustment is nowhere near similar to Emory's original makeshift design one year ago. After all, he's only a roller coaster engineer. But the framed chicken-scratch design still hangs in my living room.

I'm nervous about the impending surgery, but Emory has been staying up late with me when I'm too anxious to fall asleep. He'd be in bed before me were it not for my nerves. He's been getting up to eight hours of sleep lately, but he says he'd sacrifice any amount to make sure I'm all right.

I can't stop imagining this potential new future with him post-surgery. I dream of Emory and me running through Cedar Cliff in the mornings. I picture how my feet will feel, pumping the pavement once more. I close my eyes and try to imagine the Southern mountain breeze coursing through my hair.

I bet we'll stop to get sugar bread—of course—and then walk to Honeywood right as the sun is rising. We'll watch them test rides for the day, finding our way to The Grizzly, where we'll see our new creation soar.

I'll ride the morning's first launch with Emory by my side.

Hands high.

Screams bellowing from my lungs.

Feeling the thrill of fear course through me but knowing it's fine.

Because he's here.

And I'd ride the downhill with him every single time.

Also by Julie Olivia

INTO YOU SERIES

Romantic Comedy

In Too Deep (Cameron & Grace)

In His Eyes (Ian & Nia)

In The Wild (Harry & Saria)

—

FOXE HILL SERIES

Contemporary Romance

Match Cut (Keaton & Violet)

Present Perfect (Asher & Delaney)

—

STANDALONES

Romantic Comedy

Fake Santa Apology Tour (Nicholas & Birdie Mae)

Across the Night (Aiden & Sadie)

Thick As Thieves (Owen & Fran)

Thanks, Etc.

Honeywood Fun Park is the theme park of my dreams. But how this all came to be is still baffling to me.

I always had a very tumultuous relationship with roller coasters. I was the kid that waited in the queue line for hours only to run to the exit in tears, and I grew up to be the friend who held the bags while everyone else had fun. I was terrified of these beasts.

But in 2018, at the ripe age of 26, my boyfriend (now husband) and I went to DisneyWorld. I promised myself I'd finally ride the Rock 'n' Roller Coaster. It only took one launch from 0 mph to 57 mph in less than 2.8 seconds to send me careening into my next obsession. I, like Lorelei, have now spent far too many hours in bed watching roller coaster POV videos.

So, last year, when I stumbled through writers block, and had a lot of "None of these ideas sound interesting!!" conversations with my husband, he finally asked, "What would *you* want to read about?"

My answer was simple: "Theme parks. Always."

And so Honeywood was born.

But theme parks are built by many people, and I've got the best support network I could ever ask for.

Thank you to my editor, Jovana. You are so wonderful to work with. I knew we were destined for each other when you commented "LOL" at the cocaine joke. I want you to be with me forever and always, please.

To my dad because you deserve to be in every acknowledgement section in every book I'll ever write. I wouldn't be who I am without you.

To my mom. Sorry for all the times I cried at theme parks as a kid. But hey! Look at me now!

To my brother. I'm still in awe that you read my book every release week. I'll always be the annoying little sister who looks up to you as my hero, so it feels like a celebrity picks up my book every time.

To my sister-in-law and best friend, Jenny Bailey. You inspire me every single day with your kindness and hardwork. I wanna be you when I grow up. (You jokingly asked to be credited as: "The light of your life, your confidant, your person, the best decision your brother could have ever made, your #1 cheerleader, your biggest fan" which is all 100% true so I'm keeping it here.)

To the Avengers, Allie Giancarlo and Jenny Bunting. I live for our daily podcast. #TexasForever

My beta team! MY BETA TEAM. If I could do a standing ovation for y'all, I would. Allie G., Angie (my PT queen!), Candice, Carrie, Elizabeth, Jen Morris, Jenny Bunting ("Queen Bee"), Emily L., and Jenny Bailey. Extra special shout-out to Jenny Bailey and Allie G. who read this book TWICE. I don't know how I got so lucky with this crew, but please never leave me. This book wouldn't be what it is without you.

Thanks to Emilia Abraham for your awesome theme park knowledge! I love how our thirty minute conversation on Valleyfair ended up stretching to over an hour. You're the reason Honeywood's Employee Night exists.

To my reader group, the Feisty Firecrackers! I am so humbled by how supportive and wonderful y'all are. Not just with me, but with each other! I always look forward to our Bite-Sized Victory Fridays, and I hope we get a billion more.

To all my Instagram friends who are new or have been with me since the very first book. You make every release magical.

Finally, to The Husband. Thank you for being my permanent theme park buddy. Thank you for riding the VelociCoaster five times and laughing at my screams. Thank you for listening to my fifty thousand rants on roller coaster design. You may say you're more like BoJack but, my love, you are ooey gooey Mr. Peanutbutter at your core. Thank you for believing in me. It feels unreal that I'm living my dream—not just as an author, but by being married to you.

About the Author

Julie Olivia writes spicy romantic comedies. Her stories are filled with quippy banter, saucy bedroom scenes, and nose-snort laughs that will give you warm fuzzies in your soul. Her phone's wallpaper is a picture of the VelociCoaster. Her husband has come to terms with this roller coaster obsession.

They live in Atlanta, Georgia with their cat, Tina, who does not pay rent.

Sign-up for the newsletter for book updates, special offers, and VIP exclusives!: julieoliviaauthor.com/newsletter

facebook.com/julieoliviaauthor

instagram.com/julieoliviaauthor

amazon.com/author/julieoliviaauthor

bookbub.com/authors/julie-olivia

Printed in Great Britain
by Amazon